For the Bush girls —

Two of my favorite WOZ

↑

Look it up
pg 1

Love
Bill
AKA Parko

June 18 - 2012

THE WOMEN ONLY ZONE

Because men cause all of the trouble in the world

Parke Sellard

Copyright © 2011 by Edmund Parke Sellard, Jr.
parkesellard@comcast.net
www.smashwords.com/books/view/102045

ISBN 978-0-7414-7639-5
Library of Congress Control Number: 2012939305

Printed in the United States of America

Published May 2012

INFINITY PUBLISHING
1094 New DeHaven Street, Suite 100
West Conshohocken, PA 19428-2713
Toll-free (877) BUY BOOK
Local Phone (610) 941-9999
Fax (610) 941-9959
Info@buybooksontheweb.com
www.buybooksontheweb.com

For my wife and daughters

CONTENTS

FOREWORD

PROCLAMATION: April 13, 2050

Whereas James Whitlow, President of the United States has died in the nuclear war, Vice President Myrna Johnson is now President of the United States.

By the Emergency Powers Act of May 21, 2049, President Myrna Johnson has declared that:

Martial Law now exists in the whole country.

As males cause all of the evil the world, males are now deprived of all rights under the Constitution. All males shall be referred to as primitives.

All literary works by males and all images and statues of males must be destroyed.

Male nouns and pronouns must be deleted from all words. The archaic word woman is now wo, plural woz. The word human is now hu, plural huz.

The name of our country is now WOZ (Women Only Zone.)

The head of WOZ will be called MOTHER, as mother is the most powerful and sacred word in any language.

By Order of MOTHER MYRNA

I. Marla

It was a lovely April morning in the year 2100. The sun was still behind the hills, the breeze was slight, and hungry birds were chirping. Inside her dormitory, paying no attention to the birds, aware only of her own existence, Marla woke up. Mentally struggling to determine where she was, what the time was, she raised her head a bit. Oh, I must get up now and say my pledge, she thought. Forcing her back to raise itself, telling her arms to pull, she managed to sit up. Then on her own command, she stood and slowly walked to the mirror by the empty bunk next to hers.

That bunk had been empty for two weeks now. It had been Emily's, but one day Emily simply wasn't there. Neither were her clothes, and no one knew what had happened to her. Sometimes a wo simply wasn't there any longer and no one would talk about it. And I'd better not ask questions about her, she thought.

With a quick stroke of her left hand, she pushed back her shoulder length, straight, auburn hair. Touching her right eyelid, she was now ready to recite the daily pledge taught her when she was five years old.

Looking directly at her image in the mirror, she recited, "I pledge that I shall always be a loyal wo, complete in every way, and that I shall always love and support MOTHER MYRNA and my sister woz, and defend our country, long may it prosper."

Lowering her hand, looking at the door to the hall, she knew it was time to move, so grabbing a towel from its rack by the mirror; she opened the door into the hall. Twenty feet she must walk to the Cleanliness Room. Arriving there, and without a thought, she pushed open the door with her shoulder and made her way to the Necessary Room with its line of toilets and then to the showers.

The somewhat dull aluminum walls of the shower stall waited as she silently allowed herself to be swallowed by the impersonal enclosure. Without turning around to look, she threw her towel over the half door behind her and faced the small red light shining on a place half way between her breasts. Marla knew that the light was checking her DNA for her identity. After computing her age and her classification, it regulated the amount of cleansing spray and rinsing water allotted to her.

She held up her arms as she waited for the cleansing spray to stream down upon her. When the cleansing spray started she moved her arms quickly to spread it all over her body, for in fifteen seconds the spray would stop. Knowing that she had such a short time to make use of the spray on her body, she hand-scrubbed herself as rapidly as possible.

Patiently, and somewhat cold, she stood directly beneath the shower head waiting for the not very warm water to rinse away the cleansing spray. The thirty seconds of rinsing water stopped, though her skin was not yet free of the cleansing spray. When she had complained about the short time fresh water rinsed her body, she was told, "Marla, you are just twenty years old. You are on light duty, but if you move up among us or become a First Mother, you will get longer shower time and other benefits. Follow the WOZ pledge and you will do well."

Back in her room and dry, Marla started to dress, paying little attention to her drab blue tailored shirt, her black pants, nor the way she brushed her hair out of the way. As she looked at herself in the mirror, she thought that if this morning went well, very soon she would be wearing a yellow epaulet on the left shoulder of her shirt. That would be great so she would not be ordered around by every wo who outranked her. "Marla, do this. Marla, do that. Marla, clean the Necessary Room," she was sick of hearing. And if today went well, there would also be better food, more time in the shower, and she wouldn't have to scrub floors and toilets ever again.

She was tired of being ordered around like a primitive. At least that's the way she was told primitives of hundreds of years ago were treated, having also been told that primitives no longer existed. Making certain that her arms were nowhere near her eyes, she continued to think about the primitives. Were they real or just mythical creatures that supposedly existed centuries ago? And why are we not supposed to even think about them?

As she adjusted her shirt, trying to look neat, she wondered about the questions she would be asked today. Well, she would smile just a bit, but not grin as though she knew she was in. Oh, and the questions, she could hear them now. "Marla, did you love your First Mother? Marla, did you cry when you were eight and taken away from your First Mother? Marla, do you say your pledge every morning and every evening? Do you love MOTHER MYRNA?"

And then there would be the final questions, the same ones she answered when she had her physical examination and second interview. Interview, ha. It was an interrogation, she thought. Today I shall not get rattled, angry, or defensive. They always start the questions by asking my age. Okay, I'll just smile a bit and say, "I'm Marla 642080, born April 6, 2080 and just turned twenty last Wednesday."

She heard a low hum. Touching her closed left eyelid, she heard a voice say, "In ten minutes, Marla, you are due in room 124, building 73."

Touching her right eyelid, she thought, "I'll be there."

Touching her left eyelid again she heard, "Good, we are expecting you."

Putting both arms down, especially the right one, she remembered how much she hated the computers implanted in the lids of her eyes. Touch the left eyelid and receive; touch the right eyelid and send, just like a robot. But I won't always be this weak, she thought, looking again at her arms to make certain neither was near her eyelids.

She left her dorm building and cut across the lawn on a stone path. Several very large woz were trimming the bushes and carrying away the dead branches from a tree. Being very careful not to touch the eyelids of either eye, she thought those are some pretty big woz. Whoever they are, they're pretty big. Maybe they're primitives, sometimes jokingly called noz. No, they don't really exist.

After walking a few more steps she thought that they couldn't be. Noz don't really exist, just schoolgirl's imagination. Oh well, so what? I'm going to have my final interview and be a First Mother.

The first time she entered this white concrete building she wondered why it wasn't plain inside. Typical government buildings were nothing fancy, she thought, just plain solid will-do structures, not anything to make one smile, but not dull enough, not quite ugly enough, to make anyone throw up. The officials who worked there were enough to do that very thing; they knew it and they loved it. They knew that common woz, like Marla, would be a bit on edge just entering the building. No one ever came into a government building just to get a drink of water. All government buildings had signs all along the walls reading, Love Your Sister Woz, and, Sisterly Love Conquers All. Then she remembered this one was sometimes called the Happiness Building.

Entering the building, she smiled as she noticed the brightly painted walls, some blue, some yellow, some a deep red. Combined with thick carpet on the floor, the scent of lilacs, the building interior said to Marla, "Come on in, you're welcome here." The wall facing the entrance was painted brilliant yellow with surges of reds and greens and blues, spiraling around a large photo of MOTHER MYRNA, whose smile and outstretched arms indicated that she loved and watched over everyone. No one doubted MOTHER MYRNA in public.

Moments later, making certain that her arms were down at her sides, feeling her leg muscles tighten, and her stomach rebelling in fear that she would be rejected, she stood before the door to room 124.

She entered the room and was greeted by Anna, a Wo who said with arms outstretched, "Welcome Marla. I am so glad to see you again." In her own time, and at the right time, Anna would let Marla know why she was so interested in her and why she held her breath the first time she interviewed Marla.

Not like the last time Marla was here, when there were no outstretched arms, no smiles, no flowers on the desk, no smile on her face, but there to greet her then was the government official to ask her tricky questions. Today, it was a different Anna, not the one with the non-committal greeting.

Anna: long bright red hair, green eyes that sparkled, double Marla's age, slightly overweight, Anna was unable to hide her pleasure at seeing Marla again. She came around her desk to give Marla a brief hug as she said, "Marla, you made it. You're going to be a First Mother." Marla's arms fell limp as she smiled and then hugged Anna.

Pointing to a chair facing her desk, Anna said, "Sit down and let's talk about being a First Mother."

Eager to please now, Marla sat down facing Anna who sat across the desk from her. "I couldn't be this cheerful when you were here a month ago because you hadn't taken your tests yet." Reaching across the desk Anna took both of Marla's hands and holding them tightly said, "It hurts me to really like someone and then that someone doesn't pass her tests." And then holding up her outstretched arms, she went on. "But you did and I can be happy again."

Lowering her head a bit, still looking at Anna, silent for she didn't know exactly what to say, Marla, in an almost whisper, mumbled, "I didn't know anyone ever thought about me."

"Honey, all woz must think about each other all of the time. Remember MOTHER MYRNA taught us that we should love each other."

"I know, but sometimes the rules are harsh and seem to own us, not to love us."

Smiling slightly and lowering her head a bit, taking Marla's hands again, she turned to reassurance, "Marla, the rules are to prepare young woz for their life ahead." Snapping back to her welcome format, Anna continued, "But you came through fine."

Anna paused a moment indicating a new paragraph, a new page. "Now let's go over your program," Anna said as she turned to the large computer screen behind her. I'll send a copy of this to your eyelid computer. To review it at any time, simply touch your left upper eyelid with your left hand and think *Marla's Program* and it will appear in the vision of your left eye."

Marla simply nodded yes.

"Good. First, here is a yellow epaulet to sew on the shoulder of your new bright green shirt. Go to Clothing and draw out four new uniforms." Marla looked at her present shirt bare of any epaulet, thought how proud she would be to have one, and smiled as she imagined it sewn on her new shirt.

"Next, your nutrition will change. You'll be issued better food with much more vitamins and minerals, and it will taste better, too."

Marla more than smiled, she grinned.

"And you will get more time in the shower."

"Oh, thank you, Anna. Thank you so much," she said, giving Anna a quick hug.

Anna thought for a moment, her left arm raised, prompting the computer screen to change, and there it was, *Marla's Program*, and her appointment time to receive her injection of starter fluid, just two weeks away. Although wondering what starter fluid was, if it were painful, and how they would do it, Marla suppressed her thoughts and then said, "Fine."

Smiling from her hair to her unpainted toenails, sitting still with her hands to her side, but skipping inside, Marla thought, I made it. I'm going places after all.

As Marla started to rise, Anna, in a somewhat more serious mode said, "Let me remind you that you, and all woz as well, are complete in every way. We are so complete that if it weren't for supplements in our food we would produce a baby wo every nine months." She started to laugh as she went on. "You can see that would not be in anyone's interests. So, Marla, when we find someone like you, young, strong, willing, we cancel the effects of the supplements with starter fluid. You see, that's all starter fluid is."

She paused to see if Marla really understood. Marla did and nodded.

"Now what is starter fluid? Marla, I really don't know. I do know that it is a catalyst, something that promotes but doesn't cause some biological process to occur. Some things we don't really need to know."

Marla repeated what she had been told many times, "Starter fluid lets us have a baby; it doesn't cause us to have a baby."

"I suppose you could say that, Marla. Now if you have no more questions, I suggest that you draw your new uniforms, then go to your room and review the new material. Remember, touch your left eyelid as you think *Marla's Program*. Everything you need to know will appear to you."

That afternoon, sitting under an apple tree, watching a group of dogs play, Marla wondered why most of the dogs were built like her, but others had sort of a stick thing protruding between their hind legs. She had never seen anything like it in a wo. When she was little she had asked her First Mother about it and was told they were lower animals and walked on four legs. And if ever woz had been that way, they died off thousands of years ago.

Being careful not to touch her right eyelid, she looked at her arms, both lowered so as not to come anywhere near her eyelids. Intent on thinking about herself and her new life about to start, no thought of hers, however noble, must be transmitted to the government. Two months ago she certainly did not want to transmit any thoughts. If she had, they might have arrested her, examined her, treated her, and maybe hurt her. Every day she had asked herself if she would ever cease to be trapped in this dull routine life, frightened and confused. What's the use? Why am I here? And what's the purpose of my life? Is it to serve others? That's what I have been told, but then what is the purpose of their lives? Is it to serve the State? If so, then what is the purpose of the State?

Marla looked at the dogs again, wondering what the one with the stick between its hind legs was trying to do with the other one. Strange actions, she thought, and then wondered why she felt some strange type of a glow, one she had never experienced before.

She heard the hum. Touching her left eyelid she heard Anna say, "Marla, time to stop day-dreaming. Go to your room and review your program, please, my dear Marla."

She touched her right eyelid and thought, "Yes, Anna, right away." Quickly she pulled her hand away from her eyelid, and jerked her arm straight down to her side. Oh my, I must have been touching my eyelids when I was wondering why things are the way they are. She immediately stood up and then walked at a fast pace to her dorm.

Marla opened the door to her room. There, smiling for all she was worth, long blond hair, deep blue eyes, all the vitality of her nineteen years, sat Joyce, pregnant.

Rubbing her tummy as if her pregnancy showed, Joyce looked at Marla, smiled as she said, "Well, how did it go today?"

Acting about as nonchalant as a cat strutting into the house with a mouse in its mouth, Marla said, "Quite well, I think." And then she broke out with a grin large enough to swallow her own head, rushed over to Joyce and hugged her.

"So I assume it's all set then; you're accepted."

"Yes, isn't it great? We'll both be First Mothers soon." Sitting down beside her, Marla said, "Do you feel all right? Are you sick at all?"

"I feel fine. And I love the extra time in the shower, the good food, the whole thing. When's your injection?"

"In a few weeks, Anna told me. What's it like?"

Excited, Marla leaned closer to Joyce. "Tell me about it. Tell me everything that happens."

"All right. Well, first of all you go in and they have you lie on the same table where they did the exams."

"And then?"

"And then, Marla, they have this big tube thing they put in you."

"Does it hurt?"

Joyce shook her head. "No."

Marla breathed a sigh of relief. "I'm glad about that."

"Were you there all afternoon?"

"No, but I stayed on the table with my legs strapped up high for about an hour. I tried to sleep after the injection but my legs were beginning to ache, just a bit though."

"That doesn't sound too bad. Then you had to go back when?"

"I went back three weeks later and they told me that the starter fluid had worked and my egg was developing."

Marla lay back on the bed, looking at the ceiling and smiling. "I hope it goes as well for me."

"It will. Just do what they say and don't ask a lot of questions."

Holding her hand up and front of her, and then noticing what she had done, she quickly put it down and at her side, "But, Joyce, there is so much I don't understand; so much puzzles me; and there's so much I want to know."

Joyce stood, and looking down at Marla, as if she were the teacher and Marla were the pupil, started to pace slowly, then stopped and faced Marla. "Honey, I don't know everything. I don't even know very much, but I do know this: you can have peace and happiness or you can ask questions. You can't have it both ways. I learned what I know by creating the impression that I didn't know anything and I didn't want to know anything about what goes on."

Marla looked up. "And that's what you think I should do?"

"I think that you should just be happy being a First Mother, at least until your child is eight years old."

"I am happy; I am thrilled; but I'm also relieved that finally after waiting for three years, I am going to be a First Mother. I had almost given up any hope of ever having a baby. I felt that I might spend my whole life scrubbing floors and toilets."

"You knew you'd make it, didn't you?" said Joyce, not too sympathetic.

"But I'm so dumb. I don't know anything about being a First Mother. I don't even know how I got chosen; I don't even know who runs things. I don't even know who my First Mother was."

Joyce pointed her finger directly at Marla's face. "Fine, keep it that way." She started to walk toward the door, then changed her mind, turned and then said, "Marla, here's a few things it's okay to know: The Council of One Hundred, the U-100, run the country, really have the say about things, practically own it, though MOTHER MYRNA is above everyone. The Upper One Thousand run the country sort of, and make a few minor rules. The Upper Ten Thousand see that the laws are carried out. The rest of us are just plain woz, and we are ranked by what we do. We don't even rate the capital first letter, like Woz; we're just woz. First Mother is the first step up."

"Yeah, I guess I knew all of that. I just don't know how it all works."

"Marla, my love, here's how you should work it. Listen, but keep your mouth shut, and be good to those above you."

Looking up, holding out her hand in expectation, Marla said, "Thanks for the advice." After she noticed Joyce had smiled and touched her hand, she said, "Do you have to check in at your dorm every night? We could have some fun if you can stay here with me tonight. You know, like we used to."

Joyce made certain her hands were nowhere near her eyelids, and then she quietly said, "I remember how much fun we had when I was your roommate.

Starting toward the door, holding Marla's hand part of the way, Joyce turned and said, "Well, sweetie, tomorrow you will start getting better food. Food without those supplements that keep you from having a baby, you'll see; you'll be a completely new Marla. No more feeling sorry for yourself. Your future is about to begin."

II. First Mother

In the early morning, the sun still behind the hills, the breeze was slight; hungry birds were chirping. A new day had started and for Marla, a new life was about to start. Inside the dorm, inside her room, listening to the birds chirping, Marla smiled. Cheerfully, she got up and walked to the mirror. Looking at herself in the mirror, she smiled, and touching her right eyelid recited her pledge. "I pledge that I shall always be a loyal wo, complete in every way."

She stopped and lowered her right hand to her side, and making certain that it was nowhere near her eyelid. Now I understand what complete in every way means, she thought. Now it means that I can have a baby all by myself, providing I don't eat that supplement that stops me. And I guess today is the first time I really meant my pledge because today is the day.

The Day! In two hours she would report to the medical lab for her injection of starter fluid. Thinking of how Joyce had described the injection process to her, she felt thrilled. She also felt a bit frightened and aroused, though she didn't understand it at all.

Ten minutes later in the shower, she was all smiles as the cleansing spray poured upon her for thirty seconds, not fifteen as before, ample time for her to make herself squeaky clean. A few moments later the clear water came on. As she felt the warmth, her body wig-wagged a bit, her mouth full open as she allowed, even encouraged the spray of warm water to caress her from her stringy wet hair to her toenails. Back in her room she frequently glanced at her yellow epaulet. She was thrilled to have it, and when the starter fluid had done its part, she would have a black stripe on it. Then she would ~~then~~ be the same rank as Joyce, move to the First Mother dorm; and be on her way. There will be no stopping me, she thought. But now I must go to the Nutrition Room, eat, and then go for my injection.

Marla's thoughts were interrupted by the hum, so touching her left eyelid, she heard, "Marla, you are due for your injection in exactly one hour."

Marla touched her right eyelid and answered, "Yes, Anna, I'll be there."

Making certain her arms were at her side, she wished the eyelid computers could be removed and forgotten. But they can't be, so I'll just live with them, and then someday...

In the Nutrition Room she was greeted by Annie, dark brown hair, who was not always cheerful, not always friendly, but not ever rude. Marla rarely was able to talk to Annie who was busy selecting the packaged food for those in line. Today it was the package in the orange container, the label reading, F.M., Thursday a.m. meal. With her arms at her side, Marla said, "Oh yes, breakfast for First Mothers. Let's see, what is it today; probably the green stuff? Well, that's not too bad; better than the stuff I used to get. The line was short this morning as Marla was earlier than usual as she was excited about getting her injection. As she reached for her tray, Annie said, "Is this the day?"

Smiling the smile, Marla nodded and said, "Yes, today is the day."

As she started toward a table, Annie looked at her and with wishing eyes, asked, "How did you get this chance to be a First Mother?" Did you simply ask them if you could? How did you do it?"

"I don't know how I got picked. I didn't ask anyone; just one day I received a message to report to room 124. There I was told I could be a First Mother if I wanted and if I passed the physical. That's all I know."

"Gee, I wish I could."

Marla turned to her and grasping her hands said, "Aren't you too young?"

Standing straight, Annie looked down at Marla seated at the table. "Too young? I'm sixteen."

"Honey, I think you have to be eighteen or maybe just a few months younger than eighteen. Don't worry, say your pledge every day, and stay cheerful. Your chance will come."

"I hope so."

Marla opened the outside door and looked out at the open space between her dorm and the medical building where she was to appear. There was sunshine, but it was also hazy; there was blue sky, but there were clouds. She felt elated that she was on her way, but she felt nervous, and wondered what was going to happen that morning.

At nine that morning, the precise time of her appointment, Marla opened the door to the medical office where she had her initial exam, and now to have her injection of starter fluid. She was feeling elated, feeling that her life was about to become wonderful, yet also feeling a bit apprehensive. Suppose it hurt a lot? Suppose it didn't work? Suppose they didn't want her there after all, then what?

Before her fears could take complete ownership of her mind, she heard a wo in a white uniform say, "Welcome, Marla. You're right on time; that's great." Opening the door to the inner office and motioning for Marla to enter, she went on, "I'm Angela, the assistant." Pointing to a middle-aged Wo in a white lab coat, she said, "And this is Doctor Susan who will be doing the injection."

Marla looked at them and smiled. "Are you ready for me now?"

"Yes," said Angela. "Take off your clothes and put them on the chair. Then come back here and lie down on the exam table."

Marla smiled a bit, nodded her head. She took off her clothes and put them on the chair, and then walked over to the exam table. Using a small step stool, she hoisted herself onto the table.

"Don't be nervous, Marla. It won't hurt," said Angela.

Placing one hand behind Marla's head and the other between her breasts, Doctor Susan eased Marla down into a full prone position. "Good, Marla," she said. "Don't be nervous; think of what a wonderful life will soon be yours."

Angela took Marla's legs one at a time and placed them in the stirrups. Marla always hated this, being strung up like an animal, but she held her comments a moment, and then said, "I'm really cold. Could I have a blanket over me?

"It would get in the way, Marla, so just bear with us."

Marla stifled a laugh. "What's so funny?" asked Doctor Susan.

Marla leaned up just a bit, turned to Doctor Susan. "Don't you get it? Bear with us; that's a pun."

"All right now, Marla, we're ready to insert the injection tube. Lie still." A Wo never said please to a common wo.

"Yes, Doctor Susan."

"Now close your eyes and lie still. And don't worry, it won't hurt; I lubricated it well."

"All right," Marla said, and then closed her eyes. Suddenly she felt a sensation she had never known before. It wasn't pain; it wasn't an itch; it wasn't scratching an itch. It was just wonderful.

"Okay, Marla, the injection tube is in and we're about to inject the starter fluid. Just relax," said Angela.

Overcome by warmth over her whole body and feeling what Joyce had told her was the thunder of creation, Marla lapsed into a heavenly dream. Yes, it was as wonderful as Joyce had said. Maybe they'll let me stay here all day like this, she thought. A few minutes later Angela put a blanket over her unnoticed, as Marla was asleep.

An hour later when Angela and Dr. Susan were finished with her, and she was awake enough to leave, Angela said, "Marla, we'll see you three weeks from today for a check up.

You know, just to make certain that your egg has started its journey to becoming a fetus, and everything is all right"

"Fine, I'll be here; same time?"

"Yes."

She was on her way now and she knew it as she passed through the outer doorway and was outside in the beautiful courtyard. She saw only one puffy cloud, the haziness had gone its way, and the sun was bright. It was as a sign from the sky telling her that soon she would get a stripe on her epaulet; she would get more respect; she would move in with Joyce and be joyful. Marla, the unknown wo, had entered the building; Marla, the First Mother, had come out.

Three weeks later as Marla entered the medical office she was greeted by Angela and Dr. Susan, both wearing big smiles. "Come in, come in," said Angela. "In fact, come take your clothes off and let's take a look at your developing wo."

When Marla was on the table with her feet in the stirrups, Dr. Susan inserted a probe with a camera and computer sensor attached. "Oh, that's wonderful," Marla expected Dr. Susan to say. Instead, she heard, "Oh, oh!"

Marla's joy vanished, her leg muscles tightened, her breathing became rapid as she asked, "What's the matter?"

Neither Angela nor Dr. Susan answered her at first. Instead they looked at the computer result presented on the wall screen. "That's the third one this month," said Angela quietly.

Dr. Susan simply nodded yes.

Marla sat up a bit and turned toward them, and raising her voice a bit, said, "What's wrong? What do you mean by the third one this month?"

Angela walked over to the exam table and taking Marla's hand, in a gentle voice said, "Nothing's wrong; at least nothing is wrong with you. It's just the computer crashed again, third time this month."

Marla sat up a bit more, and turning toward them, she said, "Does this mean I am no longer a First Mother?"

"No." said Dr. Susan.

"No, dear," said Angela. "Nothing is wrong with you. It's just that darn computer or the probe." Taking Marla's hand and removing her feet from the stirrups, she added. "Come back a week from today, same time. We'll check again. I'm certain that everything is just fine."

As Marla turned to get off of the table she noticed the computer screen. She could see only part of it, but she did see: Defective conception: Reason: fault 1-a, Y chromosome. Notify Anna.

Without emotion, Dr. Susan faced Marla. "Well, you're fine for now. You may get dressed and go home now but be back here a week from today, same time."

As soon as Marla had left the injection room and closed the door behind her, Dr. Susan said, "I don't understand it. We do everything we can to insure that no sperm contains the Y chromosome."

"Yes," said Angela, "But nothing is perfect. Though you'd think that with an accuracy rate of 99.97% X chromosomes only, we wouldn't see three of these in one month."

Angela turned toward the door, but paused and looking back at Dr. Susan said, "I'll go tell Anna."

"Yes, I guess we have to, and she'll be unhappy. I know, because she told me that she wanted this wo to conceive. I remember she said, "Especially this one.""

"So, Doctor, we have to try until we get it right."

"Well, we have to follow orders. And Anna is one Wo I wouldn't want to be upset with me. After all, she is one of the Upper One Thousand."

"Why is she so interested in this wo? She never was interested in any wo before now, Dr. Susan. But you remember she told us not to abort a fetus with a Y chromosome unless we checked with her first."

"I don't know. You ask her."

"Not me, Dr. Susan. I don't ask questions from the higher ranks."

"We didn't have this conversation, did we, Angela?"

"What conversation?"

"Well, Angela, we have until Marla comes back to get her decision. Whatever she says, we'll do. In the meantime, there's no harm done, at least to us."

In the courtyard, as Marla walked slowly and with her head down, she thought about losing this chance to be a First Mother. Having seen the screen, having noticed how desperately they tried to cover up what the computer said, having practically been pushed out the door without so much as a goodbye, she knew there was trouble, and it probably was with her, not with the computer. Looking at the sky and seeing a bright sunny day, she thought she saw that haziness, that... Oh, stop it, Marla. Don't run inside from the rain just because you see a cloud.

She found an empty bench and sat down. Lost in her sorrows, she failed to hear the hum at first. Then it returned and louder and she heard Anna say, "Marla! Marla, answer me.

Quickly she touched her right hand to her right eyelid. "Yes, Anna, I hear you."

Touching her left eyelid, she heard, "Marla, Angela told me about the computer error. Don't let that worry you; everything is just fine, so do your work, say your pledge, and everything will work out fine. Understand?"

"Yes, Anna. But what is a chromosome, a Y chromosome?"

"Marla, don't ask questions about things you couldn't possibly understand, especially at this stage. Soon I'll make everything clear to you, but don't ask anyone else. Trust me."

"I do, Anna. I do."

Later that afternoon Dr. Susan and Angela were greeted by Anna in her private office and asked them to be seated around her desk. Realizing that Anna was U One K, Dr. Susan offered her regrets for injecting starter fluid with a Y chromosome. "I don't know how it happened," was her explanation.

"It doesn't matter; it happened, so now here is what we do," said Anna. "Now turn a look at the computer screen on the wall. Note this paragraph."

Due to the virus which has eliminated over 30 donors at four Starter Farms, we could have an acute shortage of donors down the road. Therefore do not abort any fetus with a Y chromosome until further notice.

Mildly alarmed, Angela spoke up. "So what do we do with them?"

"And do we tell the First Mothers that they are pregnant with a primitive?"

Anna raised her hands as if to say calm down. "The directive you just read was dated four days ago. This morning I had another directive. Here, I'll show it to you".

A special area has been established for First Mothers of these primitives. They will be given Education packet 4A-2, the limited secret information. Therefore do not abort any started eggs with a Y chromosome until you determine the suitability of the First Mother. This First Mother must be intelligent, flexible, closed-mouthed, and above all, loyal to our country. She must be carefully observed and evaluated for her first four months. On the fifth month a successful candidate will be sent to the special area for the remainder of her pregnancy. Submit name, number and date of birth to us for our approval.

Anna stood and looking directly at Dr. Susan and Angela, said, "We have a grave responsibility here. One slip-up could cause much damage to our country, and our reputations, not to mention our rank and benefits. Now I shall take care of handling Marla. You two just make certain nothing else happens, no loose talk; and keep your hands away from you eyelids when you think. Is everything clear so far?"

Angela and Dr. Susan, having both agreed to do what was necessary, quietly left Anna's office. They were both puzzled but fearful of being demoted to a common wo status, if due to their actions the public found out that primitives still existed.

A week later, mostly joyful, having been reassured by Anna that everything was all right, but also with a small bug-bite sting of uncertainty, Marla opened the door to Anna's office. Behind her desk, wearing her best deep blue uniform with the golden epaulet of a member of the Upper One Thousand, arms outstretched, wearing a big smile, stood Anna. "Come in, come in," she said, grasping both of Marla's hands.

As Marla approached, Anna let go of her hands and gave her a hug. Marla, also all smiles, said, "Angela said you wanted to see me."

"You just came from there, right?"

"Yes, and they told me that my baby is fine; I am fine; everything is fine. That's true, isn't it?"

"Yes, of course, Marla," Anna said as she led Marla to a chair next to the desk. "Sit down, dear, and let's talk about it for a minute."

Joyful but curious, Marla sat down facing Anna's desk awaiting Anna's first words. Anna took a few steps and then sat down behind her desk, faced Marla and then said, "You're a full fledged First Mother now, so go get your epaulets with the stripe, and then you can move in with Joyce."

"Oh, thank you, Anna. Thank you so much."

"But now, I have something very important to say. You're special, Marla, and you're going to have special treatment. By that I mean you are really going to be looked after. You are going to have a wonderful baby. Your baby is going to change the world; change the world for the better I mean."

Tilting her head and squinting a bit, Marla asked, "Change it in what way?"

"I really can't tell you all the things I can see happening, for the better of course, but trust me, Marla."

"I do. I said so before."

"Fine. Now just do this thing for me, for both of us; really, do it for all three of us. You know: you, me, and the baby."

"All right, Anna. Tell me what to do."

Leaning forward in her chair and once again taking Marla's hands, she said quietly, "Marla, let me tell you something. Okay, you know I am one of The One Thousand; you can tell that by my epaulet. But I was born a plain wo, like you. But I didn't like being an unranked wo, not at all, so I decided to advance myself. Here's the way I did it: I was a very, very faithful wo; I worked hard; I was very polite and obliging to those above me. Above all, I kept my mouth shut and didn't ask questions nor did I ever criticize anyone."

"I understand, Anna."

"Yes, I believe you do. And for all of our sakes, you must do the same. And you must believe that I am your very best friend, the best you ever had."

Marla lowered her head a bit and then asked, "Why are you treating me special, Anna? Other woz never said you treated them special."

"I'll tell you when the time comes. In the meantime, stay healthy, say your pledge regularly, and don't ask questions of anyone but me. For we, my dear Marla, are going places." Then looking at the ceiling she said, "UP!"

III. Let Me Tell You a Story

One morning several weeks later, the sun was just peeking over the hill, birds were chirping and Marla, lying in bed, heard them and smiled. She was also aware of the hum that meant Anna was calling her. Touching her left hand to her eyelid, she heard, "I would like to talk to you this morning. After you have eaten, meet me at the bench by the water fountain, the small one, not the one out in the open."

Marla touched her right eyelid with her right hand and replied, "Yes, Anna. Will an hour from now be all right?"

"Yes, fine. Oh, Marla, be sure to bring those eye drops I gave you."

"Yes, Anna, I'll be there and I'll bring the drops."

About an hour later Marla was sitting on a bench by the smaller water fountain waiting for Anna and wondering why she wanted to meet out here, not at her office. Perhaps it was due to the pleasant, warm weather, and the flowers in bloom. Maybe Anna just wanted to get out of the office for a while. Or was it privacy, as Dr. Susan, Angela, and other Woz might be coming by the office? That must be it. And why bring the eye drops that Anna had given her, but told her not to use them until instructed to do so?

Marla's asking herself these questions was interrupted by Anna appearing and smiling as she said, "Hello, my dear Marla," and then sat down beside her.

"Good morning, Anna, I'm so glad to see you again."

Anna immediately put her index finger to her lips to indicate silence. Reaching into her small briefcase, she took out a sheet of paper and a pen and started to write. She looked at Marla, pointed to what she had written, and then with her finger to her lips, in effect said, "Don't talk."

Marla nodded her head and looked at what Anna had written, "Don't talk, but give me the eye drops and I'll put a drop in each of your eyes."

Marla looked at her, her frowning brow and tilted head silently saying, "All right, but why?"

Anna wrote, "Trust me."

Marla nodded yes and opened her eyelids wide so Anna could put a drop in each eye. And after she did, Anna indicated that Marla should close both eyes. And then put a drop in her own eyes. After a minute had passed Anna said quietly, "Okay, we can talk now."

Marla turned to her and raising her brows said, "Huh?"

Anna put the eye drops away and then said, "Now your eye computers don't work. You can't hear incoming messages but more important, no one can hear you, except me, of course, because I am sitting next to you."

Marla looked at her again in amazement.

"Oh, it's okay, Marla, only I can hear you and your thoughts are not being transmitted either. However, just to be sure, don't touch your eyelids."

Shaking her head in disbelief, Marla said, "I didn't know that there was any way to block the eyelid computers from transmitting my voice or thoughts."

"Dr. Susan and I discovered it. She dilated my eyes once using the wrong bottle, the wrong drug, and for an hour I couldn't hear or transmit. She and I tried it several times, always with the same drug, one rarely used for dilation, and it worked every time, but just for an hour."

"So we can talk in private now? No one can hear us, at least unless she is standing next to us?"

"Right, so let's not waste any time. I only want to use this drug when it's very important to talk to you in private. And I do have something important to tell you. So, let me tell you a story. Try not to interrupt so I can tell it all before the drops lose their effect."

Marla moved a little closer to Anna, nodded yes, and then sat back to listen.

"First of all, what do you remember about your First Mother? What color hair did she have; was she tall, fat; what did she look like?"

"I don't remember very much about her looks. I know she always wore a bonnet and I think her hair was sort of red; couldn't tell much because of the bonnet." Marla lowered her head a bit and then said quietly, "What I really remember is her love for me."

"You can tell me more later; right now I need to tell you a story before the drops wear off. When I was about your age I was a First Mother and lived in a First Mother dorm in the far north part of the country. I had a roommate, Anna, and we lived with our babies until they were eight years old. We got along fine and it was a wonderful part of my life. But then many good things come to an end. We knew from the beginning that our babies would be with us only until they were eight. Then they would be sent to a dorm for an education, really indoctrination. We knew that, but we really didn't believe it.

"One night we had a birthday party for our girls. It was so great; we had managed to get some cake, ice cream, party hats, and all of us were singing. And then suddenly the door burst open and two big Woz came into the room and grabbed our babies.

Anna paused for the moment, tears forming in each eye and running down her cheeks. "Anna and I tried to keep them from taking our babies away, but they hit us, kicked us, and then they were out the door with our babies who were screaming, 'Mommy, Mommy!'

"We looked out the window and watched as they forced our little ones into a car and drove away. I swore then I would get my daughter back and I would have my revenge on this whole rotten system."

"Why do they take little ones away when they turn eight?"

"First Mothers are just to take care of the babies until they are old enough for the state to take over. Yes, First Mothers are useful in the early care of the little ones, but when the young ones start to ask questions, the government wants to supply the answers. They take over to tear down any allegiance to any other wo, especially to the First Mother. They teach them to believe that the state is their only friend. They indoctrinate them to kill any freedom of thought or action; they make robots of everyone." Then pausing a moment, she looked up and smiled. "Well, almost everyone." Then her tears started again.

"Why can't the government let the little ones make up their own minds?"

"Oh no, you can't control woz who question you. More important, the government can only control the present population. Mothers can control the next generations, that is, if they have the chance."

Marla, placed her hand on Anna's arm as tears began running down her cheeks too. "Oh, I'm sorry, Anna. And I'm sorry I touched you; I know I'm not supposed to touch an officer, especially one of The One Thousand."

Anna placed her hand on Marla's and then said quietly, "That's all right, dear, but let me go on with the story while we can still talk out loud."

Marla withdrew her hand, sat back and waited for Anna to continue. "Well, I guess both Anna and I cried all night and many nights thereafter. We knew that our babies would go to a dorm when they were eight, but we never knew it would be so heartless, just grab them and run, just like criminals."

"Did it gradually get less painful?"

"I guess it was a bit less awful for me, but only because I began to plan my revenge."

"Anna, how could you get revenge on these people?"

Anna wiped the tears from her eyes, and then with a half-smile, said, "An opportunity was just given to me. One night I looked over at Anna's bunk and she was not there.

She was nowhere in the room; then I looked in the small uniform closet and found her. She had hung herself; she put a strong cord around her neck and hooked it to a large hook sticking out of the wall."

"Oh! What did you do?"

"I tried to revive her, but she had hung there so long she was dead. I started to rush out and yell for help, but suddenly I stopped short. Anna had been scheduled for training to be an officer. But she was dead, so why not me? I quickly changed her identity tag, everything hers, and then went out into the hall and yelled for help."

"You did?"

"Yes, I went out into the hall yelling, "Marla hung herself.!"

Marla looked at her in utter confusion. "Marla? I thought your name was Anna, too."

"No, my dear, my name was Marla, just like yours. I took Anna's identity and got away with it because they didn't carefully check the DNA to see if that was her name. They recorded that Marla had hung herself. So I became Anna and was transferred for officer training the very next day."

"They never caught on?"

"Never. Well, when they came to scan her DNA, I said that I would help, but I scanned my own DNA. And for them, the case was closed."

Suddenly Marla sat up very straight, looked Anna directly in the eye and said, "Hey, wait a minute are you trying to tell me what I think you are trying to tell me? I know that the first one born takes the name of the mother. So if your real name is Marla; my real name is Marla, are you trying to tell me that ...?"

Anna, starting to tear again, but with a smile a mile wide, held out her hands and said, "Come here my baby, come here my darling Marla. Your momma wants to hold you."

After a brief but intense hug, they backed away from each other, but continued to stare at each other in disbelief. Anna realized that she had finally found her baby; Marla was trying to understand that she had found her First Mother, her only real mother.

"Our time is about up for now, my dear Marla, but before we part, I want to know if you remember that nonsense phrase I taught you when you were about six years old."

"You mean the one that starts Jacob something?"

"Yes, let me say it for you. It's really a stupid phrase, but one my mother taught me when I was little. She made me memorize it in case we got separated. Here, I'll say it for you, 'Jacob belder, belder, snelder. Q-cup, E-sup, Stee-sup ... Marla, do you remember the last line?"

Marla sat up and with a big grin said, "Sure, it goes, Ama-laza, gaza-lona, brahorn."

"Marla, no one else in the world knows that phrase. My mother made it up and taught it only to me. And I taught it only to you. Don't teach it to anyone else, except for your baby. It's a family secret."

"Anna, what's a family?'

"Ouch! You really have been indoctrinated. Well, it's just a mother and her child. That should do for the present."

"Oh, I have to get used to things now. I wondered why you were so very nice to me. No other Wo treated me very well."

Anna started to get up, but before leaving she said, "Marla, you must follow the rules. I can only help you so much right now. Be sure to say your pledge; they keep a record of how often you say it. And again I want to remind you to ask only me questions, and keep your ears open.

"I'll do what you say." then breaking into a broad grin added, "Mommy."

"I like that, but you had better call me Anna. Remember, this is just our secret; don't tell anyone, not Joyce, not anyone."

"I won't tell. I won't tell anyone."

Two days later Dr. Susan and Angela both had the day off so Anna had Marla come to her office. As Marla entered the office Anna greeted her with a hug, then said, "Let me put your eye drops in as I have a lot to tell you today and I don't want to take any chances that if you are shocked at what I tell you, you might accidentally speak out."

"Fine, Anna, I am ready to learn more about what really is, no more wondering what is really going on."

Anna put Marla's drops in then said, "Sit down across the desk from me. I wish you could sit closer, but someone might come in."

Anna cleared her throat several times, not really certain where to begin. Looking around the room, trying to know exactly where to start, she finally decided to ask Marla, "Do you know what DNA is?"

"Well, I've heard the term. I think it has something to do with what hair color you have, or maybe whether you are tall or short. Is that right?"

Anna seemed relieved that maybe she found the starting point for telling Marla the truth about WOZ. "Yes, yes," she said, raising her brows, "That's it, well, that's part of it. DNA is the plan, the blueprint for a hu's whole body. It tells the egg how to make every part of your body.'

"How does it do that?"

"Let's forget exactly how for now. Let me tell you the general idea today. First of all, the DNA is carried in cells called genes. Genes are grouped in what we call chromosomes."

"Like the Y chromosome I asked you about, like I saw on the computer wall screen?"

"Yes, but let me go on. There are a lot of these genes, and in the hu body there are 24 pairs of chromosomes."

"Sounds complicated."

"It is, honey, it is. But you don't need to know everything about genes and chromosomes, just the basics. Here are the basics of it all. Now there are 23 pairs of chromosomes that are sort of alike, but the 24th pair has two distinctly different chromosomes. Now here is a beginning answer to your question about the Y chromosome. Well, first of all there is an X chromosome and a Y chromosome. All woz have a pair of X chromosomes. Males have an X and a Y chromosome."

"Anna, what is a male?"

Anna reached for the cup of coffee on her desk. "Get ready for a shock, my dear. Males are what we call primitives."

"But they don't exist, do they?"

"Ha. Article number one of the big lie the government has forced on you woz. Of course they exist. All right so far? Can you accept, at least partly, what I have told you?"

Marla looked down for a moment, and nodding her head a bit, quietly said, "Yes, I guess so. Okay, primitives are sort of like woz, but they have this Y chromosome. Now what? Hey, why does the government lie to us?"

"Why does it lie to you woz? Control, that's why. But let me go on. Here is shock number two. Your egg has only half enough DNA to form a baby. I said that twenty-three pairs of chromosomes plus two gender chromosomes are needed."

"What's gender?"

"Oh, let me sidetrack for a moment. Remember you were puzzled about seeing some dogs that had a stick thing protruding between its hind legs?"

"Yes, but the rest were built like us down there."

"Okay, that difference is because they are a different gender. All animals and huz have two genders. Those without the stick, like us, are called females. Those with the stick are called males. In huz, they are called women, from which we get our term, wo. The other gender, the males, are called men,"

"I don't understand why the government kept all of this from us woz?"

"Control. Honey, I'll tell you all about it, how it came to pass as soon as you can absorb the truth. But now, I have to push ahead and explain the facts of life."

"Please do; I 'm so confused now I don't even know who I am."

"I know, so let me tell you about males and DNA and what your situation really is. Okay, now, Marla, when your egg was sitting in your body before the injection, it had only half of the chromosomes necessary to build a baby. A wo's egg has 23 chromosomes, not the 23 pair of chromosomes and two XX chromosomes. Your egg had only 23 chromosomes and one X chromosome."

"But the starter fluid started it going."

"Starter fluid is the name for sperm. Now before you ask me what sperm is, let me go on. Sperm is made by the males, got that?"

"Okay, I guess."

"Sperm is necessary because it contains the other 23 regular chromosomes and either an X chromosome or a Y chromosome. If a sperm cell containing an X chromosome unites with the egg, the baby will be female, a wo. If a sperm cell with a Y chromosome unites with the egg, the baby will be male. Males have 23 pair of chromosomes and an XY pair."

"But, Anna, there aren't any primitives, I mean males any more. They're all dead and gone; just a few useless primitives, if they really exist. Where do we get the other regular chromosomes and the X or the Y chromosome?"

Anna took a handkerchief and blotted her forehead. "Look, Marla, here is how it really is. And, Marla, only MOTHER MYRNA, the top ten, and the top One Thousand know the real truth here. And now you know it, and you have got to never let on that you do. Again, here is the truth: One: There are woz which used to be called women, and there are primitives, which are really males, and male humans are called men. Two: To make a baby hu, it takes an egg from a female and sperm from a male. Three: Males are alive and are kept in Starter Farms, just for their sperm. Four: You were injected with sperm, not some kind of starter fluid. And Five: Hold on dear, your baby has an X and a Y chromosome. You are producing a male baby."

Breathing heavily, looking around to see where she really was, and moving her arms across her chest, then down at her sides, she finally calmed down a bit as she asked, "What do I do now? Am I in trouble? Will they do something to me?"

Reaching across the desk and taking Marla's hands, Anna, in a comforting tone, said, "You're fine. I have permission for you to have a male child."

"You do? I can have my baby?"

"Yes, but it's going to be tricky. And you must not reveal that I am your mother. And you must not tell any other wo the truth, not until the time comes."

"When will that be?"

"I don't know, but the time will come."

Calmed down at last, Marla said, "You said that I could ask you questions."

"Yes, but as few as possible, but go ahead today."

"Anna, what I see male and female dogs do together, is that the usual way sperm is transferred?"

"Yes, it's called mating and that's nature's way. Well, you know the government's way, injection. One more thing, Marla, We do need some government. But we have a completely heartless, oppressive government which controls every wo by ignorance and fear. So I worked to become U One K to stop them."

Marla, with a hint of a smile, said, "Mating sounds interesting."

Anna laughed. "That must be the understatement of the year."

IV. An Error in Math

Partly asleep, partly awake, Marla heard the humming that meant Anna was calling her. With great effort she managed to touch her left eyelid. "Marla," she heard, "I have to go out into the country for a day. I'll let you know when I get back and we can talk again."

"Marla touched her right eyelid, "Uh-huh. Let me know when you get back," she said, and then fell back asleep.

She was awakened again a few minutes later. "Marla, this is Dr. Susan. It's time for your check-up, so come see me at nine this morning. That's just an hour from now."

"I'll be there," Marla said, touching her right eyelid as she hurried to the mirror to say the pledge, which she said in record time. Never forget to say your pledge, she thought as she rushed down the hall to the Cleanliness Room.

And at nine as she entered the exam room, Angela greeted her with a smile, but not quite her usual big smile. Marla noticed that Angela was not her usual cheerful self as she said, "Marla, the usual thing, undress, put this gown on and get up on the exam table please."

She lay on the exam table for five minutes before Dr. Susan came into the room. "Well, how are you doing now, Marla?" But she didn't say it with the enthusiasm she had shown on previous visits. Oh well, Marla thought, they're just tired or maybe it's just one of those days.

Dr. Susan took the probe she had used several times before as she said, "Well, let's take a look and see how your baby wo is doing."

"Ouch!" Marla yelled as Dr. Susan moved the probe around inside her.

"Oh, I'm sorry about that, Marla. Well, I'm all through now; you can get dressed and go home."

Five minutes later and out the door, Marla had the strong feeling that things were not exactly right. Why were they so impersonal with her? Why did Dr. Susan hurt her? Then seeing two bluebirds sitting on the limb of a bush, she felt much better about her visit. She sat down on a bench by the water fountain and let the bubbling water carry her into thoughts that soon she would be holding her baby by a waterfall, listening to her.... Oh no, it's listening to him babble on as he rolled his big eyes.

There were no chores or work she had to do and Anna was gone until tomorrow. She might as well take a walk, or maybe just go back to her room and take a nap or read a bit in the book Anna had given her, *Handbook for First Mothers*. After supper she decided to lie down and see what the handbook had to say. And almost aloud she thought, why would I trust what this book has to say? These people are such liars anyway. However, with nothing else to do, and with the feeling that she should read the book, she opened it to page one. But after trying to read two pages she fell asleep.

An hour later she woke up with a terrible pain and she noticed that she was bleeding. It's my baby, she thought. Placing her fingers over her right eyelid, she called, "Help, I think I'm losing my baby! Anna, Dr. Susan, somebody please help me."

Touching her left eyelid she heard, "This is Dr. Susan. Come to my office immediately."

Fifteen minutes later Marla was lying on the exam table, sobbing, "My baby, my baby, is it...?"

"I'm afraid so, Marla. I'm really sorry," said Dr. Susan, somewhat sympathetic.

"Did I do something wrong? Is that why I have no baby now?"

"No, dear, these things just happen."

"But I want my baby," Marla said, crying.

"I think I'll let you stay tonight in the hospital and give you something to help you sleep," said Dr. Susan. "You'll feel better in the morning. And Marla, you can have another baby, honey."

The next morning in the hospital Marla gradually woke up. At first she felt nothing, no sadness, nothing. But reality gradually engulfed her; her baby was no more. She turned and looked out the window and noticed the clouds. They weren't puffy any more. The sky was not blue, it was bluish-gray. The world was gray.

She heard the hum. Touching her left eye lie she heard Anna's voice. "Honey, Dr. Susan told me about your baby. I'm so sorry. Listen, Marla, I'll be in my office all day today, so come by when you feel better."

Touching her right eyelid, but holding back her tears, Marla answered, "I'm so glad you're back, and I'll be there as soon as they let me out of here."

An hour later as Marla entered Anna's office, she rushed over to Anna and threw her arms around her. Anna hugged her for a minute then broke loose just long enough to lock the outer door. "Now, my darling Marla, come let your mother hold you."

"Oh Mommy, I feel so awful. My baby boy, my little primitive is no more. And I hurt so much."

"Do you hurt down there?"

"Only a little bit. It's the me inside that hurts. What do I call it? But it's the me inside that hurts. I know; I once heard it called a soul. Mommy, my soul hurts."

"I know, my dear, I know. I felt the same way when they took you from me. And I know your soul hurts, but you must calm down. Go have lunch, then meet me at the bench by the fountain, the one out of the way. We have some planning to do"

Sitting side by side on the bench later that day, Marla asked, "What did I do wrong that I lost my baby?"

Anna took her hand as she said quietly, "You did nothing wrong. What I am going to tell you is going to upset you even more, but I have got to tell you. But no one else must know. Listen carefully, but make no loud response to what I tell you."

"All right, I'll try."

"And keep your hands away from you eyelids."

Marla immediately put both arms in her lap and then said, "All right, tell me the bad news."

Biting her lip and then forcing the words, Anna said, "You didn't lose your baby; it was taken from you."

Marla didn't respond for a moment; then suddenly she sat up straight and said, "What?"

While I was away an ultimatum came from MOTHER MYRNA. She was furious that someone had told her that thirty sperm donors had died of the flu. It turned out to be three donors had died."

"What does that have to do with my baby?"

"When she thought that thirty donors had died, she was alarmed as there were only two hundred and fifty available before the flu struck. With only so few our population would be seriously at risk. So she sent out a directive not to abort any more male fetuses. That's why you were allowed to keep your baby in the making."

"I hate her."

Alarmed, Anna placed her hand over Marla's mouth and then looking directly into her eyes said, "Marla, never, never say that. You could be eliminated if anyone heard you say that."

"Like Emily?"

"Like Emily."

"So she can order woz and babies killed whenever she wishes?

"Afraid so. High ranking Woz don't usually see any value in common woz. Well, maybe except for physical work and breeding stock, like farm animals. Now you may want to get revenge, but more important, do you want to change things?"

Trying desperately not to cry in between sobs Marla said, "I still …you know. How can this government just do with the souls of woz… do anything they please?"

"Go home, take that relaxing pill Dr. Susan gave you and sleep. Then tomorrow apply those eye drops to silence your eyelid computer/phone and meet me first thing at the bench by the water fountain; you know the one, and we'll make a plan."

The next morning on her way to meet Anna, she was of two minds. Suppose I just burst into Dr. Susan's office and screamed at her, "You killed my baby." I'd love to do that, but then what would that accomplish? I guess I know what would happen. She would deny everything and I would have revealed that I knew she did it. She would then figure out that Anna must have told me everything. Then what? Anna and I would be in deep trouble.

She walked a little way farther as she thought okay I'll keep silent and get them someday for this. But can I keep quiet and slowly fight this miserable government? I have to. I just have to, not only for me, but also for Anna and for all of the little, ignorant woz who suffer. Twenty feet ahead she noticed Anna sitting on the bench waiting for her. Good. Anna will have a plan. I hope she has a plan.

Anna noticed her and smiled. What would do without Anna, she thought. I guess that is what a mother is for. Government can't do what a mother can do. Marla smiled a big one at Anna and then upon reaching the bench, sat down beside her.

Anna took her hand briefly as she asked, "How are you today, Marla dear?"

"I'm angry, I'm hurt, I hate them, but I'm all right and ready to listen to you; whatever you decide I should do is fine with me."

"Marla, I see three ways that you can go now. You can have another baby. There is no record that you were ever pregnant. Myrna's thoroughness has seen to it that everything about your pregnancy has been deleted. So you are eligible to be pregnant again."

"I've considered that. Now what else could I do?"

"You can just go back to being a wo, doing light work.'

"No, Anna," she said with defiance. "Never. What's the third way?"

"I've been thinking that you are an unknown, and that's a plus for us. No one knows that you were pregnant, except Dr. Susan and Angela, and they dare not talk. Myrna would punish them. So we four are the only ones who know it was a male."

Marla looked at Anna and smiled just a bit, "And everyone knows that males don't exist." After a moment of silence, her tears began to run again as she said quietly, "My little primitive doesn't even exist, does it?" Wiping her tears away, and with a determined voice she said, "But I'll get them for that."

Anna shook her head no and then Marla added, "Someday."

"All right then, here's what I think we can do. No one knows anything about you. No one knows that you are my daughter. This is a great opportunity for you to advance. Marla, to have a baby is a wonderful thing, but to protect yourself and your next child, you must have some power. It is almost impossible to fight the system from the bottom."

"I know, Anna, so what can we do?"

Anna looked up, smiled, grinned really, as she said, "I can appoint you to Upper Hundred Thousand School."

"Do you think that I can do it? I'm not smart like you."

"I did it, and I was really ignorant then. So if I can do it, you can do it."

Marla started to tear again. "Oh Anna, what did I ever do without you?"

"My sweet Marla, for a year you will learn how smart you really are. And one more thing, you are not alone; we are not alone. We have friends in high places, but we have to be careful not to let that be known. There is much I could tell you, sweetie, but I won't. Being a simple ignorant wo knowing only what you are taught in U-100K school, is probably your best protection now."

V. How Marla Did It

On a cold winter's day in a two-story, wooden dormitory, surrounded by open fields of frozen corn stalks, stood this brassy, sassy, belligerent Wo named May. She was a member of the Upper Thousand, and often referred to as May Not for her negative attitude. Facing sixty woz, she mechanically recited her opening speech to these trainees, each hopeful of elevating herself from wo to Wo in some capacity. May looked them over, thinking what a group of nothings they were. Her thoughts were not lost on the trainees, especially Marla, who was even more determined to rise way above this Wo.

May held up her hand and all whispering and other noise stopped. "I want to welcome you woz to your first day of training. You have been chosen to be here over thousands who were not. You could have chosen not come here for this training; you could have had a care-free life taking your country's food, shelter, and care; you could have never done anything but menial work. By menial I mean stupid, easy, and of such a low grade that anyone could do it. Before today you didn't worry about anything; you didn't think about anything; and you never had to make even a small decision. You were just like farm animals. Now, if you think you like the life of a farm animal instead of being a Wo; that's spelled with capital W; let me know or see me in my office today and I shall arrange for you to be returned to your former status. Does anyone here wish to go back to her dorm and original status?"

May looked over the woz facing her, saw no movement, and so continued. "Now you are here to work, and work you shall. It's not so much physical work, such as some of you have been doing, but it is work, not play. It is brain work, and we know you can do it, but we don't know if you have the motivation, the discipline, and the patience to do it. And while it's important to do a good job, there is one thing more important than talent, discipline, or motivation, and that is loyalty. Anyone who is not loyal to MOTHER MYRNA, the officers here and everywhere in our country will find herself cleaning toilets the rest of her life." She looked down at her notes and then quietly added, "If she's lucky."

And then straightening her back and looking directly at the woz before her, said, "We expect you to say your pledge with enthusiasm and truth. Our country of WOZ can survive a bit of laziness, greed, and poor work. But it refuses to accept disloyal woz."

May walked over to a screen, pointed to it as she said, "Here is a list of the subjects you are going to study for the next four months. In a few months we can talk to each of you and find out which area suits your talents best."

"But now, as every minute counts, I'll start now and go through the organization of our government." She looked over the sixty woz seated in front of her and then said, "Most of you probably know something of the officers of your country, but I am going to take a few minutes to go over them just to make sure."

She looked around at the blank faces and thought that their minds were as blank as their faces. "First of all, there are you woz and you make up 99% of the population. Your work is planned, your food is planned; everything in your life is planned. But you are here because you want a say in your life. However, first you have to know how things are done, how things are done for the woz in our country."

No response. "Good, this is the structure that allows you to have enough to eat, a place to sleep, and work to do. Here's the table of the hierocracy with abbreviations in parenthesis. Let me put this chart on the screen for you."

MOTHER MYRNA (U One or U-1)
Upper Ten (U-10) MOTHER MYRNA's Family
Upper One Hundred (U-100) The Council
Upper One Thousand (U One K)
Upper Ten Thousand (U Ten K or U-10K)
Upper One Hundred Thousand (U-100K)
The woz

"You can see that the woz, that's you, are at the bottom of the list. You are in this room because you want to be one of the One Hundred Thousand, and as a member you must know more than the general woz population. Those of you who successfully complete this course and become one of the Upper One Hundred Thousand, will have better food, more pay, better dormitories, and longer shower time. However, you are expected to supervise the woz in your charge, make certain decisions, and you must make them correctly. But most important of all, you must be absolutely loyal to MOTHER MYRNA. Any questions?"

A wo in the back of the room raised her hand and asked, "Ma'am, Does everyone graduate?"

"What is your name, wo?"

Timidly, the wo stood and said, "June, ma'am."

"What you really wanted to know, June, is, 'Will I have to work hard to graduate?' and the answer is yes. Usually there's one or two who do not graduate and usually it is because they preferred the easy non-thinking life of a wo instead of becoming an officer and having responsibility. Only once in the past ten years was a wo rejected because of disloyalty to MOTHER MYRNA. That should tell you something about our wonderful country of WOZ."

Marla wished she could have said out loud, "Yeah, they were too frightened to say what a rotten system it is."

"The next higher group is the Upper Ten Thousand whose members run certain services. I was a member of the Upper Ten Thousand when I started here as a teacher. Five years ago I was appointed the head of this school and became one of the Upper Thousand. Other members of the Upper One Thousand are heads of schools and departments of government. Upper One Thousand members have great responsibilities which are far greater than their privileges.

The Upper Hundred are the members of the Council and write the laws that go to MOTHER MYRNA to approve. Whether she approves or disapproves, that issue is settled. MOTHER MYRNA is at the top of the chart there because she is the top. No one is above her. She is our protector and our inspiration. So say your pledge with reverence and thanksgiving.

"In closing today's orientation, I wish to say that I hope all of you will graduate and become inspired and loyal Woz. I spell Woz with a capital first letter, not all small letters as you are now. It's time for lunch, but before we go, you must stand, touch your right eyelid, and say the pledge. This is our way of thanking MOTHER MYRNA for her many blessings.

Blessings? Yeah, thought Marla, like killing our unborn babies.

"That evening Marla was lying on her bed staring at the ceiling, but not seeing the ceiling. Rather, she was thinking about today. June had been assigned as her roommate and she wondered if June were a plant. Perhaps all students there had a roommate or a classmate who was to report her impressions. Is this student bright? Is this student loyal? Will this student be a trouble maker? Especially the school administration wants to know if a student is loyal. Well, they'll never catch me being disloyal, never. They shall never know that I'm here to take revenge on them for killing my little baby. She held back a tear as she thought about Anna and wondered how she was getting along. There is no way for me to know, so I must put it out of my mind and concentrate on becoming one of the Upper... the Upper what? I'll aim for being one of the Upper One Thousand, at least.

She glanced at June. Five feet ten, 107 pounds, long dark brown hair, light skin, not bad to look at, yes, June could do well here, she thought, that is, if she keeps her mouth shut and doesn't ask any more questions. So why is it that the government does not want woz to ask questions? I think that it is because it means that wo is thinking. And thinking is not what the government wants woz to do. Yes, woz should shut up and blindly obey, and for now I shall.

Marla wanted to make some notes about what is going on, but she needed to hide them. But where could she hide them? Oh, yes, she thought, I'll hide them where I used to hide things when I was a First Mother. Some big Woz used to check our rooms when we were somewhere else, but I remember I watched them check all of the hiding places. But I fooled them; I hid everything in plain sight. Sure, I hid any writing in my *Handbook for First Mothers*. Fine. I'll just write in my *Handbook for Beginning Officers* whatever I probably won't remember, and I'll take it everywhere with me.

Marla's Notes:

December 4, 2100. Today we learned in our Food Supply class that no food is given us direct from the farm or ranch; everything has chemicals added to it. All food for First Mothers has extra nutrients added, but food for regular woz has chemicals added to it to suppress certain emotions. They didn't really say what emotions are suppressed, but my guess is that it is the urge to have babies. So certain foods for certain woz is to control them better. That's very clever. I wonder if food for the ill and old contains chemicals to kill them. I would be surprised if the government didn't feel that when you don't work any more, you're not worth the cost of feeding you or making you well.

March 3, 2101. We learned what the word tax meant. I had never heard the word before; I just thought that we had been given a little money to spend to keep us entertained. Well, it seems that we have been paid for our work. I had been paid much more than I thought, but they took out the tax before they gave it to me. For every five dollars I was paid, they kept three dollars, and that was called tax. I wonder where they got the word dollar.

May 1, 2101. Today we started part two of our training. Four were sent back to their old dormitories and will continue to be just plain woz. The rest of us are certain to graduate and starting to learn what is really going on in the government, at least something of what is going on. Poor June didn't make it. At least, I think she didn't make it. Just like Emily, she just wasn't there one day..

June 15, 2101. We have been spending a lot of time in administration duties. Most of it seems to be showing us how to control the woz. I see how we are controlled. I say nothing, but I do watch. Our food now is better and I wonder how it differs from what we were fed the first part of this training. And we are being told, directly and indirectly, how inferior woz are, probably to make it easier for us to feel superior and thus control them without feeling bad about it.

July 1, 2101. We were told about the divisions of government in which we might serve. I think we have some choice where we could go. I have decided to choose administration for that's where the power is. My whole purpose here is to get power to clean up this horrible system, but to do it I must be a super loyal Wo, and I shall. But also I am beginning to see how corrupt this whole system of government is. Maybe I can do something about that too.

August 31, 2101. Today I graduated and have become a member of the Upper One Hundred Thousand. This means I am a 'Wo,' not just a 'wo' and have been assigned to work in Population Control/First Mothers. My duties will be strictly clerical and not have much authority, but it's a start. There's no school for those wanting to become Upper Ten Thousand members, just special courses for certain Woz appointed to them. So how do I get appointed? This is the last note I need to write as I have been assigned to work not far from here in the Reproduction Department of Population Control. But I'm happy for I'm now U-100 K

End of notes.

Working with Dr. Flora for eight months in the Reproduction Department, Marla still wondered about the starter fluid. But she really wanted to know how she could get promoted, the only way she could change things. So she wrote MOTHER MYRNA a letter telling her that she was a very loyal Wo, always had been, and could she please be appointed to a special course to serve WOZ better? Perhaps that will do it, perhaps not, she thought.

When Marla told Jennie, her supervisor that she had written the letter, Jennie yelled at her, "How dare you bypass me and ask to be promoted!" Then she gave Marla extra duty and ordered her not to leave her room for 15 days, except to work, go to the Necessary Room, or go eat.

Marla then wrote in her diary:

March 27, 2102. The most extraordinary thing happened today. I was doing some boring office work when an elegantly dressed Wo came in. She was tall and commanding and I knew that she was someone important though she was wearing no epaulet, so I was very polite to her. I am polite to every Wo, but I knew this one was Upper-Upper rank, and she was. She asked to see my supervisor and I said that I would find her, and would she please be seated in the supervisor's office and I would bring her some coffee and a snack. I said that all on one breath.

Looking over the room, nodding her head, saying to herself that she was where she meant to be, this obviously high ranking Wo smiled at me and said, "Thank you, my dear, I'd love some coffee, strong, if you please."

"Yes, ma'am, right away," I said and started for the door.

"I'm Annette, and what is your name?"

I turned toward her, smiled and very politely said, "Marla, ma'am." I bowed just a bit as I reached the door and then left the room. Out in the hall I suddenly stopped as it hit me. Oh my, Annette? She must be The Annette, one of

MOTHER MYRNA's sisters, one of the Upper Ten. Am I in trouble for writing MOTHER MYRNA?

I found my supervisor, that unpleasant old pickle-puss, Jennie, and told her that she had a visitor. "How dare you disturb me just for some old Wo with no epaulet who drops by without an appointment?"

"Sorry, ma'am, I'll not let it happen again."

I opened the office door for Jennie and she stormed in ahead of me. Before I could introduce anyone to anyone, Annette stood and handed Jennie a gold business card, and I mean real gold. Now I have heard that only the Upper Ten have gold cards, and I guess that it is true, for Jennie almost fainted when she saw it. Annette held out her hand to retrieve her gold card as she said, "I've come to talk to you about a Wo who works for you named Marla."

Jennie almost choked as she managed to turn toward me and say, "This is Marla."

"Yes, we've met." Then turning to me, Annette said, "Are you the Marla who wrote MOTHER MYRNA a letter?"

Timidly, and bowing my head, I said, "Yes ma'am." I thought that this was it for me. Either I would get to go to special classes or it was back to being a common wo, scrubbing floors the rest of my life..

I relaxed a bit when Annette smiled at me, then turned to Jennie and with the authority of a lightning strike said, "I am transferring Marla to my staff, effective this minute. Any objections?"

"Of course not," Jennie stammered. "Great idea."

I turned to Jennie and said, "Good bye, Jennie. Thank you for everything." I didn't like her, and I couldn't think of anything to thank her for, but it certainly doesn't hurt to be polite to those higher in rank than you.

Out in the hall Annette said to me, "I read the letter you sent to MOTHER MYRNA. She didn't see it, and that was a good thing. If she had, she would have been furious that a 100K Wo would have dared write to her. Me? I loved it. I loved your courage, your bit of defiance, so I decided to take a look at you. And I think that you are exactly the Wo I have been looking for. Therefore, I am going to send you to several of the special courses."

I could hardly believe what I heard. Then suddenly I remembered only members of the Upper Ten Thousand or above were allowed to go to the special courses and I was just barely one of The Upper Hundred Thousand. I started to remind Annette of my lower rank when she quietly said, "I suppose I'd better make you one of the Upper Ten Thousand. Is that all right with you, Marla?"

Starting to grin the grin, starting to walk on air, starting to tear happy tears, I looked up at Annette and wiping my eyes, quietly said, "How can I ever thank you?"

"Be as faithful to me as your mother, Anna, is and I'll make your life worthwhile."

I stopped short, then looked at Annette, and said, "Anna? Oh my gosh, you know."

Annette, in an offhand manner smiled and then said, "Yes, Marla, I know. Anna called me and told me that you had sent a letter to Myrna, so I intercepted it. You were a gutsy Wo to send that letter, although it was not a wise thing to do. Yes, we are going to get along very, very well."

"And I'll never let you down, Annette; I mean ma'am."

As we walked down the steps from the building, Annette stopped, so I stopped. She put her hand on my shoulder, looked me straight in the eyes and with intensity said, "I know you won't, but we must be very careful. Not everyone who smiles at you is your friend in the Upper-Uppers. When we get to my house ..."

"You live in a house? Oh, of course you do. The Upper Ten, of course, you don't live in a dorm."

"And you shall have your own apartment, an apartment, not just a room, in my building. Yes, the whole house is mine." (End of Notes)

VI. Annette

"I can't believe it. I still can't believe it," said Marla as she woke up in the huge bed in her apartment at Annette's house. House, she thought, it's a... well, I don't know what to call it. Big? It's bigger than our whole dormitory when I was a First Mother. And the outside, it's got those large windows and doors, and those stone columns by the front doors. I wish I knew something about architecture so I would know what some of these things are called.

Well, I have to get up now, she thought. Gee, I really hate to leave this bed. It's big enough for four woz to sleep side by side and never bother each other. But I do have to get up as Annette said that promptly at seven we all meet downstairs and say our pledge. I don't really want to go down there and meet all of these strange Woz. At least Annette gave me an epaulet showing that I am Upper Ten Thousand. That should help, but I know my newness will show. Oh, so what? It's only important that Annette likes me. Well, it's important that powerful Woz like me, too. Okay, Marla, you know what to do: say your pledge, listen, and don't ask questions.

She crawled across the big bed to the edge. She looked at the drapes covering the large window and thought that in dormitories all she ever had was a cheap, wrinkled curtain covering a tiny dirty window. But look at these: red, yellow, blue swirls of patterns and on damask! I never dreamed that a bedroom like this even existed. But it does, and it is mine.

Then looking toward the cleanliness/necessary room, she remembered that she should stop being delighted for a moment and get ready to go downstairs for the pledge.

Having her private c/n room was wonderful too, she thought. And she could turn up the water as hot as she liked, stay in it for as long as she wanted, and she didn't have to share it with anyone. And when she looked at all of those heavy beautiful towels, she thought for an instant that she must have become MOTHER MYRNA, because I, me, Marla, never knew a world like this.

Just as she finished dressing, brushed her hair, and placed her Upper Ten K epaulet on her shirt, she heard a quiet knock on her door. "I've brought you some coffee, ma'am," said the voice on the other side of the door.

Marla opened the door to find a wo about 18, wearing a First Mother epaulet standing, smiling, and holding a tray with a small coffee flask, a fine china cup and saucer next to a plate of toast and butter. "I'm Jo, ma'am," the wo said.

"I'm Marla. Please come in. Thank you so much," and pointing to a small table by the window, she said, "Just put it down right there." As Jo walked toward the table with the tray Marla thought that she had never been addressed as ma'am before.

As Jo started to leave she said, "Annette said that I was to take care of you, help you obtain whatever you need: clothing, personal needs, and help you find your way around her house. So is there anything I can do for you before I go, ma'am?"

"No, I don't think so. When is your baby due, Jo?"

"Four months, ma'am," she said with a big smile.

"You should be you very happy." As Jo turned to leave, Marla asked, "How many rooms or apartments are there here on the second floor?"

Jo hesitated a moment. "I think six, ma'am, including Annette's. Of course Annette's apartment takes up half of the floor. Let's see, Annette's, then Pat's, yours, Sandy's, and two kept vacant for important visitors."

"Let's see," said Marla. "Sandy is Upper One Thousand and Annette's head advisor, but who is Pat?"

Jo frowned a bit, but after a few moments pause, said, "Pat does special projects for Annette, but we are not allowed to discuss Pat among ourselves here, nor with anyone on the outside."

Marla walked toward the door, opened it, and then said, "Thank you very much, Jo. Thank you for coming by and bringing me the toast and coffee." As she walked toward the table, Marla thought that she should remember not to ask questions. I think that I should forget Pat exists. But I wonder who Pat is and why no one should talk about her. Oh, oh, one quick gulp of coffee and I must rush downstairs for the pledge.

A minute later Marla was gently touching the white wrought iron stair rail as she came down the thick, wide, carpeted stairway. She noticed Annette and three other Woz gathered in the foyer below around a very large painting of MOTHER MYRNA next to the flag of WOZ. Annette saw her, smiled, and waved for her to come down and join them. As she approached them, Annette said, "It's seven o'clock, so let's face the flag and say the pledge. Showing no emotion, they all turned toward the flag and picture and in unison recited their pledge.

Immediately Annette turned to the others, and indicating Marla, said, "This is Marla. I have appointed her to aid us in keeping WOZ as wonderful as it is." Then indicating a Wo about forty-plus years of age, wearing the epaulet of the Upper One Thousand, an athletic, smiling, brunette with hazel eyes, she said, "This is Sandy."

Sandy stepped forward, took both of Marla's hands in hers and then said, "Marla, I'm so glad to have you with us. Annette told me what a gutsy kid you are." Marla thought the she should just smile and make Sandy a friend who would not feel that I am a threat to her.

Then Annette introduced Marla to Linda and Jill, two U-100K clerks who promptly left to attend to their duties. Finally, Annette addressed her, and with a big smile said,

"Marla, I'm glad that you could make it this morning. Now come have breakfast with Sandy and me."

"Thank you very much; I'd love to," Marla said as she and Sandy followed Annette across the foyer into an elegant dining room. She stared at the very long dining table that probably could seat two dozen guests, set with a spotless white table cloth on which were three places set with white china plates and sterling silver tableware. Marla never imagined such a display and blinked a few times. A young wo pulled the high back chair at the head of the table for Annette and helped her be seated. Then Marla and Sandy sat down on each side of Annette. Marla watched as Annette and Sandy placed their napkins on their laps, so she did the same. Wow, is this different, she thought. It's certainly not like eating in the food room at a dormitory. I wonder what color package our breakfast will come in.

But there was no packaged food. Instead they were served their choices from platters of poached eggs, bacon, ham, toast, muffins, melon, and grapes. A young wo stood by to make certain that their coffee was never lacking in their cups or became cold. Fortunately for Marla, she had learned table manners at Hundred Thousand School.

"Marla, is this the first time you have had non-packaged food?" said Annette.

"Yes, ma'am, this is the very first time."

"Those who work here of any rank, and all those who are Upper Ten Thousand and above do not eat packaged food," said Sandy. "Packaged food has chemicals to give the woz what they need, such as extra nutrients for First Mothers, or chemicals to keep the young woz from getting too excited. With food we try to make the lives of woz better"

Annette, half laughing, looked directly at Marla and said, "In other words, packaged food is to control the little darlings."

Marla smiled slightly and said, "Yes, ma'am."

Annette turned to the wo behind Marla and said to her, "Serve Marla two poached eggs and some hot toast." Then addressing Anna, said, "You can't eat poached eggs without toast, Marla. So try it and tell us what you think."

Marla hesitantly picked up her fork and cut into one of the eggs on her plate, and then tasted the egg. "Oh my, this is wonderful," she said with a closed mouth grin. After wiping her mouth with her cloth napkin, the way she was taught in school, she continued. "I was wrong about not having anything but packaged food. At one school we had scrambled eggs fresh, but I know they added something because nothing ever tasted as wonderful as this."

Annette and Sandy simply smiled at her and said nothing. Marla then remembered that she had been taught to speak little in front of those who outranked her, especially Annette. Annette out ranked everybody but an older sister and MOTHER MYRNA. "I'm sorry. I didn't mean to talk so much about myself."

"That was just fine, Marla. Now we talked about sending you to a school session when we get your work here organized. I think in the very near future there are some openings in several areas. Let's see, I think there is science, administration, and internal security, and probably a few others available. Which one would you like to attend first?"

Marla paused a moment and then said, "Science. I think. Is that all right with you?"

Sandy then asked, "Which part of science, biological, electronics, earth science?"

Marla perked up a bit as she said, "Oh biological science. I have always wondered how our bodies work."

Later as she escorted Marla through the first floor, Jo said, "This is the small dining room. Annette and Sandy usually use it for breakfast; they just used the big one today. When they use it they don't have any woz standing by to serve them. One of the woz from the kitchen comes in when called."

"Now what else is on this floor, Jo?

"Come and I'll show you." As they walked across the large foyer, Jo pointed out several offices on the side away from the dining rooms and kitchen. "There's a large meeting room to your left, and next to it is Annette's official office, next to it is Sandy's. Then ahead are Necessary rooms and storage, and I guess that's it. Any questions?"

Marla looked around a moment and then smiling said, "I think not, Jo. Thanks a lot for the tour."

As Jo was showing Marla around the house, Sandy appeared at Annette's office door. Annette looked up from her desk, motioned for Sandy to sit down opposite her, and then in a quiet, but definite voice said, "Hello, Sandy. Now let me put your mind at ease. I did not bring Marla here to eventually replace you, so don't be concerned about that. I have several things in mind for her. I have been looking for someone like her to travel for me, listen for me, and report to me. I can't send you as you are too important, everyone knows you, knows how close you are to me, and you are too high in rank. So relax, be nice to Marla. I believe that she really is what she seems to be. Oh, and remember that only you and I know her mother is Anna."

Sandy smiled and nodded yes as she said, "I'll do as you say, Annette. I guess you have to be a bit devious in this business to survive. I'll help her all I can. How much do I trust her?"

"That's a good question. I suppose trust her a bit at a time.

I should trust her in some way to test her. Perhaps send her to some class and see how it affects her. Will she talk about something secret?"

"You could tell her the history of WOZ, a little of the true history, not the official one," said Sandy.

Nodding to herself, Annette walked toward the door, and then with her hand on the knob turned to Sandy and said, "I think I know what I am going to do about her. I am not going to send her to any school, at least not now. Yes, I know what I'll do about Marla."

"You're not going to send her to school, Annette?"

"Not now, anyhow. I don't want her attendance at any school to show on her record yet. I want others to think that she is completely ignorant of our state secrets. I want her unknown; easier for her to mingle and find out things for me. Yes, I'll teach her myself; teach her what I want her to know."

"What shall I say if one of your family wants to know why she is here?"

"Tell them the truth, 'Annette didn't tell me.'"

After Sandy left, closing the door behind her, Annette touched her right eyelid and said, "Marla, you did well today; I'm proud of you. I'll see you at dinner tonight."

VII. Dawn

The next morning at breakfast Annette said to Marla, "A bulletin from the Security Department head was sent out yesterday. I would like you to look at it with me at nine this morning."

"Of course. I'll do the other tasks you set for me to and then be at your office at nine."

At nine as Marla and Annette looked at the wall screen, Annette said, "Marla, take a look at this memo and let me know what you think:

It has come to our attention that deviations from the official history of WOZ have occurred. These deviations cause doubt which disrupts the peaceful education and serenity of our young. There must be no deviation from this official history and none will be tolerated. We must encourage complete belief in the true history of our nation and work together to keep our nation strong and united.

- THE OFFICIAL HISTORY OF WOZ -

Thousands of years ago we lived in caves with some sub-creatures known as primitives. Primitives were very useful as they were bigger and stronger than woz. They were ugly and had much hair over all of their body and had little hoses where we don't. They walked slouched over and grunted a lot. We needed their fluid to get our eggs started, but when we advanced our civilization we found we could synthesize this starter fluid. They were very much like pets and prone to emotional outbursts. Some years after we were able to synthesize starter

fluid, we ceased to care for them and in three successive cold winters they all died. There have been rumors of sightings of primitives, but no evidence has ever been put forth that they still exist.

As we progressed we turned to farming and developed a language and an elementary math, science, and social structures. We think that it was decided to start numbering the years and they started with the number one, (1.) In this year of 2101, we now have had twenty-one centuries as a nation and we are doing very well.

We have successfully grown and developed despite being surrounded by barren land. MOTHER MYRNA makes certain that every wo has enough to eat, a place to sleep, and good sanitation. In addition, she sees to it that every wo has work to do in keeping with that wo's abilities and rank without the stress of making decisions. Knowing one's place and living with one's equals are keys to getting along and sharing; and this leads to a happy life. That's why everyone lives in a dormitory with woz of the same rank. The Upper One Thousand and above live in separate houses where they can give their lives managing our country without the burden of common duties.

Tayana,
Department of Security

"It's the history of WOZ as I was taught by my Second Mother," said Marla.

"Pretty much the story you were taught?"

"That's exactly the story we were taught, word for word. We were required to memorize it and repeat it back again and again."

"Did you, do you believe it, Marla?"

"I guess I believed it. History certainly wasn't important to us then. One thing I believed… that I had better believe it. But I really didn't care."

"Tell me, Marla, what did they tell you is on the other side of the desolate land surrounding WOZ?"

"Nothing. They said that there was nothing there; WOZ was all that existed on this little sphere we live on. We were told that we live on a little sphere and other little lighted spheres called stars sort of float around us."

Annette brought out a small globe of the Earth. "Look, Marla, this represents the sphere we live upon. It is called Earth."

"Oh, yes, I've heard that word. Is that what it really looks like?"

"That's what it used to look like. See the blue part; that's an ocean, nothing but water. And notice the part that's not blue; that's land. Some of the land is very green, lots of plants and trees. Some of the land, sort of colored brown here is desert, desolate land."

Annette held the globe between them and pointing to North America, said, "Marla, this is where we are. Look, see where I am pointing, it is what used to be a country called The United States." Annette then put down the small globe and picked up a book. This book shows the countries of the Earth with a few details so you can actually see where they were and how big they were.

Pointing to the American southwest, she went on, "These are called states, that is, divisions of the United States. WOZ is comprised of these former states: the lower part of Colorado, Kansas, and Missouri, also composed of the states of New Mexico, Oklahoma and Texas."

"Is the rest of the country around us the desolate country?"

"Yes, desolate, and we think that everyone who lived there is dead. According to one history book I read, the population of the United States was about 350 million. However, all but the three million who live where we do were killed by radiation from a war."

"What is a war?"

"A war is when countries fight to destroy each other. There were many countries on the Earth, but some got angry at others and attached them with large amounts of radiation. Radiation is like the energy waves that send our voices to other woz who are out of sight. Excessive radiation caused by, well, that's too complicated, but the bad things killed everyone, except us. We were saved by a wind, called the jet stream, which blew around us and did not blow the death material directly upon us. It's so complicated I'll have to explain another time.

"So, Annette, what you are telling me is that we weren't always like we are now? We were once a country called The United States. Is that true?"

"Yes, that's true, but to explain it will take days and I must leave for the southern part of WOZ in an hour. But I'll explain it all to you when I return. In the meantime, remember this is a state secret and only a few select U One Ks know it. If this were generally known, our whole society could easily fall apart. So absolutely don't talk about it, not even to Sandy."

"I won't."

"Good, I'll see you in a few days or so. There won't be much for you to do while I'm gone so just relax. I'll probably have plenty of work for you when I return."

The next morning as Jo was making Marla's bed she said, "How did you get to be Upper Ten Thousand?"

"Strange as it seems, Jo, I don't really know. One day I was sent to U-100 K School, then while working, Annette saw me and appointed me U Ten K. I never really understood it." Marla shrugged and turned toward the door. "It just happened."

"Well, I was wondering how you did it. Did you study hard, learn things... like your WOZ history?"

"No. I was just a happy little wo, I guess. I really never cared about WOZ history, or much of anything else. I just had a good time every chance I got, and never thought about history. I did what I was supposed to do and never worried."

"Never worried? I wish I never worried. How did you manage that?" Jo said as she put a pillow case on the last pillow, "Well, that's that. So tell me, why didn't you ever worry about anything?"

Marla waked over to the window and stood there quietly watching some birds chirping at each other. "Jo, you live in the best country possible. Everything is provided for you. You don't have to make any decisions. You don't have to worry about finding work; it's all provided to suit your abilities."

"Yes, Marla, but I wonder about things, like how do we know there aren't primitives any longer? How do we know what's best for us?"

Marla turned and looking directly at Jo, said, "How do we know? MOTHER MYRNA said so. Why would she lie to us? She loves us and takes care of us, just like any mother would take care of her babies."

"I guess," said Jo.

Marla started toward the door as she said, "Jo, I have to go to pledge and breakfast now. Don't worry; we are well taken care of."

Out in the hall Marla laughed to herself. That Jo is an idiot. In the window reflection, I saw her touching her right eyelid while we were talking. Probably she was sending our conversation to Sandy or Annette. As she walked down the hall, she smiled as she thought, well, they test me and I test them. Well, that's fair enough. And I was beginning to get bored.

As Marla came down the stairs to the foyer the next morning ready for the pledge and breakfast there stood Annette. As her foot touched the bottom floor she rushed to greet Annette. "I'm so glad you're back. Did you have a good trip," she said with enthusiasm.

Annette smiled as she said, "Yes, it was fine. Had a little business to do there, but it's done now and here I am. Well, it's time for the pledge, so let's do it. I'm starved."

At the breakfast table after Sandy had finished and left for her office, Annette said to the woz attending the table, "You may be excused now," and they left the room. Turning to Marla, she said, "I am not going to send you to a school just yet."

Disappointed, Marla said, "You're not? Did I do something wrong?"

"No, no, no, don't be concerned; you are just fine. Move your chair next to mine and we can talk in a low voice."

Annette continued after Marla had moved quite close to her. "I am going to teach you everything you'll ever need to know. You're going to learn a lot more from me than any school can or would teach you. I know about everything. Schools only know what we let them know and teach only what we let them teach."

"Fine, Annette. I trust you and whatever you say, I'll do.

"Oh, another reason I want to teach you myself is that I don't want any record of what you know. You see, the more you know, or rather the more others think you know, the more danger you could be in."

"Danger, Annette?"

"There are always those who want what you have for themselves. Or maybe they are afraid you could take what power, influence they have. Anyhow, I think it best that you keep a low profile for a while. We'll start right after lunch; we can go for a walk if you like."

That afternoon as they started walking on a path through the corn field, Marla said, "This is a beautiful farm you have here, Annette. It's just wonderful."

"I like it very much. My sister, Myrna, no capital letters please, likes the city. Fine, that's keeps her out of my hair, well, somewhat out of my hair. You know she seems to have the feeling that I want to take her place. I don't; I'm happy right here doing what I am doing."

They walked a few yards farther in silence, but finally Annette said, "I wanted us to take a walk so I could talk to you in private. I want to explain our world to you and there are two very important things you must know in order to understand any of what we really are and how we got this way."

"I will listen carefully to whatever you tell me. And I assume that all of it is very secret."

"Absolutely secret. As far as anyone else is concerned, we are talking about crops, flowers, the blue sky, the clouds, and things like that. Okay?"

"Yes, Annette, okay."

Gesturing toward a bench up ahead, Annette said, "Let's sit down on that bench for a few minutes and let me see if I can explain two things at once."

Sitting on the bench Annette turned toward Marla, cleared her throat several times, not really certain where to begin. Looking around the field, trying to know exactly where to start, she finally decided to start with, "I've told you a little bit about our history, but now the second thing. Do you know what DNA is?"

"Well, I've heard the term." Here we go again Marla thought; I guess that I had better go along with it. I'll just listen and act surprised as she tells me about genes, gender, sperm, and conception. "Something about DNA tells how the body is made, or something like that?"

Annette was delighted that she had found a starting place, and then proceeded to explain the whole process. "Yes, yes," Annette said, raising her brows, "That's it, well, that's part of it." Marla pretended to be amazed as Annette explained it all to her, sometimes commenting, "Really, Annette?"

As Annette went on about reproduction Marla wondered if Annette knew she had been pregnant with a male and knew the facts of life. Maybe she knows that I know and she is testing me to see if I will admit knowing anything. Anna told me several times to never volunteer anything.

Finally Annette decided that she had talked enough for one day. "Marla, I think that I have told you the basic idea of reproduction."

Marl nodded her head a bit and then said, "Yes, ma'am, I think that I have the general idea." There's a lot I would like to know and I would like to experience it for myself, she thought. When Anna told me all of this I wanted to know because I wanted to know about my baby. Now I would like to know what mating is like, and why the government won't let us do it. There must be a reason other than simply to control the woz.

"Maybe sometime I can watch and see how it's done," she said quietly.

VIII. The History Lesson

The next morning at breakfast Annette said, "I would like you to go with me to my cabin in the mountains for the weekend. Would you like that, Marla?"

"Yes ma'am, of course. That would please me very much."

"Take warm clothing; it's cold at that altitude."

Annette's cabin was a small wooden structure surrounded by a group of tall pine trees, various shrubs, and large stones scattered through the small area. No one lived there full time, but when Annette was in residence several U-100K Woz from a neighboring ranch would come over to take care of her needs. Inside the cabin was a small room at the entrance with a fireplace. There was also a kitchen, Annette's bedroom with a cleanliness/necessary room attached, two other bedrooms, a separate c/n room, and a small store room.

"This is where I come when I need absolute privacy or just to get away from it all. Sometimes Pat comes with me. "Do you know about Pat?" Annette asked.

"No. Jo told me that Pat had an apartment at your home, but that's all."

"Well, Pat is special. No questions now about Pat, so let it go at that for the moment."

You brought Pat up, Marla thought. I didn't, and I think I better not ask about Pat. Then Annette addressed one of the woz who had just arrived. "Orange, please build a fire in the fireplace. It's going to get cold."

Marla looked puzzled when hearing the name Orange, but Annette grinned. "I call her Orange as she always wears an orange colored shirt. I never can remember her real name. Sweet kid, though."

Soon it was dark and after supper Annette allowed Orange to go to bed in the bedroom in back of the house. Annette and Marla sat before the roaring pine fire drinking tea. Putting her cup down on a small table Annette said, "It's time to explain a bit about governments, especially our government and how we got this way."

"You're going to tell me the real way WOZ happened? It's different from what we have been taught all this time, yes?"

"Yes, and let me say that we do need a government to protect us and help us live together. Not 2100 years ago, but thousands and thousands of years ago we all lived in caves, males and females, and we ate whatever we could find. People argued over food and shelter and mates too. Oh, a mate is the person you have children with, you know, mate with."

"I understand."

"As we became more civilized we had to have some rules, so different forms of government were invented. First, let me tell you about kingdoms."

"Kingdoms?"

"Yes, a country ruled by a King if a male, or a Queen if a female. Thousands of years ago males were very strong physically and so they almost always ruled. Now in a kingdom the king's word was law."

Marla stared at the fire for a few moments, lost in thought. Then she looked at Annette and said, "So how did the king rule over everybody, and why didn't the people just get rid of him if he were a bad king?"

"Oh Marla, you are making it easy for me. It's because of the big lie. You see, some people rule over others because of superior strength. It's forced on them but sometimes it is by mental strength and they use what is sometimes called The Big Lie."

Frustrated a bit, Marla said, "So what's the big lie in a kingdom?"

"Marla, in a kingdom or anywhere else, it's telling something that gives someone power over others. A person or a government tells the people something that prevents them from thinking otherwise, so the people won't revolt. It controls the people because they dare not go against the big lie. The big lie, in any case is stupid, but it is told again and again and again, but speaking against it is not permitted. So eventually it becomes the truth, or rather what people believe is the truth."

"Maybe I am beginning to get it, maybe. Specifically, what was the big lie that kept kings in power?"

"The big lie was that they were appointed by God. Before you ask, God is the force that built the Earth, moon, and all of the stars. So if someone opposed the king, that person was really opposing God. And no one dared oppose God."

"Annette, why is all of this about government important?"

"Because, my dear Marla, the government of WOZ is ruled by one very big lie."

"You mean that males don't exist."

"Yes, and as a follow up lie, Myrna and the Upper-Uppers use that lie to keep control by telling another big lie, and that lie is that we live in a perfect world; everything is regulated and everybody is happy not having to make decisions."

Marla exhaled a bit forcefully then said, "But suppose people want to make their own decisions? Why does that harm the government?"

"For fear that someone's decision will lesson some official's power over them, I suppose. Marla, it's late and I'm tired, so I would like to quit talking now and go to bed."

Marla blinked her eyes a few times, shook her head, and then said quietly, "So would I."

Annette stood and stretched, and then as Marla slowly stood, she said, "Good. Marla, tomorrow we can go horseback riding early and then later I have some actual documents from the United States from the eighteenth through the twenty first centuries. We can look at them and this will help you understand where we were and how we got where we are."

"Good. I've enough to think about now."

"I guess."

I wonder what that rumbling noise is, thought Marla the next morning as she was waking up. Marla always loved the noises she heard when first awake: the birds, the wind, and the rain. Yes, that's it, it's raining. Oh, this means we won't go horseback riding now. But then she smiled inside as she thought when my First Mother, hey, I mean Anna, took me to a place when I was hardly able to walk. I remembered being strapped to that big white horse galloping around the track. Probably we were just walking slowly but Anna made me feel like I was racing other horses and winning, of course. Well, time to get up and learn more how we became the country of WOZ. I'm not sure that I am going to like this story, but let's see.

"I guess the rain takes care of the horseback riding," said Annette at breakfast. "However, it will give me a good opportunity to go over some documents from the past four centuries." She looked at Marla with a false guilty grin as she said, "I not supposed to have these papers which were destroyed." She laughed. "The big computer said that they were destroyed, but someone, no telling who it was," she said, pointing to herself, "Yes, someone just forgot to burn them, I guess."

After breakfast and sitting in front of the roaring fire again Annette said, "Let's see, where were we? Oh yes, I mentioned kingdoms where the king ruled because the public believed that God had appointed the king, and to go against the king was to be evil and go against God."

"How could they have believed that?"

"Well, Marla, woz believe that there is no such thing as a male, don't they?"

"It's easy to believe something when you are told that something again and again and no one ever tells you differently. How were we supposed to know, Annette?"

"Now let me tell you about a form of government called a republic. A republic is usually run by a group who have power given them by the people, although how much the public have to say about it varies. But the country belongs to the people of the country, not to a king. One form of republics, called democracy, is controlled by all of the people who have the say about who runs the country and what the laws are. That's what the United States was, a democracy."

"So someone was not the head of the country because she was the daughter of the leader."

"Correct, and the head of the country was called the President. There was also a Vice President, that's the person who took over if the President died. This is important to know. No one took the office of her parent unless she was voted on and won."

Annette stood and reaching a folder of papers, said, "Marla, here is a copy of a document from the year 1776."

Marla looked up. "Really, from that long ago?"

"Yes, and it is one of the most important documents ever written. You see, until that time, the United States was not a country, just territory owned and ruled by a kingdom far across the sea. The people of these states didn't like being owned by a king, especially since he was so far away and didn't pay attention to their needs and wishes. So people from all of the states, there were thirteen then, got together and decided to get rid of the king."

"Kill him?"

"No, just be free of him. No king or other country was going to own their country; they owned it and would run it themselves. So they all signed a document declaring that they were free. It's called the Declaration of Independence and here is a copy of it."

Annette then handed her copy to Marla and then said, "Read aloud this part."

"We hold these truths to be self-evident, that all men are created equal, that they are endowed by their Creator with certain unalienable rights that among these are: life, liberty, and the pursuit of happiness."

And then Marla said, "Men? Just men, not women?"

"Of course, women. In this case it meant mankind, humans, huz, but not animals. And this document was written by Thomas Jefferson, who later became President of the United States. Annette looked at Marla for a moment, a small tear starting to run down her cheek. "Isn't that a wonderful idea? First, that your life is your own, not owned by some king or some Upper-Upper. Now, Marla, let me ask you as a common wo, did you have life?"

"Not much, I guess."

"Well, you did have life. You had food, a place to sleep, a place to clean up. You had clothes, and medical care. What more could you ask? The country of WOZ gave you all of that. All you had to do was do your work, say the pledge, and mind your own business. What more could you ask?"

"I suppose so."

"All right, what about liberty? Did you have liberty?"

"Well, Annette, I wasn't locked up in prison, but I had to live where I was told. I had to get up when I was told. I had to do the work I was told. Now that I think about it, I really did not have much liberty."

"So then what about the pursuit of happiness? Could you do what made you happy?"

"No argument there. I could only have a baby if the government permitted it. Annette; many girls want to have babies. I was kept ignorant of how babies were made, so I didn't even know that mating and families existed. I was made into a bee making honey all day, and I didn't get much of it for myself. I couldn't pursue happiness because I was kept ignorant of what happiness was. Now that I think about it, Annette, the government stole my soul."

"Ah, Marla, you are seeing WOZ in a different light now, aren't you?"

Marla started to cry and through her tears said, "How did the first Myrna and her group kill the United States and imprison us?"

Annette put her hand on Marla's shoulder. "It's a sad story from what I have been able to piece together from certain documents and news clippings. Let's take a break on this stuff until after lunch, if you don't mind."

"I keep wondering what happened to all of the males. And I keep wondering why Myrna and her government didn't want the males around."

"It's quit raining. So why don't we take a brief walk around the place and I'll tell you what I know."

As they were walking through the forest, Annette said, "I'll tell you this while we're out here, mostly because it is not depressing. The Americans, that's what the people of the United States called themselves because the continent was called North America, were an energetic bunch. They started with bare land and built a country on it. Almost everyone lived in a house. People lived as families, that is, a female called mother, a male called the father, and their children. The mother and the father together were called parents, and the parents were responsible for the children, not the government. Parents kept them fed, warm, provided clothing, and loved them."

"That sounds wonderful, no dorm, but a real house, and parents to love you and protect you. What happened to all of this? Why would they give it up? It sounds like a perfect world."

"Marla, nothing is perfect; probably nothing will ever be perfect. Some families couldn't earn enough money to feed their children, and some people saw others earning or having more money and they did and this caused jealousy, anger, and greed. Some groups banded together to get more of what others had. Some put power and money ahead of the good of the United States. But basically for almost three centuries it worked well,"

"And then?

"Let's save this until after lunch and I can show you what happened. It didn't just happen over night. Briefly, some thought they could make the United States into the perfect country in a perfect world. Unfortunately, a perfect world is perfect for only the few at the top."

"Before we go in, I really do want to ask a question, even though I am not supposed to ask questions of someone with high rank. 'What would happen if MOTHER MYRNA knew you were telling me all of this?"

"You don't really want to know."

After lunch Annette told Orange that she could have the rest of the day off, "Just come back tomorrow morning." Orange thanked Annette and left. "I want to get out some papers and things that I have hidden, ones I want to show to you. If Orange were here, she might see what they were."

"You think that she would tell on us?"

"I think that anyone except Pat, Anna, and you would tell on me if Myrna or Cynthia, made the reward big enough."

Marla had been looking out the window, but she turned sharply toward Annette and then said, "You really think Sandy would tell on you, but Pat wouldn't?"

"When you meet Pat, you'll understand. But now I'll go get the things I want you to see. Why don't you sit down and rest yourself; it's going to be a tiring afternoon."

A few minutes later she returned with two boxes of papers and set them on the floor. "Now, let's see," she said.

"Oh yes, here's the first thing I want to show you and talk about."

Annette picked up an old fragile newspaper whose headline read, MILLIONS DEAD FROM NUCLEAR BOMBS. "I told you about the nuclear bomb, didn't I?"

"Yes, Annette. You said it was a massive fire ball."

"Yes, it was, but that was just the beginning. We don't know who used the first one, but then others went off until most of the Earth was ashes. Everyone died, everyone but us. It was just an accident that we were spared. The winds carrying the deadly dust were very high up in the sky and blew north of us. If they had blown over us, we would have been dead like the rest of the world. Even so, many of us got sick and died later."

"Annette, why did they have a war that kill almost everyone on Earth?"

"Greed and politics aside, for centuries the population of the world increased, and at an alarming rate. In the year 2000 there were about six billion people on Earth, but by 2050 there were about twenty billion people on Earth. Now to survive, we absolutely need two things which do not increase: land and water. The amount of land on the Earth did not increase, nor did the supply of water. So each country, each group wanted enough to survive and flourish. How did they get it? They got it the way huz always have; the strong took it from the weak. This is the cause of all wars in the history of civilization. Everyone on Earth died, except us, and we were in a miserable state.

"Is that when Myrna took over"

"It was our grandmother, Myrna. Yes, she was vice-president of the United States, but the President and all but a few of the military were killed. So then she became President."

"That, of course, was legal. Probably the only legal thing she ever did."

"What happened then, Annette?"

"She gathered her cabinet together. Oh, a cabinet, besides being furniture where you put stuff, is the group of officers who run various areas of the government. Well, half of the original cabinet were men and they had all gone with the President to see how the war was coming along. So they were all dead too. This gave Myrna an opportunity to fill those offices with her friends, all radical women, of course."

She reached into the box again and brought out a small notebook. "Here is a record of one of their meetings a few months later." Marla reached for the document and started to read:

Minutes of the Cabinet meeting.

The meeting was called to order at 10:05 a.m. by President Myrna Johnson. Lillian Goth reported that riots were getting more frequent and more violent. She asked President Myrna Johnson to prescribe specific remedies for this situation.

Myrna was in favor of proclaiming Martial Law in the country. Her request was overwhelmingly approved. She also asked that the Second Amendment of the constitution be suspended immediately.

Sara Higgins said that you can't suspend the constitution; you must amend it with approval of the states.

Myrna said that there are no states but ours and so we shall take the vote right now. Amending the constitution to prohibit the people from carrying arms was approved.

Sara Higgins said that was fine with her as long as every action is legal. She then mentioned that there are thousands of homeless and she thought that it would be a good idea to house everyone in old army barracks. The army wasn't using them any longer as 99% of the men are dead. All approved.

Then Sara suggested that we dispense with last names as they are the names of the evil men who caused this terrible war and are now dead. She said

we also don't need a male last name; we are sufficient alone. Approved.

Then Agnes of the Commerce Department said that we should go into secret session to determine what we can do about the large number of wounded army men who are not working. Approved.

"Annette, what was this second amendment to the constitution?"

"It said that the people have the right to bare arms; that means have the right to have guns. It was very important to the Founding Fathers as it means the citizens have the right and the power to stop an oppressive government."

"And what happened when their right to have guns was taken away?

Annette straightened up in her chair, frowned, and then said, "It was just as the Founding Fathers feared. Remember, the country was in a mess; war had devastated the people. There was no work for anyone unless that person was a known supporter of Myrna and her bunch.'

"How did Myrna's group keep people from working?"

"By cutting off food and supplies to businesses run by men and others they disliked. And then the only jobs were government jobs, and they certainly controlled those jobs."

"Why didn't the people riot?"

"Well, there were small riots, so then the higher ups said that only women living alone could have guns. Then they would raid houses, take away their guns, and if there was a male present they would arrest him. And he would never be seen again. The government was very afraid of the citizens having guns. They remembered when the colonies rebelled, the colonists all had guns for hunting, and they certainly knew how to use them."

"So what did the government tell the people about not having guns?"

"Well, it didn't pay to complain about it, but the government did say, "Why do you need guns? All of the men are dead or in prison. And everybody knows that men cause all of the trouble in the world."

Marla started to cry, but held back. "Annette, I think that I'm going to be sick. I just don't understand how this could have happened."

"It didn't all happen at once. And by the time the citizens realized how their country had been stolen from them, it was too late. And remember the people were starving and dying of radiation sickness. The government had all of the food and controlled the medical care."

"Annette, I was wondering where did the leaders of WOZ get the soldiers to force people to do these things. I thought that they were all dead."

"No. You see, the armed forces were about 30% female, but only the male soldiers were sent into battle. Well, they all died, but the female soldiers were here at home. And they were well armed too."

"So Myrna and her group controlled just about everything."

"Marla my dear, that was the beginning of WOZ, certainly the end of the United States, in fact and in spirit. These women wanted their version of a perfect world, and it did not include males."

"Why were they able to take complete control of the United States?

"From what I have read in all of the papers here in the box, politicians just got too greedy, sold out their country for money and power. So with so many groups grabbing what they could, it was easy to buy power, and these fanatical women played on the fears and hatred of males. The people were used to politicians paying no attention the people by stealing money, stealing votes, and not standing up for what was best for the United States. The people let them get away with anything and everything. Well, you get the crop you plant."

"What did they have against males, Annette?"

"From what I have read, several things; job competition, too much mating, not enough mating, being forced to mate with a brother, father, stranger, any number of things I guess. Maybe they just didn't want to compete against them and wanted their power."

"Gee, didn't they like mating? I think I would."

"Sometimes people just want power. These Woz also wanted a few males for themselves."

"For servants, Annette?"

"I guess you could call them that."

"Other than getting things you wouldn't otherwise have, what good is power?"

Annette thought for a moment, and then said, "You know, Marla, maybe it is the fear of death. If you are strong and have power, and others have no power, you see the weak, the powerless die. Maybe, just maybe, you think the powerless die, so if you have power you won't die. It's just a thought."

"I know that when I was a simple wo I didn't like Woz having power over me."

"Here is another document, and this one is very secret. It was written by an unknown observer at a secret meeting of Myrna and her pals:

I am not supposed to be recording this but I think it might save my neck sometime. Present are President Myrna and six members of her cabinet. I shall only identify them by number; Myrna is listed as #1.

#1: All right, what are we going to do with the men who are left?

#2: Get rid of them. Everyone knows that men cause all of the trouble in the world.

#3: Right. They all must go.

#1: But how shall we do it? Shall we just line them all up and shoot them?

#4: No, we can't do that?

#2: Why not?

#4: Because we don't have the power yet. Why don't we pass laws and charge only men with violations. People die in prison with no questions asked.

#1: Good idea. That will do for a start. Now any other ideas?

#5: What about denying them medical care? And we could poison the medications that only men take, like for prostate problems.

#1: Great idea. What about sending an expedition to the desolate country to see if anyone is still alive there. We could send thousands of men there and provide them with poisoned food. They would never come back to complain.

#2: But what about the wives and sweethearts and daughters of these men?

#1: The men would be heroes, but that's okay, they wouldn't be here.

#5: What about the orphaned boys?

#1: You know, I have been thinking about them. If we have a country of all females, how will be get our eggs fertilized? You know, we need a supply of sperm; we don't need the men, but we do need sperm, so why not keep some of the better young boys and young men for their sperm. We can just milk them for it. We need cows for milk, but we would never let a cow in our homes.

#3: I'm for all of this, just as long as it's legal.

#1: Don't be an idiot. We are the government; we say what's legal.

#4: Why don't we do away with the name United States. There are no states; there are women only. Let's call it The Women Only Zone, or WOZ, shall we?

#1: And I don't want to be called President Myrna. We are going to have a perfect world here. We are going to look out for all of our woz. Oh, I forgot to tell you that I proclaimed that all male nouns and pronouns are to be eliminated from the language. So we are woz, not women. Take the men out of the word and you get wo, plural woz.

#5: As we are going to have a perfect world for women, I mean woz, why not call Myrna, MOTHER MYRNA, all capital letters, because she is our mother, teacher, protector. We could make it the title of the head of state.

#1: Thank you. I accept. Now #4, I suggest that you form a secret committee to carry out the elimination of all males from WOZ, except for the sperm donors.

#3: I think that we must teach the young woz that males do not exist, never existed. Only a very few of the upper officials should know about males.

#4: You know, I am excited about our new perfect world. Just think, no more jealousies because some girl, I mean wo didn't get asked to the prom or didn't get to go to bed with some male. No sexual intercourse for the lower woz. It will save a lot of heartache. Of course, for those of us who want to and are strong enough to do it in secret, well, why not keep a few males for our own pleasures?"

#1: We can work out the details later. But now go to work; set the wheels in motion for our country of WOZ. #4, you are in charge of the cleansing committee. Remember, keep no notes.

"And that, Marla, should tell you a lot about how we now find ourselves in this..." Annette gave a cynical laugh... "Ha, perfect world."

"I just don't see how they could just go killing off their own citizens."

"Marla, things became too impersonal. People just became data in the government's computer. They weren't people, mothers, fathers, children, or anyone, just data. It's hard to kill someone you know, but it's easy to delete data.

"Incompetent government officials helped cause the death of the United States. And I don't want to blame it all on woz. We are all born pure and innocent, then the world happens to us. I believe, Marla, that males and females are both good and bad. Most males are good, some are not. Most Woz are good, some are not. It was not women in general who took over, just a few vicious, radical woz who used the terrible times to make their own perfect world."

"How did you learn about off of this from just two boxes of documents?"

"I brought only two boxes with me, but I have over two hundred more hidden at home. Marla, are you surprised that I feel this way as I am next in line after my older sister, Cynthia, to become MOTHER MYRNA? So if Myrna and Cynthia both died I would be head of the country of WOZ."

"I thought about that."

"Did you ever wonder how I got these boxes?"

"I have been so overwhelmed with what I have learned the past few days that I didn't get the chance to wonder. But how did you do it?"

"About ten years ago this was Myrna's house; she built herself a much bigger and fancier one. Cynthia didn't want this one, so I got it. One day I was looking around in a strange part of the house and ran across all of these boxes in a secret room. A month later I got a message from Myrna to destroy them and do it immediately."

"Obviously you didn't."

"According to the computer I did. The great thing about computers is that if you push a certain key and say something is deleted, it is not only deleted, it never existed."

"And then you started reading the things in the boxes."

"Before I knew about the boxes I had been a dedicated patriot of WOZ. No one ever questioned my loyalty to Myrna or the country. But as I read these documents, letters, and even a few novels from the past few centuries, I realized what had been done to the United States and civilization, and how horrible WOZ had been to everyone, especially young woz and males."

"I know how shocked I have been. Being so high up, Annette, I guess you are Upper Three, you must have been devastated."

"I was. I went around in a daze for months."

Annette paused a moment, gently wiping the tears from her eyes. "I wish I had lived when the United States was in its glory. But later, it was such a bad time it could easily have been any radical group that took over the United States. It could have been a radical religious group, a radical racial group, a radical political group, yes, it could have been any radical group that took over. But it was a radical group of woz that had the opportunity and seized it. Now we must correct that. If you are with me, it will be dangerous, but worth the effort and the pain. Are you with me?"

"All the way, Annette, all the way."

"Good. Now, I also brought a few novels for you to read."

"Novels?"

"Yes, stories written in the past two hundred years which will tell you a great deal about life, especially family life and the love between males and females. You should find how they were around each other very interesting."

"Do they talk about mating?"

"They do more than talk about it."

"Then I know I'll really like these stories."

81

"And, Marla, after you know a bit more about males, I shall introduce you to a few, ones that I think you would like."

Marla's eyes opened wide, her grin was from ear to ear, and she said, "Will they like me?" She paused a moment then continued, "Will they like me enough to consider mating with me?"

Annette tried to suppress her laughter and the tears that followed. But gradually she was able to say, "Will they ever!"

IX. Male Call

A few mornings later at Annette's home, after Sandy had left the breakfast table, Marla quietly said to Annette, "I read the second novel you gave me and I found it very interesting. So that is what life was like a hundred years ago?"

"I thought you might. You see, Marla, I wanted you to know how males and females got along then. I didn't want you to go up to some male and say, 'Hey, do you want to mate?'"

"Oh I won't now. Last night I was reading this one story and... here, let me read this part to you. I have a question about it."

Marla reached under her chair and brought out a book, found the page she wanted, and then looked up at Annette and said, "I think that this is about a male and a wo out on a date, if that's what you call it."

"Read it to me, Marla."

Marla opened the book and found the page she wanted. "All right, here goes:. I think the male is talking here."

"Want to get something to eat?" I asked her when we came out of the theater. What I really wanted was to be with her as long as I could.

"I really don't want anything, but if you do, I'll fix you something at my parents' house. I'm not going back to the dormitory; I'm going to spend the weekend at home," she said.

Marla put down the book and then looked at Annette. "Let's see if I understand this. I think I do, but this male and this female are on a date? Is that what it's called, a date? And she lives in a dormitory, but has two parents, right?"

"Yes, Marla, she's in college. Remember, I mentioned that young people often went away to college, but in public school, they lived with their parents. What else?"

"Oh, I think I understand going to get something to eat. They didn't go to the food room and were given packaged food."

"Right, read on."

"Let's see, oh yes, here it is:"

"When we arrived there we parked in front of her house and I was so happy to be with her alone with no one to stare at us. It was about midnight and we were sitting there in the car, her head against the back of the seat. I looked at her, thinking how beautiful she was. I used to be so shy I would plan how I was going to put my arm around a girl that I wanted to kiss, sometimes canceling out the idea because I was too nervous. But this night I decided that I was going to kiss her, even if I got slapped, even if she screamed, so I turned toward her, put my arm around her and kissed her thoroughly, not just a peck on the cheek. It was like nothing like I had ever experienced before, but the best part of it was that she threw her arms around me and kissed me back. I thought that she was never going to let go."

"You have questions about that?" said Annette.

"Well, is that the way it was, do you think?"

"Many times, and do you think it sounds true?"

"I hope so. Simply reading it I felt warm inside and wanted very much for some male to kiss me that much. And I do see what you meant when you told me not to just go up to a male and say, 'Shall we mate?' or something like that." After she thought about it for a few moments, she added, "Now, after that kiss, did they just go mate?"

"Probably not, especially in the twentieth century they got to know each other much better to see if they liked each other. And, Marla, let me explain a few terms to you about mating."

"Please do. This whole thing about males and females is a bit confusing."

"Okay, here we go. The word mating is... wait a minute, mating is not the word we want here. You see, Marla, first of all what you see dogs do, and humans did it too, is called sexual intercourse. Sometimes it is just called sex, but there are some vulgar terms for it too. Mating means having sex in order to produce a baby. If it's just for fun, it's called sex, rather having sex. If you asked a male if he wanted to mate with you, it usually meant did he want to marry you and have a baby with you."

"Annette, I'm lost here."

"I know. Marla, just file away these terms and gradually you'll understand it all."

"I'll try, but this whole sex thing sounds very interesting. I can hardly wait to find out all of this stuff for myself."

"When you're ready, my dear Marla, when you're ready."

"How do I get ready?"

"I think first I should show you some pictures of males. I have a college yearbook or two and they show males and females and the way they were together."

"Mating?"

"Oh, Marla, you're worse than a twentieth century teenager. And before you ask me what does that mean, I'll tell you it means that you're too eager."

"But, Annette, this is a whole new world to me."

"You have no idea," Annette said as she left to get a few more books. "And keep these books hidden, please."

A few minutes later she returned with a college yearbook under her arm. "Here, Marla, is a yearbook; that means it has pictures of the people in the graduating class and other classes. Open it up to the first few pages."

Pointing to a male about twenty-five years old, Annette said, "Here is a young male teacher. See, he is wearing a suit. Before you ask, a suit is a combination pants and coat, usually the same color. Sometimes, usually all of the time with a suit, a male would wear a tie, what we would call a scarf type thing around his neck."

"And look, Annette, these males have very little hair on their heads. Why is that?"

"It was just the style then, I guess. However, later in life many males lose their hair." Pointing to an older man, Annette went on, "See this is an older male and he has hair only on the sides."

"Yes, Annette, but I want to look at the young ones, can we turn some more pages so I can see lots of them?"

Annette handed the book to Marla as she said, "Here, you look though it at your own speed. You can tell me what you notice."

Marla turned the pages looking at every photo, smiling, and then moving on. Then she came to group photos. "Look, Annette, this male and this wo are standing close together and holding hands. Are they getting ready to mate? I mean are they getting ready for sex?"

Annette laughed. "I don't think so, at least not until dark. Having sex was not done in public. Now look at this male and wo sitting on the grass. He has his arm around her and she is smiling."

"Are they on a date?"

"Marla, males and woz spent a lot of time getting to know each other. They want to know if they are right for each other as they may want to get married."

"Married," said Marla, frowning. What is that?"

"It's a relationship when a male and a wo pledge to love and stay with each other the rest of their lives."

"Sounds great, but suppose they choose the wrong person, but I guess they don't, do they?"

"They date to find out if they are a match for each other, but maybe much of the time they're wrong."

A little smile made its way across Marla's face. "Well, nothing is perfect. So mating isn't all fun, huh?" Then suddenly she exclaimed, "Hey, look at the beautiful uniform that wo is wearing. I'd like one of those."

"It's called a dress and what a wo would wear to a party. Notice that she has flowers pinned on her. Probably her boyfriend gave them to her," said Annette.

"Boyfriend, her mate, I mean her male companion; what's the right term?"

"Boyfriend if they go somewhere together frequently, otherwise just a date. And look at the people in this photo, Marla. You see they are sitting down eating at a restaurant. And that wo standing next to them is serving their food. It's a common thing to do on a date."

Marla noticed a couple dancing and pointed to the picture. "What are they doing, mating, I mean having sex? Hey, do they do it with their clothes on?"

"No, my dear Marla, they are dancing, dancing to music. It's very romantic I think, and sexy too. Oh, and sex is almost always done with no clothes on."

"Wow, Annette, now I know I want to watch them mating, that is having sex."

"I'll bet you do."

Annette pointed to students in a classroom. "And here are some males and woz in class. Almost always woz and males went to school together, although there were a few males only schools and a few for woz only. Now turn some more pages. Turn to the sports section. You know, sports, playing games."

Marla turned to a page with photos of males playing basketball. "Hey, these are all males jumping around after that ball. And look, Annette, they are all in short pants. Let's look for more pictures like these."

Annette shook her head. "Well, I know one thing. I have got to let you meet some live males:

"Oh, good! When?"

"But, Marla, you have to control yourself. These males, the ones that I am going to let you meet, haven't met many woz, so restrain yourself. Remember your manners; when you meet a male and he tells you his name, you extend your right arm slightly and say, 'How do you do.'"

"How does he do what?"

"It's just an expression. Then he probably will extend his arm and take your hand gently, and then he'll probably say something like, '"Pleased to meet you,' or maybe just plain, 'Hello.'"

"Then we talk about mating?"

"No, no. If you like each other, you go somewhere and sit down, but not touching, not yet anyhow. Remember, you might end up marrying this guy, this male, and you don't want to get stuck with the wrong one, do you?"

"Well, no, but...."

"So you want to get to know him. Woz are not all alike, and males are not all alike, so play it cool. Besides, when you go on a date with a male, he pays for everything."

"Everything? I like that idea."

"It's sort of like the old idea that in marriage the males pays for everything and the wo takes care of the children, although many woz earn money too, and certainly males take care of the children too. But mostly it was that way."

Marla exhaled loudly. "Annette, enough. I've got to meet a male."

"All right, it's time you did. Just don't grab him and say, "Hey, let's mate."

Assuming a position she read about in one of the novels she was given, Marla leaned back in her chair, smiled slightly, extended her hand to an imaginary male, and said, "How do you do, Mr. Male? I'm Marla." Then after a moment to tease Annette, she added, "And I'm your dreams come true, big boy. Wanna mate?"

X. Pat

A week later on a cool but sunny, late afternoon
Annette and Marla arrived at Annette's cabin. Orange was
there and had prepared supper. When Marla noticed that
three places had been set she asked Annette, "Three? Who is
coming to eat with us?"

"You'll see, dear, you'll see."

Standing by the door and holding her coat, Orange said,
"Will there be anything else, ma'am?"

"No, everything looks fine. We can take care of
ourselves for a few days, Orange, so take some time off.
Let's see, this is Friday, so come back early Monday
morning and take care of things, please."

"Yes, ma'am, thank you, ma'am," she said as she left
and closed the door behind her.

Marla wondered about the slight smile on Orange's face
as she left. Did Orange know something she didn't? Of
course she did; she set three places for lunch and was invited
not to return until Monday. Invited not to return? That's a
strange expression for me to use.

Annette noticed the confusion showing on Marla's face
so she quietly said to Marla, "I should tell you a bit about
Orange. First of all, Orange is not her real name and I'm the
only one who knows that. Second, she is not a common wo;
she is U Ten K, and her job is to guard me. But I won't need
a guard for this weekend; I'm well protected."

Marla said nothing, simply stood there blinking her
eyes while waiting to find out what Annette was going to tell
her. She didn't have long to wait as an unusually tall wo
appeared at the hall from the bedrooms. This blond Wo,

wearing the epaulet of a U-10K, walked over to Annette, gave her a hug, then looked at Marla and smiled. "This is Pat," Annette said, looking at Pat and unable to hide her happiness.

Pat is the same rank that I am, Marla thought, so I can just greet her as a friend. "Hello, Pat, I'm Marla. I've heard of you but never met you." Pat simply smiled and nodded slightly. Marla waited to hear Pat speak, wondering why she only got a smile and a nod.

"Pat's special and doesn't say much," Annette said, and then taking Marla and Pat in arm, led them to the table set for lunch. "Let's eat; I'm starved."

"So am I," said Pat in a low, very quiet voice, as the three of them walked over to the table and sat down.

Wondering what was going on, wondering who Pat really was, wondering if Pat would speak to her, Marla sat down at the table. Turning to Pat, Marla said, "Do you have a sore throat?"

Pat looked at her and smiled. Then turning to Annette, Pat shrugged, and then waited for her to speak.

Annette started to laugh as she looked at Pat, and then looked at the completely lost Marla. Finally she looked directly at Pat and said, "Why don't you take off that stupid wig?"

Pat laughed a bit and using both hands in a hefty pull, removed the long haired, blond wig to reveal his short brown hair. He looked at Marla, who was absolutely in another world, and then said in his deep masculine voice, "How do you do, Marla? I'm Pat as in Patrick, not Patricia."

Marla sat paralyzed for a moment. Could it be? Could this be a male? Certainly didn't look like a wo, she thought. She could hear her heart beat: Bam, bam, bam! And then she started to shake, fighting hard to keep from passing out. After ten seconds of telling herself to calm down, Marla took a deep breath and started to say something. She didn't know what to say, staring at him in disbelief, choking every time she started to utter a word. Desperate to say something, a line from a British novel she had read a few days ago popped out. "Blimey, you're a big one, ain't you?" Composing herself a bit, she continued, "You're a male! And you don't look primitive to me. I've been had. We've all been had."

Annette could hardly control her laughter, bending forward and backward as she pointed to Pat and then to Marla. Pat tried not to make things any worse for Marla by being relaxed and hoping to calm her fears upon meeting her first male. After a moment, he extended his hand to her and said, "Marla. I'm really pleased to meet you."

Carefully Marla took his hand and then looked him over. "Oh my goodness, I have seen my first male, touched my first male, and I never thought I would ever meet one." Then looking at Annette, she said, "Don't worry, Annette, I'm not going to say it. But I do have a lot of questions to ask."

Pat leaned a bit toward Marla and quietly said, "You seem very uncomfortable sitting here with me. Would you like it if I were to put that wig back on?"

"Oh no, I want to study you; well, I mean I need to get used to talking to and looking at a male."

Annette leaned over to Marla and whispered into her ear, "Marla dear, he's mine and you can't see him naked. It's just not done. At least it won't be done here."

See a male naked? If that happened now, I know I would pass out, Marla thought. I'm going a million miles an hour, just touching his hand.

Annette backed away, and in a normal voice, said, "We shall arrange for you to meet and be comfortable with several males. Won't we, Pat?"

"Of course, and I know several guys you might like."

Marla's face brightened, her brows raised, her mouth opened slightly and she said, "When can I meet them?"

"When are you going back to the Starter Farm, Pat?" asked Annette.

"Tuesday, I think. I could probably bring one or 1 back here next weekend, just for the day, of course."

"See if you can bring several on Friday, on Saturday, and maybe on Sunday too," said Annette. Marla needs to meet a lot of males." Then to Marla, she said, "Honey, males are all different just as woz are all different. You need to be able tell them apart... personality wise, that is."

Marla turned to look out the window, but she wasn't seeing trees and sky; she was seeing males. She turned then to Pat, grinned as she said, "I'd like that. Yes, I would."

Annette loudly cleared her throat and conversation stopped. "Could we eat now? I'm starved," she said. "Marla, I know that you are excited, but males will still be around after we eat."

Her heart was beating slower now; things were going her way so she should be pleasant and not irritate Annette. "Yes, ma'am, should be say the pledge first?"

Annette poured herself a cup of coffee, looked up, looked at Pat, looked at Marla, and then said, "Screw the pledge; let's eat."

Marla was surprised to hear screw the pledge? Well, males can change even the most strict Woz, I guess.

After lunch Annette suggested that they go sit by the fireplace with its roaring fire and just talk a while. Pat stood and pulled Annette's chair out for her, then pulled out Marla's. "See dear, males, especially if they are gentlemen, will do these little courtesies for woz. You must allow them to do so and then smile and thank them. If we are going to build a two gender civilization, let's do it right."

Pat walked Annette over to the best chair facing the fire, then after holding her hand as she sat down, he gestured toward another chair and said to Marla, "Would you like to sit here, miss?"

"Mi~~ ~~ she said. "What's a miss?"

~~arried wo," said Annette. "Sit down, Marla,

?own and then Pat sat down between them. at shall we talk about?"

Annette said with certainty, "The weather, of course, what else?" She looked at Marla. "And, Marla, don't say mating."

"I wasn't going to, but why talk about the weather. We all know what it's like outside."

"It's just done, that's why," said Annette.

Pat spoke up and said quietly, "Marla, it's just a way of breaking the ice. That's means getting people to talk to each other and therefore get to know each other. It's called small talk."

"Okay, how do we do small talk?"

"One of us could start with, 'Nothing like a nice fire when it's raining outside,'" said Annette.

"I could add, 'Especially when you are sitting with a good-looking male,'" said Marla, turning toward Pat. "But there are other things to do."

Quickly Annette said, "Don't say it,"

"Annette, we could teach Marla to dance twentieth century style," said Pat. "That is, you and I could show her how they used to dance in the old United States. It would give her some alternative to talking about the weather."

Annette thought a moment, then stood and put her arms out ready to dance. "Pat, please put on our song and dance with me."

"All right, I'll put on the music and Marla can watch how we move and so forth. You explain it to her."

"Marla, I'll put my arms up like I showed you. Then Pat will come and stand facing me, take my right hand in his left hand, then put his other hand around my waist. I put my other hand on his shoulder." As she was speaking Pat approached her and took her hands as she had mentioned.

"Now look, Marla, Pat is standing there facing me but not close to me yet. But because we are lovers he will be pressing his body against mine when we dance. Understand?"

Marla's face lit up and she said, "Understand it? I love it! It's just like in the pictures we saw in that school yearbook. Yes, I like it!" Then quietly she added, "But I'll like it better if Pat were dancing with me. He will, won't he?"

Annette tilted her head and raised her brows. "Yes, he'll dance with you. But he won't dance close to you. Understand?"

"Yes, ma'am."

"All right then, Marla come stand like I did; Pat come and take her hands, but don't stand too close."

Marla jumped up and raised her hands waiting for Pat. Annette approached her and gently pushing Marla's hands down, said, "No. I think that we should start from the beginning. So, Marla, go sit back down. Pat, go ask Marla to dance with you."

Marla sat down and Pat nodded yes, and then standing in front of Marla, said, "Miss, would you do me the favor of dancing with me?"

"Yes!"

"No, Marla," said Annette, "You say, 'I'd love to,' and you say it calmly and smile at him."

Marla felt her heart beat running away again. She hoped that Pat couldn't hear it as he extended his hand to Marla. "Now, Marla, take his hand and he will help you up and escort you to the dance floor, which in this case is only two steps away."

"Oh, I like this." Then as Pat took her hands and stood facing her, not close, not far, she said, "Oh, I really like this!"

"Before I start the music, Pat, why don't you show her the old Box Step?" said Annette.

"Good idea," he said, then to Marla, he said, "Look, there are some simple ways to move your feet to music; it's better than just jumping around." Stepping away from her about six inches, he pointed to her feet. "Now watch and do what I say. Okay, here goes: 'Move your right foot back about eight inches, then move your left foot to the side of it."

Marla moved her feet as he had said, then Pat went on, "Now sort of slide your right foot sideways until it touches your left."

"Good, Marla, now we'll do it in reverse. I think that you'll catch on faster if you watch Annette and me do it."

"I'm good at watching, I am," said Marla as Annette gently pushed her way to take Pat's hands.

"Let's show her how it's done," she said, snuggling close to him. He smiled as they started to move and then looking at Marla counted, "1, 2, 3, 4," several times.

Their romantic closeness was not lost on Marla. She watched politely and saying nothing. Going a hundred miles per hour inside, she turned to them and started to say something. But Annette noticed Marla was about to speak and quickly said, "Marla, don't say it."

"Say what, Annette?"

"What you usually have said when you see a male and a wo together."

Marla shook her head no and then said, "Oh, that. No, I was just going to ask if I could try dancing with Pat now."

Although Annette knew that the whole purpose of this weekend was to acquaint Marla with a male, she couldn't help being a bit uneasy watching Pat with a beautiful. young Wo. "All right, I guess it's best to learn by doing. We'll dance a few more minutes, then I'll put the food Orange left for us on the table, then we can eat."

"Oh, thank you, Annette." said Marla.

As Annette and Pat stopped dancing and backed away from each other, Marla, all smiles, came forward and took Pat's hands, Annette watched them and then quietly said to Pat, "Not too close now."

Go away, Annette, Marla thought. Let Pat push against me. But I guess that it's better not close. I don't think I could stand pushing against each other right now.

Walking toward the kitchen Annette wondered why she was getting upset seeing Pat dance with Marla. I shouldn't be, she thought, Marla has just met and now dancing with her first male. I remember when I met my first male; I was stunned. I remember that it was when I walked into Myrna's bedroom and there they were, sitting on her bed. I was thirteen and she was sixteen. I ran and told my mother and she said, "Forget it, it's just Sally wearing a costume." It wasn't Sally, so I sneaked back and watched them, shall we say... mate.

As Annette served food from the stove onto the plates she stopped for a moment and then thought why am I doing this? I'm U-3, not some wo from a dormitory. Well, I shouldn't complain; I do believe in democracy, don't I? But still, Marla should be getting lunch ready, not me.

At this moment Marla, in a happy, excited voice, said, "Oh, Pat, this is wonderful. I never dreamed that dancing with a male would be so thrilling."

Then from the kitchen came, "Okay, it's time to eat, so come and get it," and she said it with authority.

Pat immediately stopped, lowered the arm he had around Marla and let go of her hand. Noticing her disappointment at stopping, he said, "I think you'll become a good dancer, Marla, but let's eat now."

Wanting to keep on dancing, wanting to have Pat hold her, but not wanting to distress Annette, Marla, all smiles, walked the eight feet to the table and sat down.

Dinner was simple; a glass of red wine, vegetable with beef soup, fresh fruit, apple pie, and coffee. During supper, Annette said, "Marla, how do you like not only talking to a male but actually dancing with a male?"

I don't want them to know how excited I am. Building up in me is a huge bubble of exploding stars. I must calm down. "Well, it's more fun than the little dances we used to do with other woz." Then looking directly at Pat, she went on, "I never knew there were males, and when I found out I never thought that I would ever meet one, talk to one, dance with one. Oh my gosh, I didn't know how very little I knew about life."

"That was on purpose, my dear, we have to keep the woz ignorant and fearful. Fear and ignorance is the way the few control the many. That's the function of a dictatorship." said Annette. But the function of a democracy is to educate the people. After all, it is the people who run a democracy."

"I'd like to meet some more of the people," said Marla. "Especially the male ones."

Annette said nothing for a few moments, then turned to Pat and said, "Honey, I would like for you to leave early tomorrow morning and go to the farm and bring back several males you think would be good for Marla to meet."

"I can do that. I should be back sometime in the early afternoon."

Annette thought for a moment and then said, "You know, Pat, if you don't get back until after noon, then there won't be much time for Marla to meet these males unless they spend the night here and it is not a good idea for them to be away from the farm overnight.:

"So what do you suggest?"

"Well, I could call Margo at the farm and have two males dropped off here on the Saturday trip to the vegetable farm. Then they could be picked up late in the day and returned to the farm."

"Good idea," said Pat. "That would give them a whole day here and save me a trip."

"So do you have any special males there I should ask for?"

"You could ask for Karen and Molly"

"Hey," said Marla. "I thought you were going to ask for two males."

Pat turned to Marla and smiled. "That's their wo names. Their real names are Ken and Michael. Every male at this farm has both a male and a female name. There is a definite reason for that."

Puzzled, Marla tilted her head a bit and then said, "Why two names?"

Annette cleared her throat a bit, and then in a definite tone said, "Marla, these males are from one of our starter farms. This one is under my complete control, so to hide what I am doing there it is necessary to give the males two names. Most starter farms don't even allow males to have a name, just a number. We give them two names for their protection and for our protection as well, mostly for ours. Tomorrow I shall tell you about starter farms and how this one is different."

Then Annette looked at Pat and faked a yawn. "All right, we can do more dancing tomorrow. But right now I think that I would like to go to bed."

Pat stood, extended his hand to Annette and then said, "Good idea. Marla, will you excuse us?"

Marla started to say, "Are you going to...."

"Maybe," said Annette, "But you may not watch."

Marla stood and then started for her bedroom. "All right." Then turning to Pat, she said, "You really do need to get some company for me."

Lying in her bed, staring at the ceiling, but seeing only Pat and feeling his hand on hers, she reached for her other pillow and hugged it. I wonder how this is the way it would feel to dance close with him, or any other male, she thought. I never dreamed that there was a world like this. And those poor woz, they don't know what there is to life, what the pursuit of happiness really means. I am just now starting to come out of the darkness. It's like I am just now starting to be born, born into the real world.

XI. Ken

It was April; it was seven in the morning at Annette's cabin in the mountains. It was cold outside and Marla knew it as she woke up. She could feel the cold sneaking into her bed so she pulled the covers over her head. Fine, but it didn't shut out the noise of someone knocking on her bedroom door. "Marla, Marla, time to get up."

Marla groaned quietly. It was Annette and Marla remembered that they had planned to go for an early morning walk. Oh, and I am so comfortable, she thought, why doesn't she just go away? Marla knew why; Annette is U-3 and Annette does what Annette wants and everyone else does what Annette wants.. She stuck her head out of the covers long enough to say, "Yes, Annette, I'm getting up."

"Good. It's warm out here; there's a fire in the fireplace."

"I'll be out in a few minutes," came a voice from the bedroom.

"Fine. Pat is outside cutting up some wood."

Marla groaned to herself as she thought someone is always telling me to get up or to go to bed. Well, might as well face the cold. Oh, my goodness, I just remembered that two males are coming here late this morning.. Well, that's worth getting up for.

A few minutes later Marla emerged into the main room of the cabin. Yes, there was a fire in the fireplace and sitting by it on the old upholstered chair was Annette. "Well, I'm happy to see you're among the living. So grab yourself a pastry, some scrambled eggs, some juice, whatever, and a cup of coffee and sit and talk to me a few minutes."

As Marla started for the kitchen she said, "What time will our visitors be here?"

"What visitors do you mean?"

Marla turned and with a quizzical frown said, "What visitors? The males from the farm."

"I know who you meant, Marla. I just said, 'What visitors?' to wake you up."

"It certainly did," Marla said and sat down across from Annette. "When will they get here?"

"In a few hours, so you have time to fix yourself up. Maybe you had better do that as soon as you finish breakfast, because before they get here I want to talk to you a little bit about Starter Farms."

"All right, I'll try to look my best. In the words of someone named Andy Hardy, 'I'll wow 'em.'"

"Where did you learn about Andy Hardy?"

"One of your old books on movies."

Forty minutes later Marla was back before the fireplace and standing at attention, waiting to see if Annette approved her appearance. "Well, Marla, I see that your auburn hair has every single hair in place, your uniform is spotless." Annette paused for a moment and then added, "And you look beautiful."

Marla smiled and turned around once to show off before Annette. "Thank you ma'am, I aim to please."

"You certainly do. I hope I don't have to chain these two males to the wall when they see you."

Marla turned quickly and stared at her. "Really, you would chain them to the wall?"

"I'm just teasing you." Pointing to the chair next to hers, Annette said, "Now sit down for a minute, I need to talk to you about these males and the different starter farms."

"I wish you wouldn't tease me about seeing males. I'm nervous enough right now," said Marla with a slight frown.

Annette continued, "First, let me tell you about the standard starter farm. In the regulation starter farm there are usually forty to fifty males and they range in age from sixteen to thirty. At the age of thirty or sooner if their sperm quantity or quality diminishes, they are then castrated completely if they are healthy. Then they are given female hormone injections, their breasts grow and they are given female names. In time they look just like woz. Sometimes they are called noz. Anyway, they are used for heavy work as long as they are healthy."

"But suppose they're not healthy?"

"Then unfortunately, the unhealthy ones are eliminated."

Marla frowned. "Eliminated? You mean killed?"

"Yes, but anyone who is useless to the government is eliminated. Our regular health plans have death panels to say who lives and who doesn't."

"That's cruel." Marla clenched her fists and tears started to run down her cheeks. "And it's against the constitution, too!"

"Maybe it's against the constitution of the United States, but not of WOZ. But that doesn't happen very often even in a regulation starter farm, never in the ones I run. Now these male donors in the three standard starter farm are fed well; they have to be in order to keep their sperm count high. They are given names, any name, taught to print their own names, but taught little else. Most of the day they work in the fields; starter farms are also regular farms and grow food. And they play games, such as basketball, baseball, and they run a lot. Physical activity keeps them healthy. They don't know about sex; they are told that sperm is poison and is taken from them to keep them healthy."

"That's terrible; their souls are being stolen."

"Yes, but they seem happy."

"Like the simple woz seem happy, but aren't."

Annette reached out and placed her hand on Marla's arm. "Dear, I agree with you and the two starter farms that I control are not that way at all."

"I should know you wouldn't be cruel."

"There are five starter farms, but in my two, as I mentioned before, each male has a male name, and then for protection a female name. I have placed at these starter farms many of the books I found, and they are encouraged to learn science, math, and history of the United States and the World. And my guys know about sex. I have heard that some have had sexual intercourse with some of the woz that work there. Officially, I don't know about it."

"Oh, my goodness, Annette, what would happen if you get caught running a starter farm this way?"

"My darling sister, Myrna, could have me eliminated. But she won't ever find out until it is too late. I have friends and sister conspirators everywhere. I have it arranged so that all of them are too deeply involved to talk about our little secret."

"Including me."

"Yes, including you. However, I want you to know for your own protection that your record shows that you are just an ignorant servant. Remember, Marla, you know nothing, get it?"

"Yes, I've got it."

"Okay, so much for starter farms, now listen to me about the males you are about to meet. They are donors, you understand, donors. But they are educated, decent guys, so just talk to them, see if you like them, or maybe you'll like one better than the other. My plan to establish the family as the power unit in the country depends upon woz and guys learning about each other and getting together."

Marla grinned. "I'll keep that in mind; I really will."

A few moments later they heard a truck driving into the yard. Marla rushed to the window to see what was going on, specifically to see if the males were arriving. She noticed two rather large woz getting out of the truck. "Oh, it's just a couple of woz," she said, not able to show her disappointment. But as they approached the house Marla's voice let out a squeal of delight, "They're males! Yes, they are males wearing wigs."

Without any encouragement she rushed to the old wooden door and opened it all the way. "Come in, come in," she said without hesitation, as she held the door open with one hand and extended her arm toward the fireplace with the other.

Pat approached them, smiled a bit and said, "Okay, guys, take off the wigs. You can cease to be Karen and Molly and be Ken and Michael now." They both pulled off their wigs and stood facing Marla and Pat, looking around the house, but mostly looking at Marla. Pat gestured toward the taller one and then said, "Marla, this light brown haired guy is Ken."

Ken stepped a few inches toward her, extended his arm somewhat and then said, "How do you do, Marla."

"Pleased to meet you," she said as she extended her arm and they shook hands briefly. Marla was happy that she could say it without trembling.

Gesturing toward the male slightly shorter than Ken but with dark brown hair, Pat said, "This is Michael."

Marla stepped forward and without hesitation, extended her arm and said, "How are you, Michael?" Ah, this is getting easier.

Michael took her hand and smiled without saying anything. Pat stepped toward them and said, "Except for me, you two are the first males Marla has ever met. Keep that in mind today, guys."

Ken and Michael looked at Marla and then glanced at each other, wondering what today would be like. Marla studied both of them, one then the other and then said, "I am really so happy to meet you." Then, as though she suddenly had a brilliant idea, she said, "Hey, wanna m..." then looking at Annette and laughing, continued, "Want to move over by the fireplace?" There, Annette! Marla thought, that'll pay you back for teasing me.

"Yes, let's all sit down and talk a while," said Annette. "Pat, could you get some coffee for everyone, please."

"Of course, coming right up."

Wondering what the day would be like, wondering what Ken and Michael thought of her, wondering which one she would like the most, if either, Marla said, "Guys, sit down next to me so we can talk. I really want to know about males and about the two of you. So, Ken, tell me about yourself. What do you do?"

He smiled slightly as he quietly said, "You mean besides what you know we do, duty wise?"

"I sort of know what your duty is, so tell me what else you do, and what you are like otherwise."

"Well, I guess I work in the field a lot, cutting weeds and that sort of thing."

"Ken, tell Marla about your music," said Pat. "Marla, Annette found some music books and from them Ken learned to read music. We found a piano in an old house, brought it out to the farm and he learned to play it."

"You learned to play it? That's great. I've only heard and seen a piano once, but I liked it very much. That awful war took so much away from us, didn't it?"

"What war was that?" said Michael.

"Michael isn't much for history," said Ken.

Realizing that Michael is as ignorant of the world as she once was, Marla decided to change the subject. "So what do you like?" said Marla.

Michael sat quietly for a few moments and then slowly said, "Oh, I like to find pieces of wood and make things out of them."

"Yes, Marla, you should see the really great birds and little animals he carves out of just wood scraps," said Ken.

"What's the farm really like?"

"I guess it's like any other farm, Marla," said Ken. "We have pigs, cows, a few dogs, and a lot of flat ground where we grow corn, carrots, and other stuff," said Ken.

"I've never been to a farm. But if I could ever go out there you could play some music for me and then Michael could show me the things he has carved."

104

"Eventually," said Annette, "I want to take you to a regular farm and then one of my special farms so you can see what I'm trying to do. That's eventually, not now."

Marla knew she meant starter farms, but to save any embarrassment she just said farms.

"Michael, did you bring any of your carvings with you today?" said Annette.

"Yes, ma'am, I have the carving of a little bird that I did. Should I get it? It's in my coat pocket."

Annette nodded yes and he walked to the rack where he had hung his brown cloth coat. He smiled as he reached into his pocket and took out a wood carving about four inches long of a bluebird perched on a twig. Marla noticed it as soon as it peeked out of his pocket and in a loud voice she screamed, "It's wonderful, it's wonderful, Michael. Bring it closer so I can hold it. Is it all right for me to touch it?"

Michael smiled and handed the carving to her.

"Oh, what a cute little birdie," she said as she held it close to her face and kissed it. "Oh, it's so sweet. I wish I could make something like this. You are so talented; I wish I were."

"And Michael sings too," said Pat.

"I brought some written music to show Marla what it looks like," said Ken. "You know, how notes are written, so she could learn to read music. She could learn some songs and how to sing them".

Breathing easier now that an ice breaker was in progress, Annette said, "Pat, you have your guitar here; why don't you get it? We could all read the music and have a go at singing together." Then turning to Ken, she said, "Why don't you get out the music you brought. Give Marla an idea of how to read the notes; I think a brief explanation will do for now."

Ken looked at Marla and smiling, went to the coat rack and got some music rolled up and in one pocket. He returned to the group by the fireplace, pulled his chair next to Marla's, smiled as he said, "Marla, this is written music."

Pointing to the five lines written on the paper and the notes arranged on and in between the lines, he said, "This tell how high the notes are,"

"How high?"

"Yes, high like this," he said as he sang the C scale."

"Oh, I understand; the higher on the lines, the higher you sing it. What about the shape of the notes, some are filled in, and some of them have some sort of poles attached?"

"Oh, that tells how long you sing them. We'll do a song and you'll catch on right away."

Just then Pat entered the room carrying his guitar. "Let's try a song," he said. "I'll play it through once; Michael can sing it and you can follow. Then we can all sing it." Pat then walked to behind Marla and Ken's chairs. "Okay, I can read the music over your heads. Ready, Michael?"

"Yes, sir, I'm ready. I know this song, so I don't have to read it."

"Good," said Pat. "Here's the first note so we can sing in the same key." And with that he struck the first chord on the guitar and sang, "I came from Alabama with a banjo on my knee, I'm going to Louisiana, my true love for to see."

Everybody applauded, and then Marla said, "Wait a minute, what's a banjo?"

Annette and the males laughed as Pat calmly said, "It's an instrument very much like this guitar."

"This song was written by Stephen Foster in the year 1847," said Ken.

Marla sat up straight in her chair. "That long ago?"

"People sang a lot then," said Pat.

I've got it," said Ken.. "Let's all sing it."

After singing it through four times, Marla said, "Yes, that's great fun. But I think I'd rather dance if we could,

right, Pat and I will dance and you can dance with
or Michael."

Marla jumped up and turning to Michael said, "Dance with me."

Annette looked at Marla. "Marla, it is customary for woz to be asked to dance."

"Well maybe, Annette, but I never got anything unless I asked for it. So may I ask Michael to dance with me?"

Annette turned toward Michael. "Is it your wish to dance with Marla?"

Michael seemed uncomfortable and lowered his head a bit. "I don't know how to dance with a Wo. Maybe Marla could teach me though. Is there any special way to ask her to dance?"

All smiles, Marla turned to him and said, "Yes, you say, 'Marla, may I have this dance?'"

"All right, 'Marla, may I have this dance?'"

"You bet you can."

"No, no, no," said Annette. "Be polite, say, 'I'd love to dance with you.'"

Sitting up straight and facing Michael with a sarcastic smile, Marla said, 'I would be honored to dance with you,' then turning to Annette, said, "That's okay now?"

Annette smiled as Marla stood, held out her hands to Michael. The music started and they held hands as Michael put his arm around her, but held her quite far away, and even at this distance, he seemed worried she was too close. After all, he thought, I've never even touched a wo, much less danced with her.

Escaping into her dreams, feeling his arm around her, trying to keep the sound of her heart beat from drowning out the music, Marla was not in that room; Marla was not in that cabin, nor anywhere on Earth. Marla was in the clouds.

Michael was aware of something stirring below his waist. He felt uncomfortable and was afraid that the poison that older wo removed from his body every week had increased out of control. So suddenly he stopped dancing, let go of Marla's hand and said to Ken, "You take over; I think I'd better rest a minute."

"What's the matter, Michael, don't you feel well?" said Ken.

Pat, who had observed everything, leaned close to Annette and whispered something in her ear and she laughed. Pat put his hand on Michael's shoulder and then said, "Sit down and take it easy. These things take care of themselves."

Embarrassed, Michael grabbed his coat from back of his chair, then holding it in front of him, sat down and held it in his lap. Ken stood and walked toward Marla who said, "Michael, I'm really sorry you don't feel well. I hope it's nothing serious." Ken and Pat suppressed a laugh.

To divert attention from Michael, Ken looked directly at Marla and then said in a high spirited voice, "Come on, Marla, let's dance." Then he stopped quickly, remembered his manners and quietly said, "I'm sorry, Marla, may I have this dance with you?"

Marla looked at Michael sitting near her and holding his coat in his lap, so dejected and embarrassed. But she had no idea what the fuss with Michael was all about but answered, "I'd love to."

As Ken put his arm around Marla and they started to dance, Michael left the room. Puzzled, Marla asked Ken, "What is really wrong with Michael?"

Ken blushed but said, "You know what we do out there, don't you?"

"Yes, of course."

"Well, when a male donor is very young he is told that he has a certain poison in his body and there is only one way to get it out, so..."

"Oh, I understand."

"Michael still believes that and so...uh, well, dancing with you made him excited and he thought the poison was going to leak out. Say, you're a pretty good dancer, Marla."

"Oh, that poor kid, no wonder he quit dancing with me so suddenly. What can I do to help him?"

"Probably nothing, at least not here and not now. It's probably best to not mention it, I guess."

"Okay, I won't. Wait, you mean to tell me that he doesn't really know why he is there?"

"He thinks he is just a farm worker and hasn't yet realized how he is being used."

"But you do."

"Yes."

"Do you understand chromosomes and sex?"

"Yes, again."

"So maybe you should explain what's really going on to Michael, you think?"

Still dancing, but silent, Ken thought about what Marla had suggested and then said, "Yes, I guess I should explain it all to him. After all, he is eighteen now."

"Ken, the only way woz and males are going to get together is for everyone to know the truth about conceiving a baby. But just about everyone has to know the truth and stop accepting the big lie we are fed day and night."

"But we are too few right now. Let's not talk about it now. We're dancing and let's just enjoy it."

"Yes, Ken, we are too few right now, but we won't always be too few if we spread the word."

Ken thought about it for a moment and then said, "Marla, I would do it for you."

No one was watching, and she couldn't resist a second longer, so she kissed him quickly on the cheek. "And I would do it for you."

Ken looked around and Michael was still out of the room, Pat and Annette were busy in the kitchen. Now or never, he thought and pulled her closer and whispered, "Oh, Marla, I could die for moments like this. Until I saw you, I lived only because it is our nature to survive."

Marla briefly pulled him even closer and answered, "I love your being close to me, but we'd better not be this close. If Annette sees us she might not let us dance together again. I would be devastated if she wouldn't let me dance with you."

"All right," he said as he backed off a bit. "Now I don't want to go back to only existing."

Marla, overwhelmed with meeting real males, touching them, having them touch and hold her, couldn't pretend to dance with her feelings so unserved. Tears flowing, she ran into her bedroom and fell across the bed. Annette observed this, looked at Ken, her expression asking, "What's wrong?"

"I don't know," he answered as Annette rapidly walked to Marla's room, knocked briefly, and then entered and closed the door behind her.

She bent over the crying Marla and said, "What's wrong, dear?"

Trying to stop her tears enough to answer, trying to understand what was wrong, trying to not appear so weak, Marla said, "I don't know." Wiping her eyes again and trying to smile, she said, "But I do know Michael and Ken are wonderful. And I do know I want them." Then sitting up, she frowned as she said in anger, "And I do know that I hate that Myrna and her bunch for cheating woz and males out of their rightful happiness with each other."

Annette immediately put her finger to her lips as she said, "Shhhhh. Remember all walls have ears. Of course you hate Myrna and the Myrnas before her. They steal our souls."

Marla gradually calmed down enough to say, "Annette, we must get rid of them. We must, and I'll help even if she eliminates me." I shall never be a passive little common wo again.

Quietly Annette said, "It will come to pass, Marla. It will come to pass."

Wiping the tears from her eyes, Marla looked up at Annette as she said, "I hope so, Annette. I hope so because I think that I'm in love with Ken. I want him."

"You may be in love with Ken; you may be only in love with having a male. There are many of them and you have only met three. Be careful whom you love."

Still drying her eyes, Marla said, "Is there something bad about Ken that you're not telling me, something I should know?"

"Pat told me that Ken was a good guy. I know nothing bad about him. I'm only saying don't make up your mind until you meet more males."

"All right, I am certainly willing to meet other males, but let me dance a while with Ken today, please. I have feelings about him that I don't have about Michael, feelings I don't understand."

Annette stood and started toward the door and then turned and said, "Tomorrow we shall have two more male donors for you to meet. They are from another farm I control. Now Ken is nice but there are about three hundred males and they are all different. So don't make up your mind yet."

Marla pushed herself off of the bed, walked over to a mirror and started brushing her hair. "All right, I won't make up my mind yet, but I doubt I'll want anyone else, just Ken."

At the doorway into the hall Annette paused a moment and then turned and said, "We are going to have lunch in a few minutes. Then you should have a few hours to be with Ken and Michael."

"Thank you, Annette. Thank you for everything."

Annette was partly in the hallway as she leaned back into the bedroom and said, "Oh, by the way, Marla, do you think Ken is fond of you?"

Marla smiled. "To quote something from one of the novels you gave me, 'He's nuts about me.'"

Annette smiled as she closed Marla's door and started for the kitchen. Then she heard the hum that meant someone was calling her. Touching her left eyelid, she heard, "Annette, this is Myrna."

Touching her right eyelid, Annette said, "Hello, sister, dear. What a pleasant surprise to hear from you, MOTHER MYRNA."

"Knock it off, Annette, I'm in a rush and don't have time for pleasantries. Can you be at my country house for lunch tomorrow?"

"Yes, of course."

XII. Myrna

In the center of five acres of flowering bushes and low shade trees, all surrounded by forty acres of pine trees was MOTHER MYRA'S little country house, a duplicate of the former White House of the United States in Washington D.C. As she climbed the steps to the elegant front door, Annette couldn't help but be impressed with the splendor and power this building represented. Nearing the end of the steps she looked up and there was MOTHER MYRNA waiting for her.

"Myrna," Annette called, "It's so nice to see you again." Neither Annette nor her sister, Cynthia ever called her MOTHER MYRNA. After all, it was just a title and the first born daughter was always named Myrna. It wasn't only that she was almost six feet tall; it wasn't only that she was the absolute ruler of WOZ; it wasn't only that others were certain she could look at them and know what they were thinking. It was every auburn hair in exactly the right place. It was that her every act, breath, head and eye movements said, "You must obey me."

At the front door Annette and Myrna put their arms around each other and kissed each other on the cheek. "I'm so pleased that you could come visit me," said Myrna.

"It's always a pleasure to be invited to have lunch with you, Myrna. Will Cynthia be coming too?"

"I'm afraid she couldn't make it today," Myrna said in a normal voice. But as they went inside, Myrna in a subdued tone said, "Why spoil a nice sisterly get-together? Even a little bit of Cynthia is much too much."

"Well, I'm delighted to be here, my dear Myrna. How are you? You look a bit tired. Have you been working too hard?"

"Oh, I'm all right, but let's do go eat. I'm starved," said Myrna and gestured toward the foyer and toward the large dining room.

"I'm sorry you're tired, but we do appreciate all the work you do," said Annette as they entered the large formal dining room. At the end of the very long lavishly carved table two places were set with fine china and sterling silver tableware. A wo stood behind each chair to seat Myrna and Annette. As they sat down Myrna said, "Annette, let's eat now and talk later. We do have much to talk about, but as I said before, I'm starved."

While Myrna and Annette were eating their light lunch, Annette noticed that Myrna seemed to have aged five years since they saw each other three months ago at Myrna's birthday party. Cynthia was almost exactly one year older than Annette and two years younger than Myrna. So, thought Annette, Myrna is fifty-six, but she looks sixty-six. I wonder why. "You seem tired, Myrna; do you feel all right?"

Myrna appeared not to hear her for a moment or two, then came to life and said, "Am I tired? You know, President Lincoln of the old United States is supposed to have said during the Civil War, 'I am the tiredest man that ever lived.' I feel the same way"

Annette moved a little closer to her and said, "Why is that; are you ill?"

"I don't think so. I am just concerned about WOZ. So many things are not going well and I can't seem to figure out why. That's one of the reasons I asked you to come and talk to me today."

Annette smiled as she said, "Anything I can do to help, I'll be glad to do. Your job must be a great burden for you."

A thin notebook of regular letter sized papers was sitting opposite Myrna and as she reached for them she looked at Annette and said, "Here are some reports I printed out to show you and see if you can help me make some sense of what's happening here."

Annette sat up straight in her chair as Myrna opened the notebook, took out the top paper and placed it between them. "Annette, when our grandmother was Vice President of the United States the population was about 350 million. That was before the nuclear war, of course. Now the war took about 90% of the population in the first five years. That would have left us with about thirty-one million. Of course radiation sickness kept killing people year after year, and then grandmother's people eliminated so many of the primitives."

Annette interrupted with, "I really don't like to think about the elimination of the...primitives."

"We didn't live then, Annette, so we can't really judge what they did. But we do have to deal with the reality of it."

Myrna reached for another paper and placing it before Annette, said, "Here is the death rate for the past fifty years. Now, of course, the death rate at first was simply estimated. Anyhow, look at this."

Annette looked at the paper and noticed the death rate starting in 2040: Notice the huge increase due to the war and then our slow recovery," said Myrna.

Year   Death Rate/100,000

Year	Death Rate/100,000
2040:	719 per 100,000
2050:	90,000 per 100,000 (90%)
2060:	35,000 per 100,000 (35%)
2070:	19,000 per 100,000
2080:	1,523 per 100,000
2090:	985 per 100,000
2100:	805 per 100,000 (00.805%)

As Annette looked at the report Myrna remarked, "Now the figures for the years 2050 to 2070 were just estimates, but I think they were pretty accurate. Notice the effect of radiation sickness and the elimination of males. Let's call them what they are: males. We can't use that term outside this room, of course. This story about them being primitives is getting more and more difficult to maintain."

"Possibly the number of males who simply disappeared is not included in these figures either," said Annette.

"That could be," said Myrna. "But I am concerned with our population in general today, specifically our need to increase our population. You know, Annette, the devastated land surrounding WOZ is gradually becoming safer and some crops and manufacturing could happen there. I want to make certain that we have enough woz to take it over."

"Myrna, I need something to drink, but I know you don't want any woz to come in here, so would you mind if I help myself for a second to some ice water?"

"Certainly, help yourself. As soon as we finish this dreadful business, I have a few bottles of real wine. There are only about a thousand bottles of pre-war wine left. Mostly we have some of that ghastly stuff we make in the southern hills."

Annette left the table and walked to a hand carved ebony cabinet on which was a bowl of ice and a silver pitcher of water. She poured herself one glassful of ice water, drank it and then poured another and brought it back to the table. "I'm sorry to interrupt, but I thought my throat was so dry that I would cough, and I certainly didn't want to do that."

"That was considerate of you, my sister. Now where were we? Oh yes, I was going to go over population projections with you." Taking another paper from her notebook, Myrna said, "Now from the Death Rate Table, you notice the death rate now is 805 deaths per one hundred thousand. Now look at the projections on this paper:

Notes on Starter Farm Statistics:

The year 2100 Estimated Population: 3,000,000

A death rate of 805/100,000, = loss of 24,150 woz/year. But we have only 18,000 pregnancies to replace these deaths: (Some loss due to miscarriages.)

Need 26,000 starter fluid donations for 25,000 pregnancies, SO: need two donations/week for 52 weeks by 250 donors. (2 x 52 x 250 = 26,000)

We have 5 Starter Farms now with 50 donors each or 250 donors, and 250 donors will only keep population steady in a good year. So need at least one more Starter Farm to increase population. And should have another Starter Farm for back up

I Recommend at least one more Starter Farm

> **Head, population control**
> **s/ Vivian**

Annette read the paper through twice and then said, "Yes, Myrna, I see the problem. I see why you are worried. What can I do to help?"

I have the paper right here with the Starter Farm comparisons, but I'll just tell you briefly what the report says."

"I'd be very interested to know how my two compare with those controlled by Cynthia."

"Well, in a nut shell, and I don't really know what in a nut shell means, but briefly let me say that I am really pleased with your two farms. Cynthia's farms have a sickness rate twice yours. Pregnancy rate from your farms is 87%, her rate is 65%. The death rate at her farms is three times the death rater at yours. So, I need to know what are you doing there that she is not."

"I really didn't realize that there was that much difference, Myrna. Perhaps the donors at mine are a bit happier. I did find them a piano and one of the donors leaned to play a few tunes. I have heard some singing when I have been there. Maybe being treated a bit less like a primitive gives them motivation to live a little."

"Well, Annette, spare me the details, I'm only interested in results. But to get to the point, I am giving you one of Cynthia's farms to manage. Would you mind?"

"Not a bit. I'll do whatever you want me to. I can see we do have a problem."

Rising from the table, Myrna said, "I'm going to get that good bottle of wine. We can take it out to the pool and just have a little sisterly talk."

Half an hour later in the changing room, the bottle of good wine noticeably lighter, the two were changing into bathing suits when Myrna said, "You know, it was better when we were kids and didn't think about the country. We didn't have to think about woz staring at us when we swam naked."

"Yes, the woz, always there, always listening to what we say, that is, if they can," said Annette as she took another taste of her wine. "Ah, that's really good stuff."

"Annette, sometimes I feel sorry for the woz; their world is full of females and no males. Well, I like the two males I have. Do you still have just the one?"

"Yes, just Pat."

"How do you do it with just one? I like having one male who just romances me and another who is crude but, well... strong."

"I guess I just don't have the stress that you do, Myrna. I don't suppose you can let up a bit, can you?"

"No, I can't." Then reaching into her handbag, she took out a bottle of eye drops. "Annette, I think that we should use the drops. The stuff we talked about at lunch, well, it's nothing that would cause us any trouble, but when we start sister talk, well, I don't want to accidentally broadcast my thoughts or feelings."

"That's a good idea. I hope that I can put mine in; it usually takes me a few times."

"Let's go on out when you're ready, Annette. By the way, do you use the drops often?"

Annette grabbed her towel and they started out the door. "Only when I have been with you, Myrna, so we can talk without worrying. That's the only time I have used them. I need to keep my communications open in case you call me or somebody on my staff needs me."

"Our sister, the great Cynthia, uses the drops all the damn time. I try to call her and she doesn't hear me, or so she says," said Myrna as they approached the table with umbrellas placed around the pool. At the white metal table and chairs Myrna arranged the umbrella so it was between them and the house.

"So do you want to sit in the sun or the shade from the umbrella?" said Annette.

"I just want to sit so the umbrella shields us from the house. It's my guess that Cynthia has someone there watching us through field glasses." Myrna sat down facing away from the house, and then said, "Do you see anyone at any of the windows, Annette?"

Annette leaned on the table with one arm so her lips could not be read from the house. She casually looked at the wall facing them, then pretended to laugh and said, "No, I don't see any, but that doesn't mean there aren't any, I suppose."

"Good, but it's possible that there is a spy with field glasses in the woods." Reaching into her bag, Myrna brought out the bottle of wine and two glasses. "Let's have some wine. And we'll not say anything that would be worth while reporting, just a lot of sister talk. Right?"

"I know that Cynthia has been a pain to you; she has been ever since our mother died. She leaves me alone, I guess, because I'm not important. She knows that I'll never take your place, and I never want to. You know that, don't you Myrna?"

"I know. I know that only an idiot would want to take my place." Myrna looked around, smiled, and took another sip of wine. "Oh, Annette, we were talking about having more donors and perhaps another starter farm, but what ideas do you have regarding increasing the number of donors?"

Annette leaned on the table again and placed her hand in front of her mouth. "I think that we could keep the present donors working a few years longer. If we keep them healthy we could keep them productive I think."

"Would that overcrowd our farms?"

"Well, I'll look into it closely, but offhand I think we could expand each farm by ten donors without much trouble. Of course, it would expand as we kept the donors longer and still accepted new donors. I'll let you know what I think after checking each of my, oh, I have three farms now, don't I?"

"I'm going to have another glass of wine." Then indicating the bottle of wine, Myrna said, "Annette, help yourself to more wine. I doubt that we can drink the whole thousand bottles up today." The raising her eyebrows and showing a big smile said, "Of course, we could try."

Wondering where this conversation was going, Annette smiled back at Myrna and sipped her wine. Then suddenly Myrna put her wine glass on the table, stood up, and said loudly and proudly, "Let's go swimming; that always sobers me up a bit." Then running over to the pool, dived in, and came up laughing, "Great, Annette, it's great;" and then swam over to the side by Annette, "Come on in!"

Annette did as Myrna asked, not simply because Myrna outranked her completely, but she always had tried to please Myrna. And she found out that by pleasing Myrna in small things, she could generally do as she liked in other situations. Cynthia delighted in irritating Myrna every chance she got. Annette had heard Cynthia tell Myrna several times, "I'll do what I want to and I don't care what anyone thinks about it."

"Let's swim around each other," said Myrna as she
ter in Annette's face.

et's do," yelled Annette, "Let someone try to
now," splashing water on Myrna. For five

minutes they churned around each other having fun as though they were ten years old, but all of the time they were talking about what a pain Cynthia was. Then realizing that they were not sixteen any longer, they migrated to the deep end, facing the pool wall and keeping their heads below the level of the deck, they paused a moment to talk without being heard or their lip movements in view.

"Did you enjoy the closet full of books and documents I asked you to burn?" said Myrna.

Annette was startled and wasn't certain what to say. Should she say that she had burned them as instructed? Should she simply thank Myrna for the knowledge about the United States and especially about males? Well, Myrna knows I didn't burn them, so why not just admit it? After all, if I lie and say I burned them without looking at them, she'll know I am lying to her. She would not like me to lie to her. "Yes, Myrna, I learned a lot from them."

"But you didn't burn them?"

"No, I have everything safely locked up."

Myrna ceased to smile or laugh. "You disobeyed me?"

"When I saw what was there, I just had to know the truth about what went on and who we really were. You know that I never could believe that story about males being primitive and all of them dying thousands of years ago."

Myrna began to smile a little now. "I never really believed it either. Grandmother ordered that this closet be given to whomever became MOTHER MYRNA. I knew that I didn't want Cynthia to ever get her claws on it, so I gave you the house, thereby giving you the closet of secrets too."

"Oh, Myrna, I'm so glad you're not mad at me for this."

"No, I'm not angry; I would have been disappointed if you had really burned the stuff. It's a valuable but dangerous closet full to have.

"Myrna, are you getting tired treading water so we can keep our head just below the deck level?"

"No, I'm fine," But finally, Myrna gave up and said, "Let's get out and lie on our towels. I need some sun."

"So do I," said Annette, getting out first and then she faced the water, held her hand out to Myrna, and helped her out of the pool. Once out of the pool they spread their towels on the deck and lay down on their stomachs facing each other.

"I doubt anyone can read our lips as we are so close to each other here, said Myrna.

"Good. We can just lie here, get dry, and almost pretend that we are still little girls hiding things from Mother."

"Wish I could pretend I was still a little carefree girl again, but I just can't shake what is worrying me," said Myrna. "In 2050 when Grandmother took over, it was thought that males caused all of the trouble in the world, so they got rid of them. But here we are generations later, no males have any power and we still have problems."

"But of a different sort of problems, Myrna. Before it was the males, but now it is the lack of males that's our problem, or one of them."

"Yes, the lack of males; actually it's males as donors, that is."

Myrna raised herself a bit, looked around, and then laid her head on the towel again. "If only I didn't worry so much, I could really enjoy the life I have." Then turning to Annette, she went on, "How long do you think we can keep these woz in ignorance about males?"

Pondering the question for a few moments, Annette said, "I don't know. The ancients did. Even until the Nineteenth Century, the royal families of Europe maintained the big lie, saying there was a Divine right of Kings. You remember from reading about it, they said that the people had no right to govern themselves, and were too stupid to do it anyway."

"Yes, Annette, and you remember that the French peasants revolted, chopped off a lot of heads, but eventually they had an emperor, Napoleon. But the United States was formed, not by uneducated peasants, but by the educated middle-class and led by well educated wealthy gentlemen, not peasants."

"I know that you're right, Myrna, but we have mostly uneducated woz, so we must decide what to do and start preparing them for the truth."

Myrna raised herself a bit and leaned on one elbow facing Annette. "And that's why we have to be very careful what we do about the males. We don't want a stampede when the whole truth is known."

Annette raised herself and leaned on one elbow too, facing Myrna. "I think that one difference between the American Revolution and the French Revolution is that the Americans were the 'haves,' and not really oppressed, they just didn't want or need a king."

"So what does all of this have to do with our eventually restoring males to citizenship, or do we have to do that?"

Annette reached for her jacket, took out her brush and starting brushing her hair. As she brushed she made certain that her hand and the brush were in front of her mouth to prevent someone from reading her lips. "And, Myrna, you know we can't just eliminate the males, we need them, and we are going to need a lot more of them if we want to grow, or even survive."

Myrna said with a bit of disgust, "So we know that. What we don't know is how and when. I don't want a disaster, such as a revolution while I'm the head Wo." She paused and looked at Annette as if to say, "So what is the solution?"

"I suppose that we first take steps to have more male donors, gradually educate them; at least teach them to read and write, and learn some simple arithmetic."

Myrna shrugged. "I suppose so."

"So, Myrna, I have your permission in the three farms I mange to start giving them a very simple and elementary education?"

"Yes, but on the quiet. Don't let it get out. Especially don't let Cynthia know about it."

"Okay, I certainly don't want those Woz living in our perfect world to know of any of this. Interesting, one Wo's perfect world is for most woz a boring worthless world. I really agree with you, Myrna, that if suddenly all of the woz found out about males, conception, and sex, our dam would break and we would all drown."

"I could probably eventually stop aborting males for a while. I'll need an excuse, an excuse better than a flue epidemic. You know, Annette, I am the head of WOZ, but I could accidentally get murdered. We are not really all sisters, so I have to be careful what impression I make with the Upper Hundred. I'm only safe if I keep most of the Uppers happy with their extravagant, carefree life styles."

"I'll do everything I can to protect you, Myrna. And please believe, I do not want your job. Of course, I don't want Cynthia to get it either. I've been thinking that if Cynthia agrees that we need more donors, she would not put up any fuss about no male abortions for a while and if she saw a good reason for me to run all of the starter farms, she would be relieved. I don't know what that good reason is, but maybe one will just show up. Maybe she would like to have more power, say she could run two new starter farms, she would not like having more work handed to her; maybe she would then dump them on me. But I'll do whatever you want me to, Myrna. I was just giving you some thoughts I have."

"Thank you, Annette. I was thinking that I might suggest that the upper hundred Woz might like to have more male, shall we say... servants. That might help break the ice."

Annette sat up straight, looked around for a moment and then leaning her head on both arms, said, "Myrna, how many woz, of all levels, do you suppose really know the official history is a lie, you know, that there are males and we conceive by having sex?"

"I don't know, probably more than we think. Let's look at it by rank. There's all of the Upper Hundred, Upper Thousand, and at least half of the Upper Ten K, maybe ten percent of the Upper Hundred K, and several hundred of the woz. So, how many is that?"

"Well, Myrna, just in my head I figured sixty-three hundred plus some unknown woz and the three of us, you, Cynthia, and me."

"I never realized that there were that many," said Myrna. "And we have to add some undetermined number of non-ranked woz, mostly those working in the Starter Farms. Well, whatever the number, none of them dare talk. Remember that our mother told us that a secret is something known only to one Wo."

Myrna lay back down, this time on her back and with part of her towel over her face. She extended her arm toward Annette and touching her hand said, "Annette, thanks for coming to see me. I feel so much better about WOZ and the future. Please consider you have close to a free hand with your three farms. But do call me before you decide to eliminate someone. I know we have to do what we have to do. You know, I am going to be much better to my two males, Ben and Larry, from now on. They help make my life be so much easier."

Smiling to herself, thinking that girls like Marla were eventually going to have a chance at a full life, thinking that maybe eventually she and Pat could get married, hoping for the best, Annette felt that it was time to leave. "Myrna, I think that I should go home now. Would that be all right with you? Do you need me or want me for anything else? If you do, I'll gladly stay."

Myrna took the towel away from her face and stood next to Annette. "No, go on home." And after a few moments pause, she said quietly, "Maybe I'll see what my… primitives are doing. Maybe…oh, go on home, my dear Annette. I'll walk with you to the changing room.

Later as Myrna was saying good bye to Annette at the front door, she said, "It's always good to see family here, Annette, so bring Marla with you next time, please."

"Marla?"

Myrna looked up, raising her brows and with a know-it-all smile said, "Yes, Marla, your new... assistant."

XIII. Down on the Farm

Whirling, whirling, whirling higher with every turn, Marla hoped they would never stop. The overpowering music of *The Blue Danube Waltz* seemed to come from nowhere and everywhere. Struggling to keep up with Ken, they spun through the clouds like a tropical storm. "I can't move my feet fast enough," Marla pleaded.

"Place your feet on top of mine and I'll carry us both," whispered Ken. She rested her feet upon his and he pulled her close, and then closer. Touching, the two were made one as they kissed.

She threw her head back and cried, "Oh, oh, oh, I kissed a male!" I don't think my heart can take it any more. Shall we dance until we are in the clouds, in the sky, among the stars? I don't want to fall back to earth."

Breathing hard, Ken whispered into her ear, "Marla, I am a male; I have no rights. I have no right to tell you that I..."

"Marla, Marla. Marla, wake up," said Annette in a loud voice. "I need to talk to you."

From under the covers a muffled voice said, "Go away."

Gently, Annette shook her and repeated, "Marla, wake up."

Again, "Go away, I'm dancing in the clouds."

Annette smiled as she said, "Have it your own way. Dream all you want," as she pulled all of the covers off and dragged them across the room. "Yes, dream you are in the Artic dancing with Polar Bears."

"I'm up! I'm up, said Marla loudly as she jumped out of bed, grabbed the covers from the floor and wrapped them around her. Then she quietly said, "Sorry, Annette, but I was having such a wonderful dream."

"Good. When you have dressed, come into the kitchen. We'll have something to eat and I can tell you about my meeting with Myrna."

Out of bed, the world of Ken and dancing gone, Marla said, "Okay, back to the real world."

"And after we eat, Marla, we are going to one of my starter farms, not the one where Ken is. And then we are going to a farm which until today was run by my sister, Cynthia, but now it is mine to run."

Awake at last, Marla said with a hint of excitement, "Well, if we're going to a farm, I'd better get myself presentable." As she grabbed a towel and started toward the cleanliness room, she said, "I'll be ready in a minute or two."

Ten minutes later she appeared in the kitchen dressed in a new uniform, her hair well brushed with not a hair out of place. "We're going to number four, that's been yours all along, right?"

"Yes, my starter farm, so sit down and eat your toast and eggs. Orange fixed those just like you like them. By the way, where is Orange? Is she still outside?"

Marla leaned a bit to the left and then said, "Yes, I see her feeding the birds."

As Marla sat down at the place set for her, Annette said, "Now let me tell you a bit about my meeting with Myrna."

"Did Myrna scold you for something?"

"No, quite the contrary, but listen, Marla, you must always say MOTHER MYRNA, never just Myrna. Now I don't care if you just say Myrna, but you could get into the habit of saying Myrna. Then sometime you might call her Myrna in front of somebody important and be in deep trouble. Understand?"

Busy eating, Marla paused long enough to mumble, "I understand; it's always MOTHER MYRNA."

"Good. Now let me tell you about our meeting. Only Cynthia and I are allowed to call her just Myrna, no one else is. Anyhow, Myrna is worried about our population not growing fast enough. You may remember I told you that the population of the United States had been 350 million, but the nuclear war, and most everyone dying from radiation, WOZ has now only about three million."

And then Annette explained to Marla about the birthrate barely keeping up with the death rate, and more males were needed. "I gave her my suggestions for increasing the number of male donors, and…"

"I'm for that," interrupted Marla.

"Yeah, I'll bet you are. Anyhow, I suggested keeping them working longer, increase the number of farms, stop aborting male fetuses, and increase productivity."

"Increase productivity, Annette?"

"Myrna has given me one of Cynthia's farms."

"She likes you more than Cynthia."

Neither of us like Cynthia, but the birth rate from her farms is lower than from mine, the disease rate is higher than on mine, so she thinks I do something different and she wants to see if I can improve the one she has transferred to me."

Gulping down the last of her breakfast, Marla said, "So what do you do differently at your two farms?"

"You tell me after we visit my number four farm and Cynthia's number three farm which I am about to take over. I have a hunch you'll not believe how different they are. Oh, and Myrna believes that we must gradually give males citizenship."

Marla gasped, "Really?"

"She said gradually, but not while she is MOTHER MYRNA. She believes it is bound to come, but she isn't one hundred percent for it. She is U-1, the head of the state, and if she acts suddenly and before people are prepared for change, we could have a revolution."

Thirty minutes later as they were going out the door, Annette said, "Sorry I had to take Pat with me, but it's the law that he may not be left alone with a Wo, except me. Also it is a rule that I may not travel alone, so his pistol hidden, he put on his wig, became Patricia, and went with me to see Myrna. So what did you do all day?"

"Orange was here for an hour, cleaned up the place, then left. I took a walk, then thought about things a while and then went to bed. Oh, did MOTHER MYRNA talk to Pat?"

"Oh, no, he sat in the car and waited for me. Myrna would never talk to a male, except her own two. And I think that they may have had quite an influence on her thinking about males as citizens, not just donors, but maybe not."

"So MOTHER MYRNA is only interested in more males because of the population problem, not that she sees that it is terribly unfair to both woz and males to be so separated?"

"I think that's it, Marla. Oh, she may feel sorry for the woz not having the pleasure of having males around for company and love. But when you are the head of state, you think of your own power first; the feelings of the woz are less important."

Annette paused for a moment. "We'll have to continue this later, Marla. I just heard the hum and my guess is my dear sister, Cynthia, is calling me."

Touching her fingers to her left upper eyelid, Annette heard, "Annette! Annette, this is Cynthia; why did you take number three starter farm from me?"

Touching her right upper eyelid, Annette answered, "Cynthia, my dear, I didn't ask for it. Myrna told me that it was not doing well and thought you were just too busy to take care of three farms, so she asked me to take it for a while. That's all."

"Why is Myrna trying to cut down on my power? Is she frightened that I am trying to be U-1? I'm not, you know. Being head of state is just too damn much trouble."

"Cynthia, I don't want to, and I never wanted to get into the competition for power. I guess I just look at it as a painful duty. Look, if you really are upset about my taking over number three farm, I'll ask Myrna not to change it to me."

Annette took a deep breath and then making certain that her right hand was nowhere near he right eye, said quietly to Marla, "We might as well sit down and relax; Cynthia will rave and rant on for ten minutes, and then she'll say she really doesn't care if I take number three farm."

Placing her left hand on her left eyelid, Annette listened to Cynthia explain that she really didn't want number three; she didn't want any of them; she didn't even want to be U-1, being U-2 was bad enough. Seven minutes later, Cynthia, quietly said, "Annette, you were only thinking of the WOZ, not power, so it's all right with me."

"All I do, Cynthia, is to try to get along and do what I can for our country and our family."

"So do I, my dear Annette, so do I."

Wearily holding her hand against her right eye, Annette said, "Well, I'll take number three then, but if you want it back, you have but to ask, that is, if Myrna says okay. In the meantime, let's just get along and enjoy life."

After saying good bye, Annette turned to Marla, "What a bunch of bull. Cynthia does not give in that easily. We have to watch our step with her. Well, are you ready to go to one of my starter farms?"

"Hoping she was wrong, Marla asked, "We're not going to the one where Ken is, right?"

Marla was not wrong. "We're going to number four; Ken is at number five, Marla," Annette said, as she put on her coat and motioned for Marla to follow her toward the door.

On the way to starter farm number four Annette explained the layout of the buildings at the farm. "There are four main building at each of the farms, and the lay out is pretty much the same at each farm. On the north end there is

Building A which is the administration offices, the food room and medical building. It's the largest building and also where the sperm are extracted."

"On the west side of the open area is the male dormitory. Usually about fifty males live there," said Annette. "Then across the open space is the woz dormitory. It is smaller as it houses only a dozen or so woz."

"So what's on the south side of the space?"

"On the south side is a large building for the vegetable farm, such as heavy equipment, grain storage, just for farm stuff. In the open space around which the buildings set are basketball courts, grass, a few trees, that sort of thing."

"Annette, I don't think that sounds too bad. But it's the males that interest me," said Marla.

"Obviously. And you shall meet some of them. But remember, even though this is my farm, the males have to do what we have them for. Almost all of them here know the real reason they are here. Some of the younger ones still think the real reason they are here is physical farm work. They think we are taking poison out of them when we are really taking their sperm."

"They really think that?" said Marla.

"They don't know any better, but usually the older ones explain the real reason."

"Do they ever run away?"

"Rarely. They know that if they do, they will either die of starvation or be caught and sent to one of Cynthia's farms where there are high fences and they have no privileges."

"No fences on your farms?"

"That's correct, Marla, no fences."

At this instant the Starter Farm #4 came into view, and Annette said, "An old song from the twentieth Century said that love makes the world go around. I don't know what makes the world go around, but starter farms keep it populated."

"That wooden building looks in great shape," said Marla. "And I really love the colors, too. This sign on this golden one says office, so it's the administration building, or part of it."

"I believe in making everything in WOZ as attractive as possible, within our budget, of course." Facing the open space in the center of the complex, Annette continued, "To your right, Marla, is the male's dorm and I had it painted white with red trim. They have a boring life; they don't need a boring dorm."

Pointing to her left, Marla said, "And this one, the green one with the white trim is for the woz?"

"Right, now shall we go into the office and meet Bonnie, the Head Wo here."

As they entered the office Annette and Marla found Bonnie, 45, blonde with short hair, sitting at a desk talking to a young wo. She immediately rose, dismissed the wo and greeted them. "Annette, it is such a pleasure to see you again. I was just getting the monthly report ready for you."

Annette smiled and said, "I just dropped by to show my aide, Marla, the farm. We'd like to look around if you don't mind."

"No, of course not. What would you like to show her first?"

"I would like to see Mac first."

"Do you want to talk to Mac with Marla present?"

"Marla has never been to a farm and I thought it would be good training for her to come to your farm, meet Mac and several other donors here."

Bonnie looked puzzled. "Annette, could I talk to you alone for a moment?"

"All right, we can go into your private office." Then turned to Marla, said, "Wait out here for a moment please."

Inside her private office Bonnie said, "How much does she know? Has she had the special classes?"

Annette quietly replied, "Bonnie, don't worry about it. She's smarter than the usual U-10K. You can say anything you like in front of her. She's with us all the way."

Bonnie smiled as she said, "I should have known, Annette, but one can't be too careful today."

Annette nodded, "Yes, or any other day."

As they left the private office Bonnie said, "I'll get Mac. I think he's at the males' dorm teaching reading right now." Picking up a microphone, she said, "Mac, come to the office please."

"Marla," said Annette, "You'll like Mac; he's the male in charge of the donors. And watch your manners; don't go overboard with this one."

"Of course not, Annette, I can quietly handle any male alive."

"Good, here he is now."

Marla felt excited for Mac might be another male she could touch. She had the feeling of fear; Mac might not want her touch. Marla felt irritation; there were too many people in the room. Why didn't they all leave her alone with Mac? Marla could hardly wait for him to walk through the doorway. Would she make a fool of herself with her first words?

Then there he was: about six feet tall, blond curly hair, a million white teeth. He entered and said hello to Annette. Flashing a huge smile, he looked Marla in the eye and said, "Hello. I'm Mac." Marla felt her legs going out from under her, but she managed to say, "I'm Marla. How do you do, Mac?"

"Let's all sit down," said Annette as she indicated a table nearby and sat down. Marla then sat next to her and Mac sat across the table from them. Marla was pleased that Mac sat across from her as she could stare at him not noticed by Annette, or so she thought.

Annette leaned closer to Mac as she said, "You may not realize how important you are, but it is time to increase our efforts to rid the country of this insane culture. So, tell me how is your teaching progressing with these young fellows? Are they really learning to read and write?"

"Very well in general, but there are some who like the easy-going life: a little work in the field, playing basketball, just lying around, and some enjoy having the "poison" removed every few days."

"You mean that they still think that poison is being removed?" said Marla.

"Yes, some do. They don't really know why they are here."

"Mac, nothing worthwhile is accomplished without effort, or without detractors," said Annette. "But we must push on; WOZ cannot survive living a lie, a very big lie."

"What would you like me to do, that I am not now doing?" said Mac.

"Things are changing and they are going to change more rapidly from this day on. For one thing, I am taking over farm number three from Cynthia. So I need a few males from here and number five to transfer over to three."

"That's great We can teach them the facts of life."

"And I'll probably send you over there as well."

Marla heard every word up to this point, but the words were simply stored somewhere in her mind while she concentrated on her big problems: Will I like Mac more than Ken? When will Annette invite him to the mountain cabin? Will I get to dance with Mac? Will Mac respond to me? Will Mac tell me that he is nuts about me? And then she saw two more males walking by and hoped she would get to meet them.

"Marla, would you like to see some of the buildings here?" said Annette.

Marla came to. "Oh, the buildings? I guess so; I might as well see everything while we're here, don't you think?" But in her mind she heard, "Marla, would you like to meet some more males?"

"All right, Mac, I'll have you transferred to farm number three as soon as I really take it over and talk to the head Wo there. I've brought you some more books and newspaper clippings to read. It's time this so-called perfect world has a make-over."

Annette stood up and the others followed. "Marla, I think we had better be going now."

Marla was disappointed as she thought, hoped that they would all have lunch together and she could get better acquainted with Mac. Maybe he would play footsie with her under the table. "Aren't we going to have lunch before we go?"

"We brought our lunch and we can eat it on the way to farm number three."

"All right," Marla said, as though she had anything to say about it. "How long will it take us to get to number three?"

"About two hours," then turning to Mac, she said, "I'll let you know when to go to number three. Start bringing those guys out of the ice age."

"I'll take care of it, Annette. I can hardly wait to see the expressions on their faces when they learn the facts of life."

On the way to farm number three they stopped under a patch of trees. While eating lunch, Marla asked, "What else do you have planned to do to make things right?"

"I was thinking that maybe, and I do mean maybe, I'd have all very young children go to school together. Males and woz together would teach both genders to accept each other."

"I see. Let them grow up knowing the facts of life. Well, I mean learn that both exist."

"Yes, and then no one would permit starter farms. And as they got older males would want woz; woz would want males. Then we could have families again." Annette exhaled as she shook her head and then said, "But it's a long way off, Marla. It's a long way off."

Annette snapped her fingers. "I just remembered I need to call Dr. Susan; might as well do it now." Touching her right hand to her right eyelid she said, "Susan, this is

Annette. MOTHER MYRA and I are concerned about the population of WOZ not growing fast enough. So for the next six months, do not, repeat do not abort any male fetuses."

Lowering her hand, she turned to Marla, "One more call and this should help jump-start the changes we want."

Touching her right hand to her right eyelid again, she said, "Bonnie, this is Annette. Starting right now you are not to radiate any sperm to kill those with the Y chromosome."

"I'll call Margo at number five and tell her the same thing," she said to Marla. "If we are going to have a free society we have to have enough males to go around. Can't let the little darling woz find out what life is all about and not let most of them have any of it. Right?"

About two that afternoon, Annette and Marla arrived at Starter Farm number three. They were shocked at the difference between it and number four. The buildings were basically the same in both farms, but none of the trim in number three was painted. The grass was mostly dead in the open space section, and there were no basketball hoops set up. There was a high chain link fence around the administration building and the woz dormitory. There was a separate fence around the dormitory for males and a few windows there were broken. All of the fences were high and all of the gates and were closed and padlocked.

Entering the main office, they were greeted by Verna, the head Wo. "Hi, Annette," she said. "Cynthia said that you were coming to look around. So come on in, look around. All of the donor creatures are locked in their dorm, so you won't be pestered by them."

"First, I would like to ask you, Verna, how do you think things are going here?"

"Okay; I guess. Cynthia hasn't complained to me about anything?"

Annette pulled a chair out from in front of Verna's desk. "Sit down, Verna, and let's talk about it." Verna sat down behind her desk and then quietly looked at Marla, then at Annette. "So when was the last time Cynthia was here?"

Verna couldn't see any reason she should take all of the blame for the poor showing here. After all, Cynthia gave the orders, not me, she thought. I'm only U-10K, so I had to follow orders; "Oh, I think it was about a year ago, or was it two years ago."

"All right, I would like for you to have some woz with the keys to open the fence gates and unlock the doors to the buildings so I can look around. I should see what your needs are here."

"I'll call Gracie who is familiar with the whole place."

A few moments later Gracie, who was U-100K entered the office. She was nineteen years old, blond, athletic, and smiling as she said, "Ma'am, I'll be honored to open all of the gates and locks and show you whatever you wish to see."

"Thank you, dear, and you may call me Annette."

Gracie looked relieved, and smiled as she said, "Thank you ma'am. What would you like to see first?"

"I would like to see the woz dormitory."

"Fine, ma'am. Oh, I find it difficult to call you Annette; You are U-3 and I am just a little Wo."

"Gracie, you are the stuff that this country is made of. You are our future and may address me either way. Now to the woz dormitory."

At the entrance to the woz dormitory, Annette asked Gracie, "Do you think the woz here are happy?"

Gracie pretended she didn't hear Annette, pointed to the doorway, "Watch your step, please; the doorstep is cracked. Don't want you to fall."

"How long has it been this way?"

"Since last fall sometime, I think."

"Well, we need to get it fixed." Then looking around inside, Annette, Marla, and Gracie entered. Stopping just inside the building, Annette said, "How many woz live here?"

"Usually ten, but two of them are in the hospital with the flu, I think."

"Anyone here now?"

"When I left here a few minutes ago there were two, Edna and Carla. They're in their room. Shall I call them?"

"No, let's go see them."

"They're in room number three. It's just the second door on our right."

They walked a few steps to the door of #3 and then knocked softly. A few seconds later a young wo, her hair messed up, opened the door and gasped. In panic she turned to another wo lying on an unmade bed, "Hey, stand up. It's one of the big ones." The other wo saw Annette, leaped out of bed and gave sort of a military salute. "Yes, ma'am, what can I do for you please?"

"Relax, relax," said Annette softly. "You woz, just sit down and take it easy." They immediately sat down on their beds and looked at Annette.

Marla looked at the woz, smiled and then said, "It's okay." Then indicating Annette, said, "This is Annette. She's U-3 and is now in charge of this farm... and of course, other farms and she wants to help things to be better. Oh, I'm Marla, and I'm U-10K.

Annette turned toward Marla and said, "Thanks" then facing the two woz sitting on their beds, she said, "I'm not here to make trouble for any of you. I simply want the truth when I ask you questions. If you wish, you can volunteer information that you think important."

Neither of the woz said anything so Annette went on. "Now I want to know what goes on here at farm number three. Are the woz here happy? What about the donors, are they happy, or at least content, or are they miserable?"

The woz who opened the door hesitated a moment and then said, "My name is Edna," then pointing to the other wo, said, "And she is Carla. I don't know about the primitives, but I think that we are all right, but really bored. We really don't understand what goes on here; all we do is to pump the poison out of the primitives."

"And then we just sit around the rest of the day," said Carla.

Annette paused a minute and then said, "Woz, first of all, they are not primitives; they are males. They are just like you except between their legs. And then shaking her head in disbelief, said, "You've got a lot to learn, and by golly, you're going to be amazed at what there is to learn. But for now, take it easy. I'm in charge now and nothing will happen to you, well, except your lives will get better."

As she started out the door Annette paused. "One more question. Tell me, Do any of you woz ever get friendly with the males?"

"Friendly?" said Carla.

"Yes, Carla, friendly. Do any of the woz talk to the males?"

"Well," said Edna. Verna said that we're not supposed to, She said it was Cynthia's orders to her that we weren't to talk to them at all, just tell them what to do by motioning to them., like, you know, lie down, sit up, stand up, and like that."

"Well, from this day on, you may talk to them." Annette started to walk toward the door, then stopped and said, "And I may transfer you two to farm number four for a month. You'll learn a lot there about the world. When you return here I'll promote you to U-100K."

Then turning to Gracie, Annette said, "Now I want to go to the males' dormitory."

A few minutes later at the door to the males' dormitory, Gracie unlocked the padlock on the outside of the front door and removed the lock. Then she unlocked the built-in lock and opened the door. "What? Annette said, "These males are locked inside?"

"Yes, ma'am, Verna's orders."

"Why would she do that?"

"To keep them quiet, I guess, ma'am."

"All right, then, let's go inside."

Inside there was one large room with 26 beds. The cleanliness room was at one end of the building. Annette looked the room over for a moment and then she asked, "Why is this place so filthy, Gracie?"

Gracie shrugged. "I don't know, ma'am; I am not allowed in here. The males are supposed to clean their own dorm."

Annette noticed three males lying on their beds asleep. "Where are the others?"

One of the males was not asleep and quietly said, "They are at work in the fields."

"Are you three sick or just tired?"

"We are sick, but we worked this morning."

Annette walked closer to his bed and then asked, "What is your name?"

"John," he said as he slowly sat up in bed. It isn't time to go get the poison removed yet, is it?"

Annette placed her hand on his forehead, frowned and then said, "John, you have a fever. Do you feel hot?"

"I guess so; I feel very weak."

"Then lie down, John, and go back to sleep."

John shook his head no. "I can't ma'am," he pleaded. "If I don't go get the poison removed, I'll be punished."

"Punished? How?"

"I won't be allowed to have anything to eat for two days. But don't let Verna know I told you that, please."

Annette smiled and then said in a quiet, loving voice, "Go back to sleep; I outrank Verna by thousands." Noticing that the other two males were awake now, she said, "Guys, things are going to improve here like you won't believe."

Once outside she stopped and said, "I've got to make a few calls. Gracie, you have been a great help to me. Now, please go tell Verna that I'll be in to see her in a few minutes."

Gracie smiled and said, "Yes, Annette. I'll tell her. I'll be glad to tell her." And with a quick and happy step she went toward the main office, whistling all the way.

Marla said nothing all of the time they were in the males' dorm. But when Gracie left, she said to Annette, "And now what?"

"A storm is coming and here is the first lightning bolt," said Annette as she touched her right hand to her right eyelid. "Sandy, this is Annette. Please call Margo at farm number five and have her rush right up here to farm number three and take over for Verna, probably for a few weeks. Then send Josie to take over for Margo. Then transfer Verna from farm number three to that outpost on the edge of the desolate area on extended leave with no duties. Well, she can send in the daily weather reports. Also I want you to send a construction crew here to make repairs to the buildings and tear down the fences."

"Wow," said Marla. "When you do something, you really do something."

"One more thing, Marla."

Marla started to say, "What's that?" but Annette answered her question as she touched her right eyelid and said, "Dr. Susan, this is Annette. I need you to come to farm number three early tomorrow morning and give all of the males and woz here a complete physical. Be prepared to treat some of them for flu or pneumonia."

Looking down at Marla and smiling, she said, "Margo should be here in two hours or less. I don't trust Verna being in charge even for a few hours. When Margo gets here we can go home and have a glass of wine before the war starts. Now let's go give Verna the good news."

Annette grinned as she threw back her head and said, "Yes!" Starting to laugh to herself, she continued, "And you, Marla, may sleep as long as you want tomorrow, for on the following day I shall tell you all about your special assignment."

XIV. Starter Farm Number Three

Warm, comfortable, relaxed, and relived that she was no longer in bed in that cold, barren cabin in the mountains, Marla woke up. What day was it, she wondered. Let's see: we went to the cabin on Friday and I met my very first male, Pat, and danced with him. Saturday, Ken and Michael came and I danced so wonderfully with Ken. Sunday, Annette went to see Myrna. Hey, in my head I don't have to say MOTHER MYRNA. Monday, we went to two starter farms and I met Mac. That was yesterday, so today must be Tuesday. Yes, Tuesday, and I'm going back to sleep; Annette said I could.

Then there came a soft knock at the door. "Who is it?" she mumbled.

"It's Jo, ma'am."

"Go away. Annette said that I could sleep as long as I wanted to today."

"Sorry ma'am, but Annette said to wake you at eleven. She wants you to have lunch with her at noon."

Well, Annette's the boss, she thought. "All right, Jo, I'll be there." And yawning, stretching, groaning she forced herself to enter a new day. Sleep as long as I wanted to, huh? That's what she said. She also said she would like for me to have lunch with her at noon. She didn't mean she would like for me to be there; she meant be there. Well, Annette is U-3 and I'm not, so I'll be there.

At 11:45 Marla stepped from the stairway to the first floor as Annette left her downstairs' office and walked to meet her in the foyer. "Let's have lunch in the small dining room and go over some reports I want to discuss with you," said Annette.

What do I know that she doesn't, thought Marla. But I'll try to help her by listening to what she has to say. As they walked toward the small dining room Annette asked, "Well, did you have a good sleep? Are you still sleepy, need to go back to sleep after lunch?"

"I'm fine and eager to hear what you have to tell me."

"After we eat. But right now I'm starved; are you?"

After they had eaten and had a cup of coffee Annette said, "What differences did you find in the two farms we went to yesterday?"

Marla quickly turned toward her. "Are you kidding? There was all the difference in the world."

"Like what, Marla?"

"Like: number three was filthy, the buildings were falling down practically, the woz and the males were bored and unhappy, there was no discipline, some were sick, no one there had planted the crops, and the whole place was a mess. Other than these few things, there was no difference."

"Good, Marla, how would you like to go help Margo change things there?"

I don't really know how to go about it; I don't know how to talk to so many ignorant males. I hope they will listen to me there; these thoughts danced in her brain, but she said to Annette. "I'd love it. Why not? Wait a minute, Margo will be there, right? I don't have to do it all myself."

"I expect Margo and you to turn that place around," Annette said at the same instant that Marla smiled as she thought Mac will be there too.

"And if you have problems, you may call me anytime," added Annette. "Someone will drive you over there early tomorrow morning. Plan to spend a few months there. Now, Marla, remember you are a U Ten K, not a helpless, ignorant wo any more. Listen to Margo and anyone else who knows something you don't. But don't be afraid to take charge and get things done."

Marla nodded yes and then said, "I'll try my best."

"One more thing, Marla: I'm not forbidding you to be friendly with Mac or any other male, but don't go overboard. You need to meet and learn about many males before you can really judge any one of them." Then Annette raised her eye brows and said, "Got it?"

Marla smiled, "Got it, Annette."

Very early Wednesday morning Marla arrived at the farm and went directly to Margo's office. On the way she noticed carpenters repairing the door to the males' dorm and two woz painting the trim on the woz dorm. Well, Margo isn't wasting any time getting this place in shape, she thought. Physically making repairs here is one thing; repairing the damage to the souls of the woz and the males is something else. How do we go about reversing years of neglect and oppression?

In the office she found Margo making a list of things that needed to be done and shaking her head and groaning, "Oh, my." Looking at Marla, she said, "How did this place ever get to be such a mess?" She really didn't expect an answer, but Marla casually commented, "Nobody cared."

Margo looked up from her paper, sighed a bit and then said, "Some do now. Sit down for a moment, Marla. Here's what I have for you to do the next few days. Every day make certain that Edna and Carla clean the woz dorm. And then make certain that Gracie gets on those males who are supposed to clean their dorm. But don't interfere with Mac when he is teaching the males to read and write."

"All right, Margo. I'll do my best," she said as she stood and prepared to leave the office. "By the way, where do I stay?"

"Oh, throw your stuff in the next room. The back bedroom is mine. Okay?"

"Sure, fine."

"Of course, you could stay in the woz dorm."

"Only if I have to."

"I was teasing you, Marla. You are U Ten K, a very young U Ten K, and need to command respect. In one way you outrank me."

Marla laughed, then puzzled, said, "Really, Margo, how is that?"

"You'll figure it out."

As Marla walked toward the woz dormitory to check on Edna and Carla, she asked herself what Margo meant. Oh well, she thought, maybe it'll come to me some day, but for now I have to get my job here done. Yeah, I can't even consider meeting males until I get these woz organized. I wonder how Mac is coming along with the males. No, I really wonder when I am going to get to see him again. Come on, Mac, let's get this place going so we can have a dance, or maybe more. Don't I wish? Yes, I do wish.

As she walked toward the woz dorm she noticed that the fence gates were still there and closed, but she couldn't tell if they were locked or not. The huz are used to the gates and if they were gone or standing open, they might enter an area forbidden to them. Probably not though, as both the woz and the males seemed somewhat subdued. As she entered the woz dormitory she noticed several woz moving beds from their rooms and toward the front door. "What's going on?" Marla asked.

"We've stripped down the beds and scrubbing down the walls and floors of all the rooms," said Edna. "Gracie told us that Margo said to get rid of years of dirt and filth here."

"Good idea. Do you have enough help?"

"Sure. It feels good to have something to do, and the place does stink."

Marla looked around for Gracie, but noticed only two other woz hauling beds from the rooms. "So where is Gracie?"

"I think she's at the donor's dorm pushing them to stop lying around and clean their place," said Carla.

Marla paused for a moment and then said, "Okay, I'll go to the males' dorm and see what's going on over there."

As she started to turn way, she stopped and asked, "By the way, are the gates locked?" Noticing Edna shake her head no, Marla left for the males' dormitory.

As she walked across the lawn between the dormitories, she noticed the large dead spots in the grass. She shook her head as she thought that this was just another example of how much this farm had been neglected. Well, things will change for the better, starting today. Two woz who were busy painting the trim on the males' dormitory stopped for a moment; wondering if they were expected to give Marla some kind of salute, they simply stared at her U Ten K epaulet. Marla smiled at them and then quietly said, "Good morning. Looks like you two are doing a good job," and then smiled again and walked through the partially open doorway into the building.

"Hello, Marla," came from a male voice behind the door. She quickly looked around and saw Mac standing there smiling. "Sorry, I didn't mean to startle you," he said.

To the casual observer, Marla only smiled. In her mind, she screamed to herself, "Mac! Don't just stand there, hug me." But to anyone else she simply extended her hand and said, "It's so nice to see you again. How's it going here?"

He gestured toward the end of the large room. "You can see that the beds have been stacked at one end, the floor has been scrubbed and is drying."

"Yes, it looks fine. And you, Mac, you look fine too."

"We did have a bit of a problem earlier this morning. Two of the males did not want to get up. I ordered them get up or I could have them sent to another of Cynthia's farms. So one said, 'You're just a male like us. You have no power.' I decided that he was just ignorant as they come and I should try to reason with him. So I said, 'As soon as this room is clean I am going to start to teach you guys to read and write. But I can't do that until the room is clean.' Then I raised my fist and yelled, 'So move it!' and he did. I am just about to start our first lesson. Do you want to observe?"

"Yes, but I won't. You need a free hand with this. However, I would like to say a few words to them before you start."

"Fine, go ahead, Marla," he said and then sat down facing the males.

"Are these all of them?"

"No, half of them are working in the field today working with George. You never met him, Marla, but he's the other male; the one who came from farm number four with me. Two are in the hospital."

Marla looked at the males; what a bunch of lost children they were, she thought.

She looked at each one of them for a moment and then looked at them as a group. "Males, we are about to do things for you that you never dreamed would ever happen to you. We are going to let you in on secrets kept from you, and from the woz too. However, you must pay attention to us and believe what we tell you. It is your chance to have a soul. If you don't know what a soul is, you'll find out and be amazed at who you really are."

Most of the males simply sat there with a blank look on their faces. Marla watched them for a moment and then added, "Mac is in charge. He has full authority, so believe him, and obey him. Good things are about to happen." Marla smiled at Mac, then at the males, and then she walked out the door.

Mac wasted no time in standing up, and with a stick about three feet long, pointed to the row of capital letters tacked across the wall, said, "Now, guys, these are the English letters used to form words. There are twenty-six of them. Most of you should know some of them as all of you have been taught to print your own name."

"I know all of them," a male named Greg said.

"Good, you can help out, Greg." Then taking the stick and pointing to the letter, A, he said, "Here's a little jingle, a little song to help you learn all of them. Greg, do you know the song?"

"I think so."

"Good. Now everyone who knows it, or any part of it, help us sing it." Then singing softly he started, "A, B, C, D, E, F, G. Good, some of you know it, so we'll do it again."

After an hour of work, almost everyone knew the whole jingle, and Mac said, "That's great, guys. Now let's go out and install the basketball hoop we just received from Annette."

From the doorway of the woz dorm that afternoon, Marla could hear the males out in the open space shooting the ball at the hoops and everyone yelling with delight every time the ball went through the hoop. Mac blew a whistle and the noise stopped. She looked at them gathered around Mac as he said, "Now I am going to teach you to play a game called basketball.

As she heard him say, "We split up into two teams now," she turned and walked inside and toward twelve woz seated in front of her. "Woz, how many of you have ever heard of chromosomes? Hands up if you have," Marla said.

No one held up her hand. "Okay, well, how many of you know what a baby is?"

"Trying hard not to laugh, everyone held up her hand."

That's something, Marla thought. "Now, how many of you know what starter fluid really is?" Every wo held up her hand so Marla went on, "Well, now we have a starting place." But I can't tell them everything at once; she thought, they would be at the males like crazy. Most of them would mate here and get pregnant. Wow, would I be in trouble then! We have to go slow for the sake of restoring a two gender world and perhaps the Good Old USA, as it was called centuries ago.

I might as well keep going for now. It will take them some time to get it anyhow. I know it took me a while to learn about mating. I don't think that these young woz will be as eager to learn 'first hand' as I was, as I am; they have mating-suppressing material added to their food. I don't now and I don't think I ever did.

The males and the woz had packaged food which was given to them in their dormitories. Two U-100K Woz cooked fresh food for Margo, Marla, Mac, Gracie and the kitchen staff. That evening at supper in a small dining room in the north building Margo asked, "So, how do you think it went today?"

Marla looked at Mac. "I heard your guys singing the ABC song. Are they catching on?"

"To the alphabet, yes, but tomorrow I start arithmetic, and then I introduce the concept of chromosomes and gender."

"We have to be careful there, Mac. When all of the males realize it wasn't poison we were taking from them, eventually they might riot," said Margo.

"And the woz might cause a lot of trouble too," said Marla.

"How so?" said Gracie.

"When it comes to extracting the sperm, males have no privacy. And the woz who do the extracting may see this as their opportunity to get pregnant without being appointed First Mother. We want the males and the woz to be friends, but only friends, not mates, at least not until the time comes. It would ruin all of our plans."

"You're right, Marla. If we get a lot of hot blooded males and woz together too soon, we could have boycotts of the system, maybe even riots."

"What do you think would happen then, Mac" said Marla.

"I know what would happen," said Margo. "Annette would be forced to restore this farm to what it was last week, a mess. Actually, she would be forced to eliminate us."

"Yes, or be eliminated herself," said Marla.

"If Cynthia ever took over she would eliminate Annette too; maybe not forced to, she would enjoy it," said Margo. "So let's all be very careful and simply concentrate on teaching the males to read, write, and do math. Then gradually let the males and the woz be friends, like little children."

"Is that possible?" said Marla.

"Time will tell, dear. Time will tell," said Margo. All was quiet for a moment, and then she said, "It seems to me that the reason MOTHER MYRNA gave Annette this farm and the authority to change things is the low ratings. The pregnancy rate of sperm from this farm was much too low, and the health problems here were much higher than the farms of Annette. I think we need to work to improve those items."

"Yes, we must work on that," said Marla. "But we must not neglect our own mission. There is no point in our taking risks things if we don't make progress in eliminating this oppressive government, and restoring citizenship and rights for both genders."

"So how do you want me to proceed with the males?" said Mac. "How much do you want me to teach them? Rather, I should ask, "How fast do you want me to proceed?"

"Why not start by explaining chromosomes and why two sets are needed? I mean just basic science, no details," said Marla. "And I have another suggestion: Why not have a dance before either gender knows too much about sex? They could learn to talk to each other, and they could touch each others' hands but not press against each other front to front."

"Eventually that's a good idea, Marla. I said eventually, not now. First, they have to grow to like each other and respect each other. They need to talk to each other socially, not just in the extraction rooms. Let's think about ways to do that before we try having a dance..

"The fact that the males are pretty ignorant about life in general and about woz makes them rather shy. But that should work in our favor as we have many m
woz," continued Margo. "We have males of
ages so some will be more interested in talkin
than others. I also think that if the males and

abo

151

another's names and establish friendships, it will help control any tendency to riot or mate when they all find out the facts of life," said Margo."

"I think that we should spend some time teaching each about the others' gender, and explain good manners too," said Marla. "We can have both woz and males learn how to talk to each other. I'll teach the woz and Mac can teach the males. I can see it now, "A male approaches a wo and says, 'Would you do me the honor of dancing with you?' or some such."

Margo smiled and then stood up and with a serious face said, "Dancing probably will be all right eventually, but it must not interfere with sperm extraction. That's our job here, like it or not. When the males fully realize why they are here, in fact the only reason they were allowed to survive, then what? They must be made to realize that nothing is free, and that the world will not change without a lot of thought, work, and discipline, and probably pain We didn't have much trouble when they thought that sperm removal by the woz was medical, that is, keeping them alive."

"Well, Margo," said Marla, "We must convince them that our purpose is to eventually free them by making more males, enough so every wo who wants a male can have one."

"And that's a good argument to convince the woz to cooperate," said Margo. "I remember reading about slogans from centuries past. Two of them were, 'A chicken in every pot,' and 'A car in every garage."

Immediately Marla burst out with, "Yes, and we could say, 'And a male in every...' never mind," and laughed almost beyond control.

Mac started to laugh. "Oh, Marla, you are too much!"

Marla leaned back in her chair, stared at Mac and then said, "Really, Mac, too much what?"

"Just too much sweetness ought to cover it."

"Okay, let's settle down a minute" said Margo. "How this? First we allow them to talk to each other, but only in groups and only with one of us there. Then we teach dance manners and then a dance. Finally we teach the males what is really going on, but as we don't want the woz to participate in sperm extraction, we give containers to males and let them do it themselves. But we must, absolutely must have everybody sign on to our plan to liberate them and all of us."

"I'll tell Annette what we are doing," said Marla, "But all of this stays here. We don't talk about it to anyone at Annette's other two farms. Remember the old saying, 'A secret is something that only one person knows.' In this case, I think it should be something that is known only at this farm. We have no control over what is said at other farms."

As they were leaving the office Marla said to Mac, "Let's have the dance before you have to go back to farm number four. I can't dance with you if you're way over there."

By Friday the males' dormitory and the woz dormitory were clean and painted. Saturday morning Mac said to the males, "You guys have done well this week; none of you missed you extraction times, all of you have worked very hard in the fields, so we are gong to have a little chat about life."

Mac looked around to see if anyone wanted to ask a question. All he found were blank stares, so he continued, "Each one of you look around; you are all pretty much alike, but you're not alike completely."

Puzzled, they looked at each other, but didn't seem to know why Mac wanted them to do this thing. "Why did you ask us to look at each other?" said Jim, blond hair, blue eyes, age 15, and only five feet three inches tall.

"Jim, you are the same age as Robert, but he is three inches taller than you, has dark hair and green eyes. But you are both males the same age. Why are you different?"

No one had an answer so Mac went on, "All r ⌐ ' ¬ take a look at the different buildings here. This k different from all of the rest of the buildings here. All of the buildings were built from a drawing, a plan."

Mac held up the building plan for various buildings at the farm. "See these drawings show what the building should look like, what size it should be, and the arrangement of the rooms. Now your bodies were built according to a plan also. Does anyone know what the plan is called?"

Freddie, 17, dark hair said, "I do. It's called the DNA."

"Right Freddie, we get our DNA part from our father and part from our mother."

"I don't understand," said Jim. "What is a father? I only remember having a mother. Until I was ten I lived with her, then I had to come here to work. I don't remember anyone called a father."

Mac looked at the clock on the wall. "Guys, I notice that the basketball hoop has been put up. So, we can continue this now, or we can go play basketball for a few minutes before supper. I suggest we continue all of this another day. Is that all right with you?"

"Let's go play basketball," was heard from several of the males as they eagerly they moved toward the door and were soon outside.

After supper Mac and Marla stood outside by the door to the main building. It was almost dark, Gracie had gone to the woz dormitory. Margo was busy in her office talking to Annette. "I'm glad we could stop there," Mac said. I don't want to bring up mating just yet. I don't want them thinking about sex until after they have been able to talk with some woz and we have had the dance."

"Do you think some have it figured out now?"

"Some probably have, Marla, but hopefully not the details yet."

What a shame to keep it from them, she thought. What a shame it was kept from me. What a shame Mac and I can't find out for ourselves right now. That's what Marla thought, but she said, "When should you go to the dorm for the night?"

"Was that a hint that I am late in doing my duty to the guys?"

"I'll take off my epaulet and then ask you the same question." Golly, are some males dumb, she thought.

"Well, maybe we should inspect the grounds before it gets completely dark," said Mac as he grinned the grin of expectancy.

"Yes, we should all do our duty," Marla said as he took her hand and she held on to his, wondering if this is how they did it a hundred years ago. Could this be called a date? If there were someplace they might stop unseen by male or wo, would he kiss her?

"We shouldn't hold hands where we can be seen," Mac said as he let go of her hand and gestured to point out the way they should go.

"I suppose not, Mac, and both of us could get in trouble."

"Especially me," Mac said. "I'm basically a slave and you are U Ten K, though a beautiful U Ten K. If Cynthia or someone like her found out we even went walking they would have me castrated or eliminated. Probably just scold you."

"I can't put you in jeopardy, but Mac, if we can find a dark corner, would you kiss me?"

Mac said nothing, but took her hand and led her behind the woz dormitory and to a dark area not seen by any window or doorway. He put both of his arms around her, looked into her eyes and said, "Marla, you are worth any trouble that finds me," and then he gently kissed her. She felt his kiss down to her toes and felt that she was going to pass out, so she held onto him to prevent her from drowning in her joy.

With arms still around each other, they backed away a few inches. Mac looked at her face brilliantly glowing with smiles; she looked at his face too, smiling, but with a hint of sadness. "In three weeks I am supposed to go back to farm number four. Will I ever see you after that?" he said quietly.

She lost her smile for a moment, looked away, and then looking at his eyes, said, "Tonight makes me want to change things more than ever, and we shall change things." Taking his hands in hers and squeezing them, she said, "And I shall never rest until it is done. Our souls belong to us, not to the government. I shall never rest until woz and males have their own lives." Leading him by the hand she said, "Let's go in now. We need to be rested for the next three weeks of living to the fullest while we start to undermine the status quo."

Looking into the distance, Mac said, "I remember reading about a flag in the American Revolution. I remember this flag said, "Live Free or Die," and now I can understand what it meant. I would rather live free, but we males are physically slaves, and you woz are slaves of ignorance. Our revolution is coming, but a political revolution, not an armed and deadly one."

Mac put his arm around Marla as they started back to their reality, but she stopped in a shadow just short of the office door. Pulling him back to her, said, "Mac, is there such a thing as love? Is love, is everything, just the urge to mate?"

"You're asking me, a slave, whose only use here is to donate sperm. I am not allowed to think, just produce." Then changing his facial expression from stress to joy, he said, "But to answer your question, if there really is such a thing as love, then I love you, Marla, dear."

Marla threw her arms around his neck, pulled him down to her, and kissed him fully on the lips. "There! That should hold you until tomorrow," and then she disappeared into the office.

Spring had certainly arrived Saturday afternoon; leaves had returned to the trees and bushes; daffodils were blooming. Even the laziest wo and the most bored male wanted to be outside doing something. A basketball game had started in the open space between the dormitories and most of the woz were sitting on the grass nearby watching the males try to make a basket. Marla approached the woz and said to those sitting nearby, "I'd like to talk to you woz for a bit. I'd like to get your opinions on a few things."

Carla looked away from watching the males and said, "Fine, what shall we talk about?"

"I'm trying to help you, but I need to know where you are, that is, how much do you know about things, such as, do you know the history of WOZ?"

"I guess so," said Gracie.

"You mean about how we lived in caves, and about the primitives?" said Edna.

"That's what you know?" said Marla.

"Sure," said a wo named Elsie. "We were taught the official history by our Second Mother."

"And do all of you believe it?"

"Why shouldn't we believe it, Marla?" said Edna.

"Let me ask you a question." Pointing to the males playing basketball, Marla said, "According to official history, all the males, sometimes called primitives died. If so, then who are those creatures out there playing basketball?"

"Well, maybe all of them didn't die," said Elsie.

"Maybe they are not primitive, maybe they never were primitive. Maybe the whole story is a lie."

"But, Marla, they don't know anything; they can't ever read or write. And if they're not inferior creatures why do we have to remove the poison from them every few days?" said Elsie.

"Did you woz ever stop to think that if it were poison you were removing, why would the government spend a lot of money to keep them here just for farm work? Did you ever wonder if what you were removing was valuable?"

Marla stopped a moment and looked at the woz sitting around her. She started to walk away, her job done for now, but then she knew there was one more thing to say today. "Woz, I don't want to go any farther with this discussion until I explain something else."

"Okay, Marla, most of us know it isn't really poison, it's starter fluid, some kind of fluid that starts a wo's egg to develop," said Elsie. "Verna told me so."

"That's somewhat the truth, but still a bit misleading. Margo and I are here so that you and the males can have a better life. And you can't have it living a lie, so we are here to liberate you by teaching you how to be free of lies." Marla stopped here and looked at each wo sitting around her.

The woz around her seemed to be quietly confused, even tired of listening, so she said, "That's all I want to tell you today. But do think about the males: you know they seem a lot like you, not exactly like you. After all, you extract their poison as you call it, so you know they are built different. But except for that, aren't they much the same? Tomorrow we shall have a lesson showing you what the truth is about males and woz and why both are needed for life."

"Marla," said Gracie, "Some of us were wondering if we could use the new hoop and play basketball too, or is it just for the males?

"Gracie, I think that is a great idea. We have another hoop stored in the farm equipment shed. I'll ask Margo to have it set up for you. I'll get Mac to teach you to play."

That night at supper, Margo said, "I'm glad you brought up the woz playing basketball too. If we have woz shooting baskets at one end of the ground between the dorms and males playing a game at the other, it won't take long before they start talking to each other."

"Especially if we put some benches around the field, because they won't all be playing at once; some will sit and watch," said Marla. "And then some males and woz will sit together. At least, I hope so."

"If we put a hoop at each end of the field it would then be a basketball court. Of course we have to tear down the fence around the dormitories. Do you think we could do that?" said Mac.

"The woz and males here are used to the fences," said Margo. "What will happen when the fences are gone? Will that be an invitation for undisciplined behavior?"

"We could ask for more woz to be sent here to help control both sides, said Marla.

"But we want woz who know the score. Perhaps we could get five woz from farms four and five. Then they could get replacements they could train. Ten woz with empty heads would be more of a problem than help, don't you think, Marla?"

"All right, I'll call Annette and get her approval, and then I'll call and get more woz sent here from the other farms."

The next morning it was raining hard. Mac and the rest of the males were looking out the windows to see if it were about to stop. It was not, so Mac had the males gather around as he said, "Hey, it doesn't look like it's going to quit raining for a long time today. We can't go work in the muddy fields, and we can't play basketball, so I'm going to have a little talk with you guys. So gather around, sit down, and let's talk a bit."

"About what?" said Freddie.

"Are any of you friends with a wo?"

"I wanted to be friends with Cindy and Edna, but they said they were not allowed to be friends with males," said Freddie.

"Why do you suppose they couldn't be friends with you?"

"They said we were different from them and we were primitive."

"All right, let's talk about differences.. First of all, what difference is there between the males and woz here?" Mac looked around and then looked at Freddie. "I'll bet you have an opinion or two, Freddie. So what do you think?"

"Well, their faces are smoother than ours."

"Is that it? Is that the main difference? Do you just see someone with a smooth face and say to yourself, "Oh, that's a wo?"

Eddie, a male in the back, 16, spoke up. "Freddie, you must be blind. They're completely different from us. For one thing, their chests stick out in front. Ours don't.""

"Okay," said Mac. "Anything else?"

The males simply sat on the benches and on their beds smiling. Mac looked around and could hardly keep from laughing as he said, "Any other difference?" Still there was no response from the males. "None? Then let me ask you a question, you guys tell me that the woz extract the poison from you. Do you think that any of them have poison extracted from them? Okay, Freddie, answer that one, please."

Freddie bolding stood up and laughing, said, "They ain't got a place to extract it from," and then he sat down as most of the males laughed.

"How do you know that, Freddie? Have you seen any of them without clothes on?"

"No, I've not seen any of them without their clothes. Clara told me that woz don't have that thing we do."

"You're absolutely right, Freddie. If anyone here doesn't know what we are talking about, we can talk later. For now, let's just say that woz and males are built differently" Picking up some drawings he had on the chair beside him, he went on. "So we know that we are different from the woz? And how are males different from each other?"

Holding up a drawing of the twenty four pair of chromosomes, Mac explained about chromosomes and how a woz and a male each had twenty-four, but twenty-four pair were needed. It only matters that you understand it takes chromosomes from both a male and a woz."

Eddie held up his hand and asked how do those from the male meet those from the woz?"

"According to what woz are told, you males are supplying the necessary chromosomes in a form called starter fluid, and that's really sperm that has your chromosomes. Then what they take from you is injected into willing woz to make a baby."

"So it's not poison they were taking from us!" said Freddie quite angry.

"Right! All right, guys, now you know. But for your sakes you must not fuss about this. Margo, Marla, and I don't like this system of stealing from you at all. And we are trying to change things, but you must cooperate with us. And you must keep your mouths shut about this to anyone outside this room."

Two weeks later the courtyard looked completely different. The fences had been removed; there was a basketball pole and hoop on the north and south ends. There were six benches around the basketball court, three on the woz side and three on the males' side. It was late afternoon and noises could be heard coming from the north end where woz teams of five players each side were yelling and scrambling around trying to get the ball through the hoop.

It was quiet for the moment on the south end of the court and the males had just finished a game and were wiping the sweat from their foreheads and/or drinking water or sitting down watching the woz frantically trying to get the ball away from one another, then flinging the ball toward the hoop, sometimes going through it. Often a wo watching the game would yell, "Come on Carla, throw it," or scream, "Get the ball away from her!"

"I've never seen them so animated," said Margo as she watched from her office window.

"It's one way to control young woz; keep them having fun and worn out," said Marla. And then turning to Mac, she said, "Let's walk down there by one of the benches. I'll go over to the woz side; you take the males' side. That way we can sort of listen to comments."

"Have you noticed that all of the woz are still on the woz side of the hoop. None have crossed over to the males' side of the north hoop to watch their sister woz play," said Mac. "I wonder how long it will be before they are on both sides of the hoops."

Marla looked at him and smiled. "I wonder how long it will be before they choose mixed teams, males and woz on each team."

"When that happens, we will know that real progress has been made, Marla."

Marla thought what about progress with us? What about...? Never mind, Marla, your day will come. Stepping away from him, she smiled as she said, "Mac, I guess we'd better split up here; I'll go over to the woz side."

He nodded yes, smiled and then said, "All right, I'll see you at supper."

Standing behind Edna and a young wo named Jane, Marla tried to appear to pay attention only to the game and not to what these two woz were saying, but she did manage to hear, "Oh, Jane, Look the males are starting to play another game. What do you think of that tall one? I get strange feelings every time I see him."

"What kind of feeling?" said Edna.

"I don't know, just feelings."

I know, Marla thought, believe me, I know. And someday we shall all know, and not from books either. I wish that I could run away with Mac or Ken. I don't know which one. It's like Annette told me, don't make up your mind yet. But really, how is a wo to know which one?

The woz game was over and some of them went into the woz dormitory to take a shower. The rest wandered down to the south side and watched the males still playing. They were not cheering the male players, but they were watching them intensely, laughing and staring at certain of the players. Marla heard one wo say, as she indicated a certain player, "Oh, I would like to take him home with me."

"What would you do with him?" said a wo standing next her.

"I'd figure out something, I think."

We're close to ready for socializing, Marla thought. And I'm glad we took Mac's advice about extractions. "Marla, I think that changing the extractions so that each male did his own will help males and woz see each other in a different light," he had told her. Yes, knowing about chromosomes and that starter fluid was not a poison really helped them think about what could be.

Two days later while helping both woz and males learn and practice passing, dribbling the ball, and shooting baskets, Mac called both the woz and the males to gather around him. "I was just thinking, would you all like to play a game with both woz and males?"

"Yes," said Edna, "But it wouldn't be fair because the males are stronger and taller than we are."

"That's true, but suppose that we had mixed teams. You know there are about twice as many males as woz, so suppose each team could be made of three males and two woz?"

There was some discussion by both woz and males, and at first Mac thought that some from each gender would not like to play on the same team as the other. But finally Carla said, "I think we would like to try it. We have just been shooting for fun and haven't been told how to keep score yet."

"Good. You'll like basketball much more when there is an objective, that is to win. Now here's how it is scored and the rules. Does everybody understand how it works?"

Everyone there seemed to understand the rules, but about half of the males wanted to play on all male teams. "That's fine," said Mac. "That eliminates the high number of males compared to woz, so how about three woz and two males on each mixed team?"

This arrangement seemed to please all, so Mac said, "Okay, we can have four teams of three woz, two males. I think we can have some really fun games."

Four days after the first games, Marla asked Mac how the games were coming along. "I think they are having fun. At first males would only throw the ball to another male; woz would only throw to another wo. But the next day males and woz started throwing the ball to whomever was open. Now they are starting to work as a team."

"Any trouble during the game or after?" said Marla.

"Yesterday, Eddie was a bit rough when he took the ball away from Carla. I blew the whistle, but before I cold go over to him and explain that Carla got a free shot, Freddie walked over to Eddie, stood close to him and said, 'Hey, watch who you're pushing. You're bigger but that's doesn't give you the right to push her around.' Eddie backed away, turned to Carla and said, "Sorry, Carla. I guess I got carried away.'"

Marla smiled, looked around, no one was watching, so she squeezed Mac's hand as she said, "Great, sweetie, it looks like they are about ready for the big dance. Let's have it while you're still here."

XV. La Danse

Marla had only taken a few steps toward the office when she heard the hum. Touching her left eyelid, she heard Annette say, "Marla, I just wanted to tell you that one of the woz at farm number three is not just a low ranked Wo. She is on Cynthia's staff and was transferred there two days before Cynthia was forced to give that farm to me. You can check the records there and find out who this one is. So you and Margo watch your step because Cynthia has spies everywhere."

"Thanks, Annette. We shall be very careful and we are concentrating on making the donors here healthier and sperm production increase. That should please MOTHER MYRNA."

"So how are you getting along with Mac? Isn't he adorable?"

"Adorable."

"As adorable as Ken?"

"Gosh, Annette, how am I to tell?"

"Slowly and carefully, my dear Marla."

"Oh, Annette, we want to eventually have a dance. We think it would be a good way for woz and males to meet each other. Is that all right with you? If so, could you find me something that plays music we can dance to."

"I think a dance is a step in the right direction, but remember, Marla, no touching except for touching hands. We can't let woz and males get excited, well, not yet. It's important to have educated males on our side, but just as important to have many of the three million woz living in dorms and in ignorance to understand what their lives could be like. I have a few ideas for this, but I really don't have a master plan yet."

"Thanks, Annette. Margo and I will look into Cynthia's plant. We shall be very careful.

At the males' dorm, Eddie asked Mac. "So what are you going to do for us that we should trust you?"

"We are going to start to make you free."

"Fine, but what are you and Marla going to do for us right away?"

"Freddie, we are going to teach you to dance."

"Dance? What's that?"

"Dancing is moving to music. You'll see. We are going to start tomorrow or the next day. Freddie, do you think you are okay with that?"

"I guess."

"Good," said Mac. "Then we are going to start in small groups of ten or so. We are going to teach you about how to move when you dance. And no less important, we are going to teach you dance manners. That is, how you behave, what you say, what you do not say."

"Why is that important?" said Glen, a sixteen year old male who was sitting on his bed in the back of the room."

"Why?" said Mac. "You are going to be dancing with woz; that's why. Tomorrow afternoon half of you are going to start your dance lessons while the rest of you will go to work in the field as usual. The day after tomorrow the group that worked in the field will start the dance lessons. Are there any questions?"

"Suppose I don't want to do the dance lessons?" said Jim.

"You come to the lesson. If you don't want to learn to dance, then just sit quietly and watch."

The next afternoon was sunny so half of the males left to work in the fields. The rest gathered around Mac. "Listen now, we won't have any music until tomorrow, so we are just going to practice moving our feet to a beat. What's a beat? It's just what it says, a hit or beat on a drum or table or most anything." Mac picked up a ruler and started to regularly hit it on the back of a chair. As he hit the ruler on the chair he counted, "One, two, three, four. See, that's called rhythm."

He then faced the group and facing them squarely, said, "Now line up on me and face the same way I am facing."

Slowly they did, finally forming somewhat of a straight line. When Mac was somewhat satisfied the line was a good as it would ever be, said, "Now watch me. I will move to the beat. I shall take a step every time I hit the ruler on the chair now watch."

He took one step forward with his left foot as he hit the chair and said, "One." And then he stepped forward and toward the right as he said, "Two." Then he slid his left foot to meet his right foot as he said, "Three. Now I shall pause as I hit the ruler on the chair for four."

Stepping back in line he said, "Now let's all do it. One, left foot forward, two, right foot forward and to the right, three, move the left foot to the right, and four, pause."

Out of the twenty-four males present, only three got their feet tangled, none fell down. "Great," said Mac. "Let's do it again and again. It's very simple, just something new to you."

"That's dancing?" said Freddie sarcastically.

The next day Mac went over the same lesson with the males who worked in the field the day before. The results were the same. The same time that Mac was teaching this second group, Marla was explaining to the woz how the wo Vice President of the United States and her friends took over the war-torn USA and turned it into the country of WOZ.

"You mean that there used to be as many males as woz?"

"Yes, and almost every woz who wanted a male had could have one."

"I'd like that," said Edna.

"I want one for myself," said Gracie. "And I know which one, too."

Marla held up her hand to quiet them. "This is what Margo and I, and many others are working for. But those in power are working hard to keep things the way they are. So we must be very quiet about what we know and how we are going to change this government so that we can have males and our souls. Now you must all pledge to keep what you know to yourself until the time is right."

"When will that be?" said Carla.

"I don't know, but I do know that the music machine and the music I asked for is here. And now we can go over to the males' dormitory and start to learn to dance, not just do that boring exercise, the one where we moved our feet and count one, two, three, four."

A half-hour later, as twenty woz and forty-eight males were gathered at the males' dorm, Marla said, "Now before we begin, I should say a few words about dance manners. First of all, woz and males are equal in the dance. And all dancers must be polite and cheerful. It was the custom, and we are making it the custom again, for the male to ask the wo if she wants to dance with him."

"What does he say?" said Freddie.

"He says something like, 'May I have this dance?' Or he may say, 'Would you dance with me, miss?'"

"What's a miss?" said Edna.

"A miss is an unmarried wo."

"What does unmarried mean?" said Edna. I never heard that word before."

"Marriage is a legal and moral term binding a wo and a male together. We'll go into that another day. But okay, the wo replies, 'I'd love to dance with you,'" said Marla.

"Now Marla and I are going to show you how dancing is done." And then turning to Marla, he said, "Would you dance with me, Marla?"

Marla stood up and grinning answered, "I'd love to dance with you, Mac."

And then she turned on the music machine, put in a disc and the song, *Long Ago and Far Away*. Marla waved at the woz and males gathered around them and said, "Move back a little bit, will you. Mac and I need some room."

Mac took her right hand in his left; Marla put her left hand on his shoulder as he put his right hand on her back. "Now this is the correct position for our dance. First, we shall simply move and count the beat out loud, such as one, two three, four."

"Ready, Marla? Here we go; One, two, three, four," he counted as they moved and counted a dozen times. "All right, "said Marla, "Now we shall dance to the music. Unless you are tone-deaf or have no sense of rhythm, you woz and males should catch on really fast."

The music started again and Marla and Mac danced as Marla whispered into Mac's ear, "Long ago and far away, I found a dream one day," as they danced on and on.

As the song was about to end, Mac very quietly sang in Marla's ear, "And now, that dream is here beside me." His words and being so close sent chills up and down her spine.

The music stopped so Mac and Marla disengaged themselves. Marla then turned to the woz and males there and said, "Now, you males go over to the woz and ask one of them to dance with you. Remember, you say, 'May I have this dance?'"

"Suppose I don't want to dance with the male who asks me," said Edna.

"Then, my dear, you politely say something that won't hurt his feelings like, 'Not right now; would you ask me later?'" said Marla.

"Hurt his feelings? Ha, ha," said Jody, a slim, dark haired wo. "He's a primitive; he has no feelings, he's just a starter fluid machine."

"Then you are excused, Jody," said Marla glancing at the U-10K epaulet on her own shoulder.

Turning to the group, Marla said, "Anyone else feel that way?"

Marla looked at the woz, but there was no response, so Mac said, "Okay, we are going to have a few more practice sessions after work, and then on Saturday we are going to have a dance. Wear your best clothes, uniforms and prepare to have fun."

And start the revolution, thought Marla.

"Just where do you propose to have this big dance?" said Mac as he walked with Marla to the office building for supper.

"I've seen pictures of great waltzes in the old books, large marble palaces, ladies with full skirts, jewelry in their hair, and the males in very formal wear. I doubt we can have anything like that here, but we can make it special, considering what the usual Saturday is like."

"After supper let's walk down to the farm equipment shed. I think it's large enough, has electricity, and a wooden floor. The guys and I can fix it up."

Noticing that Marla's enthusiasm seemed to wither away, Mac said, "Why so pensive? Are you beginning to let the coming problems get to you?"

Walking with her eyes lowered in thought, Marla said, "Annette told me that Cynthia had transferred one of her staff here, supposedly just a 100K Wo, but Annette thinks she could be a spy for Cynthia."

"So do you think we should cancel the dance for now?"

"Maybe, Mac, but we can't be timid forever. Maybe she isn't a spy; maybe Cynthia transferred her here just to get rid of her, maybe."

"This Wo, is she Jody who made a scene about dancing with a male?"

"Margo couldn't find any record of anyone being transferred here recently, so we don't know. It could be Jody, but if she is a spy, would she call attention to herself?"

Remembering to not be negative while Mac was still at Farm #3, she said, "Anyhow, Mac, let's go after supper and look at the farm equipment shed" Just being with Mac gave her spirit a lift. Use this time, enjoy this time, treasure this time and all time with Mac, she told herself. We are now starting a war on oppression. There could be casualties; I could be one; Mac could be one; Ken could be one; we could lose this war.

Later at the equipment shed on the south end of the courtyard, Marla was a bit disappointed at its appearance. It was not clean; it had an old tractor, several hand plows, and stacks of seed bags on the old wooden floor. "What a mess," said Marla to Mac.

"Well, I don't know. The guys and I can get in here tomorrow and clean it all out." He looked carefully at the wooden floor, sitting on it and scraping it to see if it could be cleaned. "Yes, I think this place will do nicely, Marla. We can start on it early tomorrow morning. By Saturday you won't know the place." Pointing to the old tractor, he said, "It won't be a palace, but no one will care. You and I will dance and you will be the Belle of the Ball."

By Saturday afternoon Mac was right; the farm equipment shed didn't look like a Roman palace, but it did look like a country barn palace. The wooden floor was absolutely clean; there were benches and chairs set up around a small area for dancing, with colored paper streamers tied on them; the music machine was set up near the large door; large bare light bulbs were glaring through the red, white, green, blue streamers around them.

Marla, Mac, and George stood at the doorway and surveyed the masterpiece. "You guys did a wonderful job," said Marla. "And I was pleased that woz and the males worked well together to get this all finished."

"I hope that the dance goes off as well," said George. "Mac and I have to go back to farm number four in a week. "I guess Margo is going back too."

"When Annette finds a replacement," said Marla.

Hearing young woz and males approach, some chattering enthusiastically, some not so enthusiastic, the three turned to see the potential dancers arrive. "Take a seat, everyone," said Marla in a loud happy voice. "Woz sit on the small benches, males sit on the long benches, the ones from your dorm."

When all were seated, Marla stood, faced them and announced, "I know most of you are looking forward to dancing with a member of the opposite gender. Some of you would rather die. However, I want all of you to try dancing at least once. If after one time you don't want to dance any more, you may sit and watch."

Marla nodded to Edna who was in charge of the music machine on a small table by the doorway. As the music started Mac stood and said, "To start things off, just watch this first dance. I am going to dance with Marla and George is going to dance with Margo. This is a regular song like we practiced and has four beats, just like we practiced. Now here's how it is done," he said as he approached Marla and said, "May I have this dance, Marla?"

Marla turned toward him and as he took her hand said, "I'd love to dance with you." Then they walked to the open floor area and began moving to the music.

A few seconds later, George said to Margo, "May I have the pleasure of dancing with you?" Margo smiled, said nothing, but placed her arm on his shoulder as he took her other hand and they moved away. "It seems like old times, doesn't it, George?" she whispered in his ear. He smiled and squeezed her hand a bit.

It was a brief dance, too brief for Marla, but she knew that it was not a dance for Mac and her; it was for the woz and males. Marla turned to the woz and males. "All right, now it's your turn. Ten of our woz are here, and thirty males are here too. I've given each male a tag that says A, B, or C on it. So here we go. I want all of the males with the letter A on his slip of paper to dance this first number. I expect all of you to ask a Wo to dance with you."

She looked around and saw little inclination to stand and walk toward the woz, so she said, "All right, do you want to choose your dance partner, or shall I assign partners?"

"Then Freddie stood up and said, "I want to dance with Carla."

"Don't tell us, Freddie," said Mac. "Go over and ask Carla. Do it the way you were taught."

"And will you dance with me, Carla?" said Freddie as he walked right up to her.

"Of course, Freddie, I was hoping that you would ask me."

Freddie took her in his arms, closer than he had been taught, but they were not exactly strangers. After a few moments of rather awkward dancing, Freddie whispered into her ear, "I missed you."

"Missed me?"

"Don't you remember that you used to extract the poison from me?"

"That was strictly medical, Freddie, not personal."

"Yeah, I'll bet. You know I'm built differently than you."

"Freddie, please!"

"Come on, Carla, loosen up. One time you even showed me how we were built differently."

After a moment of quiet, Carla looking into his eyes, but saying nothing, she smiled and said, "I do like you, but this is not the time to talk about it. Please."

Mac looked at Eddie standing next to him. "Eddie, go ask Marla to dance." Eddie froze in his tracks.

"Marla, Eddie wants to dance with you, but he has forgotten how to ask you."

She looked at Eddie, gave him a big smile and said, "Eddie, I'll just assume you asked me so I'll just say, "Eddie, I would love to dance with you." Taking his hand she led him onto the dance floor and proceeded to lead him saying, I'll help you with the steps for a moment, and then you take charge, okay?"

Eddie smiled and did his best to follow her.

Gracie looked at George as they were dancing, and then said, "We're too far away for me to follow you well. Would it be all right if you held me a little closer. I can't follow you very well at this distance.'

With an unemotional voice, he said, "Gracie, I wish that you could follow me back to farm number four." And then he smiled, looked her in the eye, wrinkled his nose, and said, "One never knows what tomorrow will bring." When he urged her toward him each knew that the other was the opposite gender.

During a break in the dancing Mac turned to Marla. "When we started tonight all of the woz but one were here, and now I count twelve here. I wonder why Jody decided to come. I thought that she hated males."

"I'll find out," said Marla as she casually wandered over by Jody who was talking to Carla and Edna. Marla heard her say, "Well, I still don't like it, but maybe I could be wrong. Maybe there is more to males than just sperm machines."

"Well, I think there is," said Carla. "And it looks like a few of the woz think so too. Why don't you choose one to teach you to dance? You might find it sort of interesting."

Jody looked around for a moment, then indicating George, said, "I think I'll ask that one. He seems to know more than the others, or at least as much as Mac. Yes, he's not bad looking... for a male, that is. Yes, I'll get George to ask me to dance."

After almost two hours all of the males but two had danced at least one time; all of the woz had danced several times. Noticing that most of them, males and woz were getting tired, and noticing that several males were getting too interested in a few woz, Marla said, "All right, guys and woz, there is punch and cookies in the food room. So, let's all go there to celebrate our first dance party."

Margo with George nearby led the group to the Administration Building and the food room. Marla walked with Mac and she noticed that Freddie and Carla walked together to the food room as did several other males and woz who had danced more than once with each other. But most of the woz and males walked in groups of their own gender.

At the party Margo said to Marla, "How do you think it went? It looks like the males are talking to each other and the woz are doing the same. I don't see any wo-male couples standing here talking."

"Time, Margo, give them time. Seeds have been sown, plants will sprout and grow," said Mac.

"It would be interesting to know what these people will dream about tonight. I doubt that it will be basketball," said George, looking at Margo and smiling.

"Maybe we can do this every Saturday evening," said Margo. "But let's see if we hear from outside the farm. Maybe I am in for trouble. After all, I am supposed to run this place and produce crops."

"I would like to suggest that we have a meeting and plan our strategy," said Marla. "We need to really consider what steps to take now and we need to agree on whom to take in with us. I'll bet that there are thousands who feel like we do, but feel that they are alone."

At that instant the door opened and Glen came running into the room. Excited, he yelled, "Mac, Marla, one of the males sneaked out and ran over to the woz dorm."

"Why?" said Gracie.

"Why? He said that as it wasn't poison one of the woz was taking from him, he wanted her to do it again. He really went wild and said he wanted to make a baby himself."

The room was suddenly vacant as Mac, George, Marla, and Margo rushed out the door and ran over to the woz dormitory. They rushed in the door to find Freddie trying to put his arms around Carla. As they entered the building they heard him say, "Come on Carla, let's make a baby the right way. You know what I've got and I know what you've got"

"No, Freddie. I took the poison out of you and I kissed you a few times, but that's as far as it goes."

Just then Mac was close enough to grab Freddie's collar and pull him away from Carla. Freddie then collapsed and started to cry, "But I want to do it. It's not fair that we are slaves with nothing to live for."

Margo stepped forward and said, "Close the door." When it was closed, she continued, "Now listen, everyone. Nothing happened here. Nothing, because if something did happen Cynthia would take back this farm, maybe she'd get all of the farms. She could eliminate all of us, too."

Turning to Mac, she said, "Let him up."

"I'm sorry," said Freddie. I just couldn't help it."

"This time, Freddie, it's okay. I guess the dancing got you too excited," said Margo. "But for all of our sakes, it must never happen again. Someday males and woz will make babies as nature intended. But we must work hard and be very careful to see that our someday will come."

"Suspend all education but reading, writing, and math until we can work out a program," said Margo. "I don't think that we had better have any more dances for a while."

"I suggest that we increase work time and basketball time for everyone," said Mac.

"And will that keep them more tranquil?" said Marla.

"I don't know," said Mac, "But it should make everyone more tired at the end of the day."

"Fine," said Margo. "Monday morning we shall have a meeting to determine what we should do and how we should do it. I'm going to ask Anna to come down and join us. Tomorrow we can rest and I would like everyone to think about our plans, make suggestions, but for now, good night. Mac, Marla, please go check and make certain all of the woz and the males are in their dorms. We don't need any more excitement tonight."

XVI. The Best of Plans

At 9:50 Monday morning Anna arrived at Starter Farm Number Three and went immediately to Margo's office where she was greeted by Marla with a hug. "Hello, Anna, so nice to see you again." Marla wanted to greet her with more intensity, but no one knew that Anna was her mother and they wanted to keep it that way.

"Well, Marla," Anna said, "You've done well since the days when you were a wo at one of my dorms."

"I've tried."

Margo heard Anna and smiling entered the reception area to greet her. "Anna, it's been a long time since I have seen you. How have you been? Shall we get some coffee and go into the other room and get started. You probably don't have a lot of time."

"I don't, so I guess we should get started."

"All right, let's go into my office." Turning to Gracie, Margo said, "Would you bring some coffee and cups into my private office, please?"

As they were sitting down at the table Marla heard a hum and said, "Excuse me, Annette is calling me."

Then touching her left eyelid, she heard Annette say, "Marla, you are to run farm number three as Margo is going back to farm number five. Oh, head of a starter farm requires the rank of U One K, so you are promoted. Oh, and you can keep Mac there to help you if you wish."

Marla touched her right eyelid and said, "Thank you, Annette. I'll do my very best here."

With a big smile on her face, Marla said to the rest, "I've been promoted to U One K and in charge here so Margo can go home to number five."

"Congratulations," said Anna.

"Congratulations, and I suppose that you would like to keep Mac here to help you," said Margo.

"That's a good idea, Margo. I guess I will keep him here, if it's all right with Bonnie."

A few minutes later, and with the door closed, Anna said, "Now, how can I help you? Marla has filled me in a bit about what you are doing here, the fraternization between the woz and the males, the dance, and the disturbance Saturday night. Where do you plan to go from here?"

"From what I have learned from the dance and the disturbance right after, I think that we have to be very careful what we do. The woz are beginning to want males. Okay, that's fine, except for one thing. If we have many more woz wanting males than there are males, then we are going to be in a bind. How do we keep them patiently waiting until there are more males, many more males? We also don't want Cynthia to know what we are doing until it is too late for her to stop us."

"I see the problem, Margo," said Anna. "After all, you can't just buy a million males at the store."

"So we have to produce a few hundred thousand males before anyone knows about it," said Marla. "Too bad we can just go off into the desolate countryside and do it."

"MOTHER MYRNA wants to increase the population, but the vast majority of new ones would be woz. We want to increase the population, but mostly males. I assume we are agreed on that. Now as head of population control, I can help you some, but you must be careful," said Anna. I am U One K, but I am not head of state, so you must do as Annette ᵒᶠᶠⁱᶜⁱᵃˡˡʸ told you; that is, to increase the sperm output and expenses here at farm number three."

)icked up several sheets of paper as she said, "I . rather sketchy list of things to do to educate the woz about males. Most of them believe that there are no such creatures or that they are primitives in cages somewhere."

"Why don't you read the list, Marla," said Anna.

"All right, here are some possible things we can do:

"Let woz teach each other the truth. We can do that if we:

"Routinely transfer woz between regular dormitories and starter farms.

"Transfer woz between Cynthia's farms and ours.

"Assign first mothers with male children and female children to the same dormitory. This enables children to learn that there are two genders and what the other gender is like.

"We can produce more males if we:

"Stop killing sperm with the Y chromosome.

"Stop aborting male fetuses.

"Establish new starter farms.

"Teach all males to read and write.

"Here's two ideas for later on. We have to be very careful on these two:

"See if there is an old law on marriage still legal.

"If so, have Annette appoint a marriage official to marry the woz and males.

"Allow woz on starter farms to get pregnant nature's way."

Nodding her head yes, Anna said, "Those are good ideas, Marla, but the main thing is to protect the males we have, utilize them to the max, and keep Cynthia and the U-100 committee off of our backs. Some of them might believe as we do, but no one likes to give up power."

"Providing we don't have any interference," said Anna. "How long will it take us to have enough males to really be able to satisfy most of the woz who want one?"

"I've done some calculations," said Margo, "Although I'm not certain about the numbers: We are now getting about 18,000 woz pregnant per year with our present supply of sperm. If we extract sperm three times a week instead of two, we can in theory get about 27,000 pregnant a year.

That's in theory. If we stop killing the Y chromosomes and stop aborting males, we should increase our male population by 9,000 a year. I read that in the old USA there were 102 males born for every 100 woz."

"But they won't be able to produce adequate sperm until fifteen years later," said Anna.

"I know, Anna, but in fifteen years we shall have 19,250 males producing sperm. The next year we shall have 38,750 males producing sperm, and the next year almost 60,000 males. By that time we should have many of the younger woz knowing the true history of WOZ, and ready for natural conception, not conception by injection. Even now a large number of our population should be past the child-bearing age, so we don't have to worry about males available to produce their children. Maybe they'll want them for fun, but first things first."

Marla spoke up. "But it's the fun part that will produce the instant motivation, not the probability of producing a baby. And I doubt you can stop an idea whose time has come."

"Okay," said Margo. "What do we do now?"

"The way I see it," said Marla, "We have to take over the other two starter farms as soon as possible. All starter farms must work together; all males and woz at the farms must know the truth and be willing to work with us. We need to educate those males at farms one and two, increase production there, and we need them to do farm-dormitory transfers. And we certainly don't want to worry that the Upper-Uppers will find out what we are really doing, trying to establish a two gender country again."

Anna held up her hand, touched her left eyelid, and then put her fingers to her lips. "Shhhhhhh, I am getting a message from Annette." Anna frowned as she listened, then touched her right lid and said to Annette, "That's terrible. All right, I'll go back to my office immediately."

Marla and Margo sat in silence waiting for Anna to speak. After twenty seconds she did. "MOTHER MYRNA is dead!"

All gasped. Finally Margo said, "How, why?"

Quietly Anna said, "Annette thinks Cynthia had her killed. The official story is that one of her male lovers stabbed her. But Annette thinks Cynthia had someone else murder her."

"So now we really have to be careful because if Cynthia gets away with this, she is now U-1. I mean she is MOTHER CYNTHIA."

"Margo," said Marla, "What do you mean if she gets away with it? Who is going to arrest her? We three are U One K and we can be demoted in a split second if Cynthia says the word."

"There's Annette, next in line."

"When U-1 has all of the power and uses it in any way she pleases, there isn't much Annette can do, at least legally," said Anna.

"Anna, she does everything she can," said Marla. '

"Well," said Anna, with a slight smile, "That leaves the other way, illegally and quietly. I guess that I had better get back to my office now. Keep in touch; but not electronically; we should use trusted messengers."

As she started for the door all three of them heard a hum, touched their left eyelids and heard, "This is Cynthia and this is an announcement to all U One Ks. I am now U-1; I am MOTHER CYNTHIA. My darling sister, Myrna, was brutally murdered by two males who have now been eliminated. This should be a lesson to all of us that my grandmother, MOTHER MYRNA The First, was correct when she said, 'Males cause all of the evil in this world.' I know that some of you have gone soft on males, but that must cease immediately. We keep them alive for one purpose only, and my administration will be diligent to guarantee that they remain inferior creatures. I am going to keep WOZ pure. I hope that I have made myself clear on this."

XVII. Mother Cynthia

Tuesday morning, the sun was just peaking over the hill, and hungry birds were chirping. Inside her apartment at Starter Farm Number Three, Marla woke up. Her first thought was that she was now one of the Upper One Thousand. Yes, I'm now U One K, and she smiled inside.

Her next thought quickly dissolved that smile as she remembered that Cynthia, who was against everything Marla believed, was now the head of WOZ. Cynthia could destroy all of her dreams; Cynthia could eliminate her and all of her friends, even Annette.

It was time for her to get up and say her pledge, but to whom should she say it? Not knowing what she would really say, she got up and stood by her bed as she had done thousands of times, and said, "I pledge that I shall always be a loyal wo, complete in every way and that I shall always love and support MOTHER...." Oh, my gosh, she thought, do I have to say MOTHER CYNTHIA? I don't know if I can, but I suppose I must. What I must do is find out what Cynthia is going to do, and then I must figure out what position to take. Do I openly fight her or do I appear to support her publicly, but work for my own agenda quietly? I must talk to Annette, and then decide what we shall do to not only survive, but eventually defeat Cynthia.

Was I happier when I was just a wo with no status, but no worries? No, I was not. I am U One K and I love it. Ignorant, common wo Marla is going to make history in WOZ. So watch out, Cynthia, here I come. First thing after I've had my coffee, I'll meet with Gracie, Mac, and George. We've got to hide what we have done from Cynthia.

Annette was so wise not to send me to Ten K School and keep me unknown.

An hour later, seated at a table in Marla's office were Gracie, Mac, and George. "Close the door, please, Gracie, and let's talk about the situation. First of all, Gracie, how long have you been at this farm?"

"About three years."

"In these three years has MOTHER CYNTHIA ever visited here?"

Gracie looked up as though the answer were written on the ceiling. "I don't think so, however, I was gone for a month one time, Marla."

"Has she sent anyone here to inspect the place?"

"Marla, I mean Ma'am, she has sent a Wo with the epaulet of an U-100K several times, but I suspect her rank was really much higher. She asked a lot of questions, mostly about whether males could read or write, and how they were treated. But as far as Cynthia, she wasn't MOTHER CYNTHIA then, she never saw the place."

"Well, Annette told me that MOTHER MYRNA thought that Cynthia was lazy, only interested in her own fun, not in how farms were run. Of course now, she is U-1 and she may feel differently. At any rate, we must make her happy with us."

"Marla, what should we males do now?" said Mac.

"You, George, and the guys must go back to being just ignorant donors, at least as far as anyone can tell. You may go on educating the males, but you must not do it openly. Hide the books when not in actual use. You must also explain all of this to the other males. It's for their survival and their future. My guess is that she does not care about the survival of WOZ which depends on having a sufficient number of males. Annette described her to me as a spoiled brat"

"One question, please, ma'am. You command this place, so I guess that we should not call you Marla. Should we address you as ma'am?" said Gracie.

Marla exhaled loudly. "I suppose that in front of anyone, especially woz and the males, you should not call me Marla. I must obey those above me, and those below me must obey me. I intend to really run this place and I shall set the tone of this farm, not to please my ego, but to guide us so we won't be eliminated. However, in private we are just friends and I prefer that you call me Marla."

"So what would you like for the males and me to do right now?" said Mac.

"You and George need to explain to the males what has happened and what they should do. We'll keep self extraction of sperm for now for those who are doing it that way. Then I want you to replace some of the fence and return locks to the gates. And there must be no fraternization between males and woz for the time being."

"The woz are certainly not going to like that," said Gracie.

"Gracie, you have got to explain the situation to them. They have to be patient if they ever want to be with males again. And they must address me as ma'am."

Frowning, Gracie said, "Well, I'll try."

"When they complain, ask them if they would like Verna to return as head Wo?" said Mac.

"Do any of you have anything to add?" said Marla.

No one said anything, so Marla stood and said, "Look, we are all in this together. We must have discipline and do what we have to do in order to survive. So go give the bad news to the others and tell them to cheer up. Cynthia can't live forever."

As they were going out the door of the office, Marla said, "Gracie, please ask Jody to come to the office."

Ten minutes later, Jody entered Marla's office. In the week Marla had been at Starter Farm Number three she had never seen Jody smile. She wasn't scowling, but her jaw seemed hard set and she didn't appear to socialize with the other woz.

Marla smiled and greeted her by saying, "Sit down please, Jody. Let's have a chat."

Expressionless, Jody sat down at the small conference table, looking for Marla to set the tone of this conversation. Marla placed a few papers in front of her and then said, "Jody, I know very little about you. According to my information you arrived here just a few days before I did. I would like for you to tell me about yourself please."

Jody looked down, and brushed some crumbs from her shirt, or seemed to do so. After a moment, she said, "Ma'am, I don't really know what to tell you. I was transferred here because I had terrible allergies, you know, sneezing a lot, at farm number one. What else could I tell you?"

"You are not wearing an epaulet so I don't know your rank. You could tell me that."

"I'm just a U-100K."

"I see. You have allergies; is that the only reason you were sent here?"

"As far as I know."

Marla looked through the three sheet of paper in front of her and then said, "Are you certain you are not U Ten K?"

"Does it say that on my paperwork in front of you?"

"I haven't read it all yet; I thought that you might save us some time here."

"Ma'am, I'm sorry I called males primitive last week. I don't really feel that way now, not since I danced with George. Dancing with him was so... well, it made me feel alive."

Marla said nothing but only faced Jody with an expressionless look. "Please don't hold my blurting out about males and leaving the dance lesson against me."

"Jody, let me tell you two things. I expect to be told the truth and I do not punish someone who may disagree with me. I am here to run this farm and I expect to be obeyed as I must obey those over me. It is not going to be an easy job and what I really want to know is will you work with me. If you don't want to work with me, say so and I shall transfer you where you will be more comfortable."

Jody started to tear and then broke down into a full fledged cry. "Please don't send me away. I want to stay here." And then after wiping her eyes, she went on, "Ma'am, I'll tell you everything I know, just let me stay and help you."

"Tell me."

"I am really U Ten K and I was sent here by Cynthia, er, MOTHER CYNTHIA, now. She sent me here to report on Verna because she thought Verna was not doing her job at all. I never had time to send any report as Verna was sent somewhere else."

"Fine, Jody, you may stay." Marla handed her a tissue as she said, "Dry your eyes; we have work to do. We have to at least appear to follow what Cynthia wants. So you and Gracie must keep the woz in check. I hate it, but I must follow orders; I don't want to be a common wo again."

"Thank you, ma'am."

Right after Jody left the office, Gracie entered. "Ma'am, there is a messenger wo here to see you."

"Do you know this wo?"

"No."

Marla walked into the reception office and looked out the open door. Marla grinned and yelled, "Pat. I'm so happy to see you. Come on in." Then turning to Gracie, "This is Pat; and she is an old friend."

As Pat entered Marla gave him a hug and then they walked into Marla's private office. After the door was closed, Pat took off his wig and smiling said, "Marla, it's so great to see you again. It's only been just a few weeks, but it seems like years since we left the cabin."

"Sit down, won't you, and tell me why you're here."

Pat still standing said, "I can't; I have to get right back. I bear a verbal message from Annette. She said to tell you not to call her or write her. She does want to meet with you tomorrow, so have Mac take you to that place where you and

Annette had lunch by the side of the road not long ago. She said you should remember what she taught you."

Marla smiled and hugged him. The she touched her finger to her lips and said, "She means I am to listen and play dumb."

"Pat laughed a bit. "That's what she means." Turning toward the door, he put on his wig and adjusted it, leaned toward her and kissed her on the forehead. "Keep dancing, well, dancing in your dreams."

As he walked away from the office to his vehicle, Gracie said, "So that's Annette's male, huh?"

Marla turned and looked amazed. "How did you know?"

"Ma'am, his wig was on backwards when he left."

The next day Marla and Mac, wearing his blond wig and assuming his wo identity as Myrtle, were approaching a small group of pine trees on a hill surrounded by freshly planted corn. As they slowed their approach the dust from the road caught up with them and blocked their view of Annette and Pat standing by the road. As soon as the car had stopped Marla jumped out and hurried to Annette. "I'm so glad to see you, Annette," then turning to Pat, added, "You, too, Pat."

Annette gave her a hug, but said, "Let's get away from the road and this dust. I have only a few minutes before I have to get back to my house, so forgive me if I am a bit brief, even a bit rude. But, Marla, we have trouble living with us now."

"I know, Annette, and I need you to help me to think about what I should do."

"Do? Cynthia is the head of the state. We obey her. Well, obey her up to a point. We put her at ease, but we don't forget our mission."

"I know, but how do I put her at ease?"

"Let's go sit on that log over there and talk a bit," said ~tte quietly, her face showing wrinkles of concern.

ided and following Annette to a large pine log

hidden from view from the road. Pat, carrying a picnic basket, followed them to the log and handed each a sandwich and then poured them some coffee. "Marla, you eat while I say what's on my mind."

Marla took a bit of her sandwich and then turned toward Annette who said, "Marla, what you have going for you is that you are an unknown Wo. There is no record of anything about you except your birth and your attendance at 100K school. No one knows that Anna is your mother."

"It's on the computer that I was on your staff, isn't it?"

"But that's all."

"Suppose Cynthia asks me how I became U One K?"

"Tell her the truth, in fact always tell Cynthia the truth because if she catches you in a lie, she'll have it out for you. Of course, you don't have to tell her the whole truth, just don't lie. And do not volunteer anything."

"So I tell her I was appointed to run farm number three and probably that's why I was promoted to U One K?'

"The main thing to do about Cynthia is to be really supportive of her. She wants and needs Woz to like her and flatter her a bit, not too much now, she's not stupid, but she does want to be thought superior."

"I'll try."

"And, Marla, she likes Woz to do little favors for her, unexpected favors, unexpected compliments. But don't overdo it. Don't be a push-over. In the language of the Twentieth Century, 'Don't be an ass kisser.'"

"Annette, let me tell you what I have done since I heard that Cynthia had taken over. I put the locks back on the gates; Mac hid all of the books and the music machine; stopped the fraternization of woz and males. I also had Mac and Gracie caution both woz and males to keep to themselves and not talk about the dances. They weren't thrilled, but I told them that if Cynthia knew what was going on in our minds she would probably bring back Verna or someone like her."

Annette quickly put down her sandwich, took a sip of her coffee, put her fingers to her left lid and said, "Hello, Sandy. What's on your mind?" She listened quietly for a moment and then touching her right eyelid said, "Thanks Sandy, I'll start back right now."

Annette ate the last bite of her sandwich, finished her coffee and then turning to Marla, said, "Sandy tells me that one of our friends who works for Cynthia told her that Cynthia is going to visit all of the starter farms starting tomorrow."

"So soon? Ouch!"

"Ouch is right, Marla. We both should get back to our jobs right now. I don't know what tomorrow will bring, but it won't be singing and dancing until we can convince Cynthia that we are not a threat to her."

"I'll do my very best acting. When I was a common wo I learned not to ask questions, keep my mouth shut, and listen."

As Annette started to walk toward her car she stopped and turned toward Marla. "Oh, I almost forgot one of the reasons I wanted to see you." Reaching into her pocket she brought out a key and offered it to Marla. "This is the key to the closet where I have all of the books, papers, and photos about the United States. There are two keys only. I have the other one hidden in the ground at the cabin."

Things are getting serious, Marla thought. I wonder if Annette feels in danger. I know I fear for her and for myself too; wish I didn't. "In case of an emergency, Annette?"

"We can afford to lose this evidence of who we really were, and who we really are, too. Keep this hidden just in case... well, just in case."

"I shall guard it always." As Marla entered her car she turned and said, "Good bye, Annette. We'll win yet." Under her breath she added, "I hope."

Wednesday morning Marla found herself being shaken Wo with a deep voice saying, "All right, Marla nd get up. You have a lot of explaining to do."

Marla didn't know where she was, but this deep loud voice kept yelling at her to get out of bed and face her. As she opened her eyes she wanted to run as this Wo shaking her was tall as Mac, muscular as the largest male she had ever seen, and ready to tear her to pieces.

"Who are you? What have I done?" cried Marla.

"I am Cynthia, ruler of WOZ and you are trying to destroy me, but I shall destroy you. Confess how you and Annette are trying to kill me, but I shall eliminate you and all of your male friends anyway." With that, the horrible Wo grabbed Marla by the throat and reached for a large knife, its blade shining brightly in the sun. Marla closed her eyes and as she did so, the ceiling of her bedroom slowly appeared.

She sat up in bed thinking, goodness, what a dream. She began to realize that she was shaking and breathing rapidly, so decided to get up and regain control of herself. It's light out now, so I should get rid of my panic and get moving, she thought. I'd better check the farm and make certain that it would meet with Cynthia's approval, or at least not displease her too much.

As she raced through her bedroom and office, she hastily gulped a cup of coffee, briefly thinking that she wished she were back at Annette's having poached eggs at the elegant diving room. Well, she wasn't, so time to make one last check to make certain some wo or male hasn't really messed things up. As she passed through the outer office, Gracie was cleaning the windows in the upper half of the outer door. "Great, Gracie. We must make a good impression, especially if MOTHER CYNTHIA didn't like the way Verna ran the place."

Marla left the administration building and walked to the fence around the male dormitory. At the gate Carla unlocked the padlock and let Marla through the gateway. "Thank you, Carla. You're very efficient. Sorry we have to go back to the locked gates, but what is, is, and we may be inspected any time now." Carla smiled and said, "Yes, ma'am do fine."

Entering the male dormitory, she noticed Mac in his work clothes lining up the bunks in a straight line. "I thought it should look very military, like these males were common soldiers following orders," said Mac.

"Yes, Mac, let everything look as though they are just unthinking, unfeeling canon fodder."

"Canon fodder?"

"Oh, that's an old term for soldiers sent into battle to die and no one cared."

"Okay, ma'am, canon fodder."

"Everything looks fine here. So, how are the males taking the changes we had to make?"

"They were just getting used to being worth something and now they are depressed."

"I don't blame them." After a moment's pause, Marla smiled a bit, took two steps toward Mac, put her arms around him and kissed him. "It's not easy for any of us to go back to the old ways, but we have to do so, at least for a little while. We are giving up a little bit so we don't have to give up everything we want. They have to understand that and accept it."

"Mac, one more thing: If you or they ever think that I have changed my mind about anything and thrown in with Cynthia, don't believe it. I do have to follow orders, but I also may only be appearing to follow orders. The woz and males here have to work with me in what will probably be a trying time."

Mac put his arms around her and kissed her not lightly, not briefly. As he let her go he said, "Now to battle. Watch out, Cynthia, your days are numbered."

Marla wiped a few tears from her eyes as she stood her full height and then marched out the door, felt the warm sunshine, and headed for the woz dormitory. As she entered the dormitory she heard Jody yell, "All right woz, stand by your beds; Marla is here to inspect."

Jody then appeared from the nearest bedroom. "Good morning, ma'am. I hope that you will find everything to your satisfaction."

"Thank you, Jody. It looks fine. Now relax and tell me how the woz like the change since Saturday night."

Jody thought for a moment then said, "Well, some never understood what you were trying to do anyway. Several of them didn't care if males were huz or still primitives, but most liked the idea of dancing with males, and most liked the idea of natural, what should I say, the natural conception of babies."

"Do you think that they can take a change back to the old way of thinking, at least for a little while?"

"I don't know, but probably they will cooperate."

Marla exhaled, looked up for a moment as though her next words were written on the walls. "Jody, this is for information, certainly not a threat from me, but if MOTHER CYNTHIA thinks these woz will cause trouble, trouble for her, she could easily have them eliminated. Many woz have suddenly disappeared when they have caused trouble."

Jody looked down a bit. "Yes, ma'am, I know of some who just weren't around one day."

"And Jody, no one is to mention dancing with males unless asked. Then, don't lie, but don't volunteer information or opinions."

Well, back to the office now. I guess we are as ready as we can be, Marla thought, as she turned and smiled at Jody. "Remind the woz that I have to follow orders, but I don't intend to be a fanatic about it."

So today is Wednesday, she thought. Will she come today? Will she come next Wednesday, or Friday, or not for a month? I wish she would come right now so I can get this over with. Suppose she comes in two months after we have relaxed a bit and finds the woz and males in a basketball game or worse? Come on, Cynthia, come soon so we'll know where we stand.

After lunch Marla sat at her desk starting to check some figures on production and expenses. Unable to hold her eyes open a second longer she put her head down on the desk and instantly was fast asleep. A few minutes later she felt someone tapping on her shoulder saying, "Marla, Marla, someone just drove up."

Struggling to not only wake up, but to appear to be wide awake and alert, Marla knew what she must do. Woz do not wait for high ranking Woz to come looking for them. Woz rush to greet the visiting Upper-Uppers. Stealing a moment for a quick glance in the mirror, Marla rushed through the outer door and down the steps to the car. Standing by the rear door were two large Woz who probably were males wearing wigs, and a average sized Wo whose epaulet signified that she was U-100, a member of the ruling council.

Marla held her breath waiting to see who then exited the vehicle. It must be Cynthia. Goodness, she thought, I must remember to say MOTHER CYNTHIA. After a moment, a short, blond Wo stepped out of the car. My goodness, Cynthia is short and blond, a real blond. She's not big or ugly at all. She's very pretty and not some huge monster who is going to grab me and twist my head off. No, she'll get two big males to do it. Cynthia stood for a second beside the car and then looked at Marla. I'd better greet her immediately, Marla thought, so she took one step toward Cynthia, and with a broad smile, bowed slightly and exuberantly said, "MOTHER CYNTHIA, I am so pleased and thrilled to see you. Thank you for visiting us," and then she stepped back slightly, still smiling, and bowed again.

Suddenly Marla had a flashback to one day when she was in 100K school. She had poured quite a bit of gravy on the potatoes. The cooking teacher was standing beside her and said, "Marla, that is much too much gravy." Marla remembered very well that she had answered, "Better too ᴸ than not enough." So here she was pouring out a ed amount of greeting on someone she feared. Was too much better than not enough? Powerful Woz like to be recognized, she thought.

Cynthia smiled slightly, looked at Marla closely, but finally said, "You're Marla?"

"Yes, MOTHER CYNTHIA."

"I would like to look around."

"Yes, ma'am. Would you like something to drink or eat first?"

"Perhaps after I have finished inspecting this farm."

Good, thought Marla. Let's get this over with and done. "Where would you like to start first, ma'am?"

"The donors' dormitory."

Marla turned to Gracie who was by her side, "Gracie, run and tell Carla to unlock the gate so that MOTHER CYNTHIA doesn't have to wait to get to the donors' dorm."

Gracie bowed slightly to Cynthia, then ran to give Carla the order. Carla was standing at the gate and immediately unlocked and opened it.

Cynthia turned to her two large males posing as woz and said, "You stay with the car, and then said to the U-100 Wo standing by her side, "Betty, why don't you go look at the woz dorm while I look at the donors' dorm."

Betty started for the woz dorm as Cynthia said, "Come, Marla, show me how the donors live here at farm number three."

"Yes, MOTHER CYNTHIA, happy to show you whatever you wish to see." Happy to get this over with, thought Marla.

On their way to the donor's dormitory Cynthia said, "I never heard of you, Marla, until yesterday when I saw that you were U One K and ran this farm. Where did you come from?"

"Ma'am, I'm not certain I know what you mean. Do you mean?"

"I mean who was your First Mother, how do you know Annette and why did she promote you to U One K?"

"My mother's name was also Marla; and I am twenty-two years old. For some reason Anna liked me and sent me to 100K School. I was working after graduation and decided to write MOTHER MYRNA and ask her if I could go to Ten K school. For some reason Annette got the letter, scolded me for writing that letter, but assigned me to her staff. We came here about three weeks ago and Annette saw the dirty, run down farm, fired Verna, then had Margo run the place for a few weeks. Then two days ago Margo went back to farm number five and I was told I was in charge and promoted to U One K."

"Marla, several times, you said, 'for some reason.' What reason do you think you have been promoted several times?"

"Ma'am, I was told when I was a common wo to never ask questions, so I have tried to follow that advice."

"Marla, who told you never to ask questions? Was it your First Mother?"

"MOTHER CYNTHIA, I was told that my First Mother had killed herself by hanging."

"Yes, that's what my record shows."

At this point they were at the doorway of the donor dormitory. Cynthia stopped at the open door, frowned as she looked at the freshly painted trim. "It looks like it has just been painted."

"Yes, ma'am. Margo ordered it painted when we first inspected the farm. Margo also ordered that broken windows be replaced and a hole in the roof be repaired."

"Is that too much catering to the donors?"

"MOTHER CYNTHIA, I think that we found several donors ill; two were in the hospital, others were sick here. Annette said that sick donors give very little sperm, so we should keep them healthy."

"Quite so. What else was done to promote their health?"

"A donor named Mac suggested we install the basketball hoops that were kept in the storage building. He said that exercise makes them healthier and makes them tired at night, and that makes them easier to control."

Cynthia walked inside the building a few steps, noticed the beds lined up in a straight row and said, "Very interesting, is it your idea?"

"No ma'am. Mac's. He has been much help to me in controlling the donors." Immediately Marla realized that she had volunteered information and should not have mentioned Mac in any way. Well, too late now.

"Yes, very interesting. Mac is not the average donor, is he?"

"I don't know much about donors, ma'am. He just seems useful in getting donors to do what I want them to do."

Any smile that Cynthia might have had disappeared as she looked Marla in the eyes with intensity. "Tell me, Marla, I had a report that there was a dance here last week. Donors and woz were dancing together. Is that true?"

"Yes, ma'am, it is true."

"And how did that work out?"

"Some woz liked it, some refused to dance with a donor."

"And did you like it, Marla? I want your honest answer."

"Ma'am, it was fun. At that time I didn't know your strong belief and rule about males. I do now. It will never happen again. But let me tell you that when I was six or seven years old we used to play with dogs. That was fun too, but we knew they were dogs, not woz."

"Hmmmm," said Cynthia. "Well, no more dances here. Do you understand?"

"MOTHER CYNTHIA, I understand and I shall obey you."

"Marla, I think I have seen what I came to see. So I think I shall leave now." Turning to walk away she said quietly, "Well, I shall watch your progress in making this farm efficient and profitable."

At the car Marla with a smile said, "MOTHER CYNTHIA, thank you for coming to see us. I appreciate it," and then she raised her hand and waved as the car drove away."

As Marla watched Cynthia's car fade from view Jody then appeared. "That Woz who came to inspect the woz dorm simply looked around inside at the building, looked at Edna and me, then without saying a single word, just walked out. She's a strange one, she is."

"Well, Jody, I think that they knew what they were looking for. I don't know if they found out what they wanted or if they liked us. I only know that they are gone, at least for now."

Marla exhaled and slowly shook her head. "She is no dummy; she investigated the farm and me and knew exactly what to ask. She wanted to leave here with us feeling we had nothing to worry about, but I think she is going to watch us like a hawk watches chickens."

"She really looked me over, too," said Mac who had come up behind them. "But she didn't say anything to me."

"Of course not. She would never talk to a male in public; probably talks to her male lovers though." But if she takes Mac from me, I'll kill her, thought Marla.

XVIII. To Hear is to Obey, or is it?

The sun was peeking through the tree tops; hungry birds were chirping; and in the distance tractors were noisily digging into the earth making it ready for seed. Marla was not asleep, but sitting at her table drinking coffee, thinking that it's been two weeks now and she had not heard anything from Cynthia. Good, she thought, maybe she has forgotten about me and the dance we held here. Of course, she has not forgotten, she's simply going to deal with me when she feels like it. She's knows I'm waiting to see if she will let it pass, and then go on doing what I want to do when I feel the heat is off. But I won't. I'll just be a good Wo in every way she wants; yeah, I'll be a good Wo except for planning how to get what I want.

Hearing a hum, Marla touched her left eyelid. "Marla, this is Dr. Susan. It's time for your yearly physical exam and shots. Can you be here day after tomorrow at one in the afternoon?"

Marla thought for a few seconds then touching her right eyelid answered, "How good of you to remind me. Yes, I think I can be there day after tomorrow at one."

Well, that's one day I won't be able to do things here, so I'd better get today's work and the next few day's work done. Wait a minute, I just had my physical and my shots two months ago. Well, maybe I'm wrong, but even if I am right, I'll stop and see Anna. I'd better go see Mac and make certain he can take me to see Anna. It's against the rules for any Wo, U One K and up to travel alone. I assume he has a proper wig to wear.

Two days later at one in the afternoon Marla opened the door of Dr. Susan's reception room and was met by Angela who greeted her with a smile. "Marla! It's so nice to see you. And you're now U One K. Oh, I guess I have to address you as ma'am, sorry."

Marla gave Angela a brief hug, "Angela, unless there are Upper-Uppers around, just call me Marla, like you did when I was a common wo. My rank has changed but I haven't.

"Good, Marla, but now go right in; Dr. Susan is waiting to see you."

Smiling, Marla opened the door in anticipation of seeing Dr. Susan, and there she was sitting by the side of Anna, both having a cup of coffee. They both rose to greet Marla and gave her a brief hug. Then Dr. Susan said, "Sorry, Marla, I got your last physical and shots dates confused, so you don't really need either; sorry to drag you away from your work"

"By the way, Dr. Susan, Did you get an order from Annette that you are not to abort any male fetuses?"

"Yes, and I have not even seen any male fetuses, but I did get the order."

"Good, because Annette and MOTHER MYRNA were alarmed at the low birth rate and felt that we needed more donors. Annette told me that we are not even keeping up with the death rate."

"Yes, I understand."

Marla paused for a moment, then said, "You know the woz who work at the starter farms are at considerable risk of getting pregnant handling sperm. So what can we do if a wo at my farm gets pregnant?"

"How can handling sperm cause a pregnancy?" said Dr. Susan.

"I guess that I was being too subtle. I meant the sperm might go into an unintended container and cause a pregnancy," said Marla.

"Oh! Yes, I get it now."

"There are ways to satisfy the computers. Don't worry about it; just let me know if it happens, Marla. Sorry, let me know, ma'am."

"I knew that I could depend on you," Marla said, then turning to Anna, said, "Anna, "You're head of population control, so I have some questions to ask you. If you have the population charts in your office, could we go there and talk about a few things?"

"Of course. Will you excuse us, please, Dr. Susan?"

As the door closed behind them in Anna's office, Marla threw her arms around Anna and in tears said, "Mommy, I've missed you so much. And even when I've seen you, there have been woz around and I had to act like I hardly knew you."

Anna shed a few tears too as she held Marla tightly. After a few moments she said, "I'm so glad to see you. And I want to tell you how proud I am of you. You are not that fearful, ignorant wo of two years ago. Imagine, common wo to U One K in just two years. It took me ten years."

"But I had you. You did it all yourself."

Relaxing her arms around Marla, Anna said, "Now let's go over these population figures and talk about what we can do."

"All right, here's the way I look at it. First of all, Annette told me that she and Myrna were alarmed that the death rate was higher than the birth rate, and that the desolate land around us was getting safer to use. Therefore we needed to increase the woz population and this meant increasing the donor population."

"I know, Marla"

"Now I think that if Annette can convince Cynthia to go along with this, we have our chance to increase the male population."

"You're right, Marla, and we don't want riots. We want gradual acceptance of a two gender civilization."

"Anna, we should work on two projects at the same time. First, we must gradually inform the woz about males.

I have been working on the population groups and think that we can pretty well ignore the old retired woz. They have lived all of their lives believing that males don't exist. Besides, we need babies and they are too old to have them."

"What about the middle-aged working woz, Marla?"

"Yes, inform them, but I think the priority group to inform is the common woz. I can tell you most of the ones I knew were restless. Yes, some of them like playing around with each other, and I did it now and then, but mostly it was boring. We had strong feelings, but didn't understand them and didn't know what to do except try to get some satisfaction with each other."

"So what's your plan, Marla?"

"There are several things we can try and hopefully not get in trouble with Cynthia. One thing we can do on a limited basis is transfer woz from dormitories in return for transferring woz from the starter farms to dorms. Even with no special instructions from me, woz from the farms are going talk about males, in secret, of course."

"Oh, I see, Marla. When the woz spend some time at a farm and get to know males, transfer them back to the dorm," said Anna. "You know, we shall have compound increase, not just arithmetic progression. But increasing the number of males is much more difficult."

"I know, Anna. We have to increase the number of starter farms, and perhaps Annette can persuade Cynthia it is necessary. And there is one other thing we can do. Annette told me that in searching the records, she found that the law permitting marriage was never repealed. Perhaps Annette can quietly appoint someone to marry woz who want a particular male. They can have babies nature's way. Probably begin this at starter farms. Quietly, of course."

"That makes me very nervous, Marla."

"Me, too. Do you think that pregnancies resulting from these marriages can be put on the computer as by injection? think that Dr. Susan and Angela will go along with

"I think so, but I don't know. They still don't know that you are my daughter."

"Should you tell them?"

"Remember what I told you, Marla. Once you tell someone something, you can't get it back."

Marla shook her head in agreement. Then wiping tears that were rolling down her cheeks, she said, "I don't know, but I have to get back now. Give me a big hug, Mommy."

As Marla started out the door, she paused, then closed the door and said, "Anna, the Upper 100 is another group we need to work on. They all have male lovers and they can depose Cynthia by voting her out. The problem is most of them are her close supporters."

"What can we do to change that, my dear Marla?"

"Maybe MOTHER CYNTHIA will do it for us," said Marla, smiling as she closed the door behind her.

That afternoon Annette heard a hum; touching her left eyelid she heard, "Annette, this is your darling sister Cynthia," and then laughed slightly.

"Cynthia, I'm so glad you called. I wanted to talk to you, but I knew you must be swamped with work and people wanting things from you."

Cynthia, in her gravel-sweet voice said, "Annette, I ran across some notes of Myrna's in which she seemed very upset about our population. What do you know about this?"

"Well, MOTHER CYNTHIA, I…"

Cynthia came right back at her. "Annette, we are sisters, so forget the MOTHER CYNTHIA crap except in front of the peasants. Now, what about the population?"

Annette hurriedly looked through the mess of papers on her desk; finding what she wanted, she touched her right eyelid and said, "Sorry for the delay, I had to look for some notes I made about our population." Looking at one particular paper, she said, "Now, what's on your mind; and what can I do to help you?"

"Annette, what was Myrna worried about? Do you know?"

"I think I know. Myrna thought our population needed to grow because the desolate land is getting safer to use, but we don't have enough woz to use it."

Surprised, Cynthia said, "That's it? That's all she was concerned about?"

"Not really. It seems that we aren't replacing the number of woz who die each year with the number of babies born each year."

Her voice saturated with a noticeable lack of concern, Cynthia said, "Really?"

"Yes, in 2101, 27,604 woz died and only 25,997 baby woz were born, and 103 of them died within six months of birth."

"Then, Annette, we need to do four extractions of starter fluid a week instead of two or three."

"We could. However, Dr. Susan did studies regarding three versus four extractions per week. She found that the sperm count and the quantity of the fluid decreased to the point that there was better production with only three times a week."

"So are you saying that we need more donors?"

"Probably so. Myrna thought we needed at least two more Starter Farms and let the donors work until thirty-five instead of thirty."

"That's all right with me. In fact, why don't you take over all of the farms? Do you have time to take charge of all of them?"

"If that's your wish, I shall be glad to do it."

What else did Myrna suggest?"

"Well, this won't affect us this year, but eventually we shall need more donors, so probably we should stop the aborting of male fetuses for a year or two."

"I'll think about it. Anything else?"

"Cynthia, there is a source of adult donors we have never tapped. Among the U-100 Council there are 140 adult males, intact males. The U One Ks have 472 adult intact males, shall we say, servants."

"Are you suggesting that they give up their personal servants?"

"Well, not give them up permanently, but perhaps some could volunteer their servants to be donors at a farm for a month or two. That would increase the number of sperm donations, but not the number of males, just utilize more. It's just a thought."

Cynthia was silent for a moment and then she said quietly, "Yes, it is a thought, isn't it?" But with an irritated voice, said, "Annette, I didn't like that Marla having a dance at farm number three. I don't like that at all."

"Cynthia, I had a long talk with Marla and explained it was not funny. She was very sorry and apologetic and promised to never do that again. I picked her as I thought that she had a lot of talent and really believed in WOZ, so I hope that you will forgive her this one time."

Cynthia paused a moment, and then irritated, said "Oh, all right. I suppose I could forget the incident, but I shall watch her."

"Just one more thing, Cynthia, if we are going to have another farm or two in the near future, we are going to need a few more trained woz to help out. What about transferring a few more woz from the dormitories and transfer some of the lazy woz from the farms back to the dorms. That should help prevent any attachments to the donors, don't you think?"

"Sure, I don't care much about transfers just as long as they don't get attached to the donors."

"Perhaps keeping the woz moving between farms or between farms and dorms can help discourage any attachments, don't you think?

"Yeah, sure, Annette, I've got to go now. Take care of it yourself."

That same afternoon Marla was sitting on a bench between the two dormitories. She had been looking at the unused basketball court and the locked gates and thinking how wonderful it was before Myrna was killed. But now her eyes were closed as she felt the warm sunshine on her face. Wonderful, she thought, it's the first day of May and I'm just sitting here as though I hadn't a care in the world. She gradually became aware of a gentle tapping on her right shoulder. Opening her eyes and slowly turning her head she noticed Carla standing beside her. Forcing herself to return to the real world, she smiled slightly, "Carla, is something wrong?"

"No, I don't think so. I'm just a bit confused about things."

"I'll scoot over if you would like to sit down and tell me about it."

Carla's mood picked up a bit. "Oh, yes I would," she said and promptly sat down.

Marla said nothing, simply waiting for Carla to think about what she wanted to say. Finally Carla said, "Ma'am, I don't understand what's going on here."

Marla interrupted with, "MOTHER CYNTHIA wants no interaction between woz and males. Regardless of my own feelings, such as dancing together, I have to follow orders, and I am. Does that help you understand what's going on?"

"No, I'm really confused, like why do we have four new woz here? And they are so dumb; they didn't know there were males. And that Rosemary, she's so dopey. Oh, did you like the word dopey I used?"

"Dopey?"

"I learned it from one of the novels you let me read. Anyhow, she started laughing and carrying on so when she was shown how to do her first extraction. She came back to the dorm saying, 'And, I had to handle that funny hose thing that donor had. It's weird.'"

"What about the other three new woz?"

"Oh, they didn't seem to think anything strange at all. At least, they never said anything about it if they did."

"I'm glad that you came to see me as I want to ask you a question or two. No, you're not in any trouble; I simply want to learn more about the woz here. Now, you don't have to answer if you don't want to, but I hope you will. Anything you tell me will not go any farther than my ears. Okay?"

"I guess so, ma'am, so go ahead and ask."

Marla sat up straight and then smiled as she said, "The night of the dance Freddie rather came after you. How did you feel about that?"

"I was upset. I like Freddie; maybe I like him too much. After all, he is just a donor."

"Suppose he were on your level? That is, suppose males and woz were equal in WOZ, Would you have responded differently?"

"I don't know, ma'am. Maybe I would. But we're not equal. Even if I wanted him, even if I wanted him to impregnate me, or whatever you call it, it could never be, so why go through a lot of pain wishing it?"

"Now, let me ask you a question, and it's a question you may not know the answer to at this moment. Take some time; take a day; take a month until you really know the answer. Here's the question. Would you be willing to work for that day when you and Freddie, or some other male could form your own family and have a baby the natural way?"

"Ma'am, if I say that I would, then what would you have me do?"

"We have transferred woz here to learn about males. But it is equally important to transfer some woz from here to secretly tell the common woz in the dormitories about males and what the government is doing to make all of our lives very dismal."

"So would I volunteer to be transferred to spread the word? Is that it?"

"That's it."

"But ma'am, I would be leaving Freddie. I don't know if I can stand that."

With a big smile, Marla exclaimed, "Ah, ha, you just told me what I wanted to know. You do care about him; you do love a male."

Carla lowered her head a bit and Marla could see tears in her eyes. "Yes," she said very softly.

"The question is, how much you care and what you are willing to do. You need to take time and give me your answer based on deep thought, not just an impulse answer. If you decide to work with us in making WOZ into a two gender country, you might not ever be able to change your mind."

"Thank you, ma'am, for talking to me about this. I'll think about it very seriously."

Marla stated to rise and as she did she said, "Carla, you must excuse me now; I heard a humming and I must answer this call."

Carla stood and then walked toward the woz dormitory. Marla touched her left eyelid and heard Annette say, "Guess what? Cynthia has given me all five farms to run and approved starting a sixth farm. Isn't that great?"

"I'm happy that she can see that we need more woz and more donors, Annette. Is that all you have to tell me?"

"Yes, that's it, Marla. I just wanted you to know. I've got a lot of work to do now, but day after tomorrow I am taking a few hours off and going on a picnic."

"Lucky you."

"True. Well, take it easy, Marla."

"Good bye, ma'am."

As Marla walked back to her office she thought, what a boring, impersonal call that was. But Annette did need to tell me that she is in charge of all five farms. And I'm happy we can start another one. I couldn't seem too happy on the phone; Cynthia probably monitors Annette's calls, and probably mine too. But Annette and I can talk easier day after tomorrow when I meet her at our picnic spot.

A few feet from the entrance to the Administrative building Marla turned sharply and changed her course to the male dormitory. She walked in just as Mac was telling one of the donors about the United States. "And that's how the United States became the country of WOZ."

When he noticed Marla, he closed the book he was holding and immediately approached her. "What may I do for you, Marla?"

Quietly she said, "Mac, I would like for you to deliver a note to Anna tomorrow early. I'll give you two notes. One you must give only to her, not to anyone else. If she is not there leave note number two for her which is a simple production report. Oh well, give her both notes if she is there. Understand?"

"Of course, but why don't you call and see if she is there?"

"I don't want anyone snooping on my calls."

"If she is there and wants you to wait for answer, you may wait for two or three hours, but no longer than that, please."

"All right," he said, and then taking a step closer to her, added, "Marla, I miss you very much."

"If I started thinking about what might have been, I would fall apart, so I can't go into all of that now. Let's keep our feelings under control; we have work to do."

Two days later Mac and Marla met Annette and Pat at the usual group of trees in the midst of acres of farmland. After greeting each other with hugs and smiles, Annette said, "I am pleased that you were able to make it today."

"So am I," said Marla as she reached into her pocket brought out a sheet of paper and handed it to Annette. "Here is the list of First Mothers whose male babies were aborted." I had Mac go to Anna's and get it without anyone knowing why he was there. I hope that I'm not getting paranoid, but I do feel Cynthia is out to get me, no matter how forgiving and sweet she is to me."

"Thanks, Marla. We can't be too careful in trying to keep on Cynthia's good side."

"Annette, do you think she has a good side?"

"Maybe, but if she catches on to our long term plan, we're in for it. I got along with both Myrna and Cynthia, but they did not get along with each other. Perhaps being the third wo born made them think I was never a threat."

Marla turned toward Mac who was talking to Pat and they both were laughing about something. "What did our cook make for lunch for us?"

"The usual boring two pieces of bread with one slice of ham in between," said Mac.

"Forget that," said Annette. "We stayed at the cabin last night and Orange fixed us one of your special salads."

"Great, let's eat."

"Marla, why do you want to staff farm number six with these First Mothers?"

"I know it's not on my record but you know that I am still sore about having my baby aborted because he was male. You do know that, don't you?"

"Of course I do."

"All right then, probably at least some, if not all of them are unhappy about it too. Now they are on the computer as having had their male baby aborted. That means they are not allowed to be injected again. We know that it is the father's sperm that determines the sex of the baby, not anything the mother can do to change that. But our leaders don't care; if you conceive a male child you are not permitted to be pregnant again."

"So, Marla, you think that they are probably on our side?"

"Not only that, but perhaps they just might accidentally get pregnant handling the donor's sperm."

"Do you think that you are going too fast again, Marla?"

"Maybe, but I think that if we have control of farm six and all of the woz are with us, we can increase the population of males."

"How do you propose having more male babies born?"

"We don't have to do anything. In the old USA, the normal ratio was 102 males to 100 females. Nature will provide males for us."

"Fine, Marla, and then what do we do with the male babies?"

"We'll bring them up at the farm. Each one will have a mother and a father."

"And if you get caught?

"I'll pay for it, I know. But suppose it works; then think how much we have done to free WOZ from tyranny?"

Later, as she walked toward her car, Marla wished she were certain this would work. But she smiled as she walked knowing it was a blow against this insane government oppression.

As she stepped inside the car, she remembered she was going to remind Annette to try to find that ancient marriage law. It supposedly said marriage was legal and males were "legal by marriage," citizens.

At that instant both Marla and Annette heard a hum and touching their left eyelids heard Cynthia say, "Attention all Woz Upper One K and above; For this minute on, all males, except personal servants of those with rank of U One Hundred must be shaved bald. No hair is permitted longer than one half inch long. This rule will be strictly enforced."

XIX. Catch Me if You Can

The sun was still behind the hills; no birds were singing; all was quiet, but Marla was awake. Why am I awake? It's July and it's still dark out. She managed to turn on a light, looked at her clock, and thought that it's only a bit past three in the morning. I've got too many things on my mind to sleep very long. When I was a common wo I could sleep forever. Back then I had nothing to think about, nothing to worry about. Would I like to go back to those days? Absolutely not. I had nothing to think about, except how bored I was. I had nothing that gave me any joy. Now I am not bored; I have purpose. Yes, now I am someone and I have a soul. Of course, nothing is free.

It all started sometime in May. Molly, a U Ten K, who was also a First Mother had been appointed by Annette to be in charge of the new starter farm, number six. She had been chosen for her initiative, a record of diligent service, and because Anna knew that she hated the system. All of the other Woz appointed there were U-100K. Molly was none too keen about this assignment as she was in contact with the male donors without let-up. This continued to sting her as she could not forget her own male child being aborted by the state. However, being the senior Wo there, she was not required to do extractions from the males. All of the Woz knew exactly what they were doing and were way past the sweet explanation that they were extracting poison from the males.

A month after Cynthia became MOTHER CYNTHIA, she said that she agreed with Annette that more male donors were needed temporarily to keep the general population from decreasing. Annette was then given complete authority to do what was necessary. Marla assumed whatever was necessary meant not telling Cynthia things that would make her be upset. I'll be calm if Cynthia is calm, Marla thought. One morning a month later, Molly told her, "I think that I am pregnant."

"How?" asked Marla.

"I don't want to talk in your office, so could we go sit on one of the benches outside?"

Marla stood and started toward the door. "Sure, tell me about it on the way over to that bench by the woz dorm."

Arriving at the bench and sitting down, Molly started, "Marla, you know that I don't need to do fluid extractions, but two of the woz weren't feeling well so I filled in for one of them. We're trying to keep out production up to please MOTHER CYNTHIA. I started to do the so-called volunteer males of one of the U-100 big shots. The first time I was supposed to extract from him, he said, 'Molly, have you ever had a baby?'

"I didn't want to talk about it, but finally I told him that two years before I had been pregnant by injection, but it was aborted because it was male.

"He said that he thought that was terrible, not only losing the baby but injection was cruel and without feeling. I told him that he was probably right but that's just the way it was."

Marla remembered what a cold miserable time she had; first she had the cold injection tube, then her baby was taken from her. "I understand," she said, but she did not mention her own experience.

"That's all that happened that time, but I was scheduled to do him again three days later. This time he put his hands on my breasts and said, 'Do you know why the U-100 Woz have male servants?' I knew, but I wasn't going to admit it, so he went on, 'You know there is a natural way to have a baby, don't you?'

"I simply smiled. 'Of course, Dan, but I never heard of a U-100 Woz having a baby.'

"'Do you think that all we do for them is carry heavy things?'

"I laughed. 'Oh, really?'

"He said, 'They have us for sex. That's unfair for the millions of common woz who are told that males don't even exist.'"

"And what did you say to all of this, Molly?"

"You know, Marla, the rest of our visit together is not really very clear. I do remember that he had his hand on my left breast, then I remembering feeling ignited, or excited, or turned-on. I also remember I stopped extracting his fluid and then it seemed that I was in fog, but we both did have our clothes off."

Marla's first thought was lucky you, Molly. But then she remembered why Molly told her about this encounter. Her pain showing, Molly looked at Marla with tears in her eyes. "Can we do something about this, Marla?" Molly asked. "I refuse to give up this baby so the Upper-Uppers can go on lying to us about males."

Marla looked at her and taking her hands said, "My dear Molly, I shall do whatever I can so that you can have your baby. But you must join us in fighting this corrupt regime."

"I'll be happy to join in any group that wants to bring reality and love to our country. Just tell me what I can do."

Marla turned and looked directly into Molly's eyes. "That's wonderful, but don't tell anyone that you are pregnant, not even Dan, especially not Dan. Oh, I need to know how you and Dan feel about each other. Do you feel that he is special? Does he feel that you are special or that you were just another woz he had sex with? Think about it nber he has to go back to his U-100 Wo.

and Molly gave each other a brief hug then "I have to be getting back to my own farm now. know if you can help me."

214

That same day at the Townhouse of Iris, the U-100 Wo who volunteered her servant, Dan, to do starter farm duty was waiting impatiently for his return. She had not wanted Dan to leave her for two months but MOTHER CYNTHIA put pressure on several U-100s to help out increase the population. There was not much discussion about this as no one wanted to displease Cynthia.

When Dam entered the lavishly decorated townhouse, he was met by Mary Anna, a U-100K assistant to Iris. Her long blond hair, her general beauty and charm had interested Dan since the first day he came there to serve Iris. Two years ago Iris had picked him one day as she inspected farm number five. She simply said to Margo, "I want him for my servant," and that was that. There was nothing Margo or Dan could do about it. When a member of the Council of One Hundred spoke, one listened and then said, "Yes, ma'am."

"Iris is in her bedroom, and wants you to join her as soon as you get here, stud."

"Oh," he groaned, "Why now, why me? That farm really wore me out." As he started for the bedroom door, he looked back at Mary Anna. "I'd rather join you in yours."

She frowned as she said, "Ha, fat chance. You want me to be sent to the desolate exile farm?"

"Sugar, we would never get caught."

"That's right, we won't," said Mary Anna quietly, but not politely, "Because we will never play sex games together. Now go in there and take care of Iris Hot Pants."

Giving up, Dan walked over to the bedroom door and knocked softly. "Is that you, Danny Boy?" said Iris hopefully.

Dan slowly opened the door, then looking around with a big smile said, "Ah, there you are, my fascinating Wo, fulfilling my every dream."

Iris opened her arms widely, and then smiling said, "Come here; your pleasure is waiting for you," and with that he rushed over to her, picked her up and laid her on the bed.

"It's about time you got back; you don't know how I suffered without you."

As he started to unbutton her top he said, "Tell your Dan all about it."

"Oh Dan," she whined, "You don't know what I had to put up with."

"Didn't Cynthia let you have a substitute?"

Still whining, she went on, "Oh, he was terrible. He was a very young donor fresh from starter farm number two, or was it one? Anyhow, he didn't know anything."

"He didn't?" Dan said in his best imitation of sympathy.

"He was so stupid. When I finally got him to take off his clothes, he asked me, "Are you going to pump out the poison from me? What did he mean by that?"

"Iris, I think that they tell the younger donors that they are pumping out poison from them."

Iris frowned a bit more. "Dan, stop talking so much and touch me, get my clothes off and hurry."

"Yes, ma'am, nothing would please me more."

"And get yours off too. And Dan, this male was really dumb. He didn't know what his thing was for."

"But you told him, Iris, didn't you?"

"Told him, of course I did, and then he didn't know where to put it."

"Oh, you poor darling"

"Iris smiled slightly. "But he was a fast learner."

"Well, Dan's here to make everything right."

Several hours later when there was calm about, Iris asked him, "How was it for you there? What did you do all day? Were the woz there pretty? Tell me."

"Oh, it was terribly boring. Every other morning an ugly wo would come get me at the donor's dorm and then we had to walk to a room in another building where she would say, "Now I have to extract some fluid from you so pull your pants down to your knees and lie down there."

"Was she good looking, Dan?"

"No. I think they chose the ugly ones for this."

"Good, and then what happened?"

"Well, she would grab me and pump it out into a container of some sort."

"That's it?"

"Oh, she would throw me a towel and say, 'Wipe yourself, and then go back to your dorm.' Then she would turn and leave by a different door."

Iris got up from her chair and sat down on Dan's lap. "So it wasn't fun, just a duty."

"Just a duty, my dear. Well, twice I had a different wo, actually, she had rank and so she was really a Wo spelled with a capital W. Anyhow, she was very nice to me. She made me want to do my duty for a change."

Iris smiled a bit and placing her arm around his neck said, "Tell me about this one."

Dan shrugged. "Not much to tell, but she did talk to me a little bit. She told me that she had been pregnant once, but it didn't live. I felt sort of sorry for her."

"So what did you do to make her less unhappy?"

"Oh, I just listened to her a bit."

"I have never seen you do anything for anybody but your own self, Dan, unless you got something out of it. So what did you do for her? You touched her didn't you?"

"Well, just a tiny bit."

Iris jumped off of his lap and facing him said in an angry voice, "You creep. You had sex with her, didn't you?"

"Of course not."

"Dan, I have ways of making you tell me everything, so make it easy on yourself and tell me now.'

"I know you have ways and I know about your ways, so I'll tell you. Yes, I had sex with her, but only one time. She never came to extract me again."

Iris started walking the floor and muttering, "That Cynthia, always wanted to take you away from me one way or another. Well, I'll fix her... sometime." Then turning to

Dan she said, "It's not your fault, honey, but go to your room for now."

An hour later at a townhouse a hundred yards away Ursula, 42, a slim, red headed, tall U-100 Wo, heard a humming in her ear. Touching her left eyelid she heard Iris say, "I'm really upset. You knew that Cynthia had me volunteer Dan for farm duty for two months."

Touching her right eyelid, Ursela said, "So how did that work out? Is he back now and all is calm?"

"Yes, Ursela, Dan is back, but all is not calm. It turns out that he had sex with one of the woz there. He said that he couldn't help it because he felt sorry for her."

"You're kidding, aren't you?"

"No, I'm not kidding. I got him to admit it."

Ursela was not pleased when Cynthia asked her if she would volunteer her servant, Guy, to be a donor at a starter farm for two months. Ursela was not pleased when he said he didn't mind working there for a few months. Ursela was definitely not thrilled to hear about Dan having sex with a common wo. Dan was the property of Iris and she certainly would talk to a few other members of the Council about this. Was Cynthia imposing on their right to have a male servant of their own?

Two days later Anna came to farm number three to see how things were going. Marla greeted her at the door of her office. "Anna, I'm so glad to see you. Come into my private office and let's have a chat." Then inside the office with the door closed she said, "Mommy, I really am so happy and also relieved to see you."

Anna smiled and hugged Marla and then said, "You mean this thing about Molly is getting to you too?"

"Yes, what can we do?"

"Do you have any coffee? If so, let's take our coffee and go sit on one of the benches outside."

In the outer office Marla said to Gracie, "Would you pour us some coffee? We'll take it to one of the benches outside."

Gracie smiled. "It's still brewing; I'll bring it out to you when it's ready."

"Thank you Gracie," said Marla. Turning to Anna she said, "That Gracie is a wonder."

Outside sitting on the bench Anna said, "I guess Dr. Susan could abort it."

"No, Anna, no more abortions. We need the population to grow and poor Molly has had one child taken from her. It's time we think of the person, not promoting the big lie!"

Taking Marla's hand and squeezing it a bit, Anna said, "Of course, I agree. I just mentioned the easy way out, but I am tired of the easy way out. In the long run, it is not the easy way out."

"You don't want to take the easy way out, Ma'am," Gracie said looking at Marla.

"Gracie," said Anna, "We didn't see you appear."

"Ma'am, I heard Marla say, 'No more abortions." You see, when I was just a common wo I had a roommate who was deaf and I learned to read lips. Sorry, I didn't mean to listen, but it's just second nature with me now."

"Gracie," said Marla. I think that you can be very helpful in a way I never imagined."

"I serve you, Marla."

Turning to Marla, Anna said, "Why don't you ask Annette to promote Gracie to U Ten K? You need someone with rank to help you here."

"I'll do that, unless Gracie objects."

"Well, I really would like to be a U Ten K if you don't mind, ma'am."

"Fine," said Marla. "I'll do that today."

"I'd better get back to work now," said Gracie, smiling as she started to walk toward the office.

As soon as she had gone Anna asked, "And what about the male who got Molly pregnant? Is he still here?"

"No, yesterday he went back to Iris, the U-100 he served before he came here."

"It would be interesting to know how she felt about his being volunteered by Cynthia to be a donor for two months," said Anna as she stretched a bit. "I get really stiff from riding in that lousy car they let me use."

"Anna, do you suppose that Dr. Susan would inject Molly with water and enter it on the computer so that no one would know she became pregnant the natural way?"

"I think so. She could do that, and if it is entered on the computer, then no one would question it."

"Annette should have to authorize her pregnancy. No, better, as head of Population Control, I could fake a previous authorization from Myrna. No way to prove she didn't."

"I hope you're right, Anna."

"Marla, listen closely now and keep your hands nowhere near your eyelids." As Marla put her head very close, Anna looked around and then very softly said, "You know Annette has been digging through old records of early WOZ."

"Yes, I know, for anything like a marriage law, if any."

Excited, Marla said a bit too loud, "What did she find out?"

"I have a copy of the marriage law of 2057 hidden at my place, but basically it said that any Wo, rank U One K or higher could have a male as a husband."

"Seriously?"

"Seriously, Marla, I think it was because certain high ranked Woz back then were beginning to rebel against the first MOTHER MYRNA. She made this law to please them, so the ones who were married before WOZ took over the USA would support her."

"And it has never been repealed?"

"Annette said she could find no evidence that it had. But, Marla, the law also said that the males, the husbands, were not citizens of WOZ, only tolerated, you know, like saying you can have a dog as a pet, but he is still a dog."

Marla's face lit up with one huge smile. "So I am allowed to marry Mac."

Anna, not smiling, not frowning, pressed her hands against Marla's arms and said, "Marla, because it is presumably legal, doesn't mean that you should test it, at least as long as Cynthia hates males. Let's keep her happy and believing that we are all just good little woz."

"You're right, Mommy, let's keep her happy and away from us while we play 'Catch me if you can.'"

XX. Marriage Has Many Pains, but Celibacy Has No Pleasures.

Rasselas, Samuel Johnson, 1719

At three that afternoon Carla and two other woz from one of the common wo dormitories arrived at Starter Farm #3. The two new woz were taken to Marla's office and greeted by Gracie who pointed to several chairs by her desk. "Sit down; Marla, the head Wo here, will be with you shortly."

Carla walked into the office also and said to Gracie, "Well, here I am back at the old farm."

Gracie looked up, smiled and said, "I'm glad to see that you're back with us." And then looking around for Marla, and seeing her in the courtyard by one of the basketball hoops said, "Carla, quickly now, come into Marla's office with me for a moment," and then hastily entered that office. Carla followed her immediately. Gracie opened a drawer of Marla's desk, took out a very old book whose cover title, *Book of Rituals,* was faded to near invisibility.   Gracie shoved it into Carla's arms and said very rapidly, but quietly, "Here, take this, read it, bring it back before nightfall. And listen, I read Anna's and Marla's lips while you were gone. You should know that marriage to a male is legal and always has been."

"Really?" Carla said as she grabbed the book, hid it under her shirt, and beat a hasty retreat to her dormitory. Ten minutes later she saw Marla walking toward the car and waving goodbye to Edna and Cindy leaving for duty at a common woz dormitory. "Carla, I'm so glad to see you back here," said Marla, as she gave her a brief hug.

Smiling, almost laughing, Carla cried, "Not as glad as I am to be back here. It's really dismal and boring at the dormitory. It's like having no life. And those woz are so stupid, well, I guess that I should say ignorant."

"Come, sit on the bench and tell me all about it."

"Marla, I mean ma'am, the woz there have no idea of what life is really like."

"I know, Carla, believe me, I know."

Carla raised her voice a bit as she struggled to find the words, "They don't know anything! They don't even know what a male is. And, and, and they…"

"Okay, calm down a minute."

Carla took a deep breath, and then slowly said, "I just mean to say talking to one of them is like talking to a butterfly."

"Do you think that you got through to any of them?"

"Yes, ma'am, one or two seemed to understand and maybe they believed me, especially when I described touching a male, dancing with a male, and uh, well, you know…"

They sat in silence for a few moments, each one waiting for the inevitable question. Finally, Carla asked, "Do you think Freddie missed me?"

"Mac told me that Freddie was really irritable all the time you were gone.. Why don't you ask Freddie? The gate will be unlocked for two more hours, so maybe you would like to see if he is in the male dorm."

Carla jumped out of her seat and as she started to run toward the gate, turned and yelled, "Thank you ma'am. Thank you," and then ran through the gate and on to the male dorm.

Freddie heard her yell and came out the door just as she arrived. With no hesitation, they flung themselves at each other, holding on as though they were adrift in a rough ocean and hanging on to a floating log for dear life. "Carla, please never leave me again. You're the only wo I ever cared about, the only source of life for me, the only, the only... I guess, just the only."

"Freddie, let's get married."

"There is no such thing as marriage in WOZ. And if there were, there is no one to marry us. And if there were, remember that I am a male and males don't exist in WOZ."

Carla backed away a moment, then wiping her eyes said, "Freddie, we will do the wedding ceremony ourselves."

Freddie looked down a bit, wondering if she was right. "How do you know what the marriage ceremony is?"

"It's in one of the books Marla had and Gracie told me it was legal now." Then standing straight, determined, she said, "I'll get the book and be right back. Meet me behind the seed storage barn in ten minutes and we'll marry each other."

Freddie stood wide eyed, motionless, and dumbstruck as he watched Carla run toward her dormitory. Ten minutes later they stood behind the barn holding the old book of church rituals with their outer hands and each other with their inner arms. "We'll take turns reading," said Carla. "You go first."

"Dearly Beloved, we are gathered here in the sight of God and these witnesses to join this man and this woman..." Freddie stopped and then asked, "What's a woman, Carla?"

"That's an old word for wo and man is an old word for male."

"Oh, I see; it means to join this man and this woman in holy matrimony. I guess that means marriage. You read now, Carla."

"We don't have but a few minutes so let's just answer the questions," said Carla, and then went on to say, "Freddie, do you take me, Carla, to be your wedded wife, to have and to hold, to comfort me, honor and keep me, in sickness and in health, and to love and to cherish, for as long as we both shall live?"

"You know I do," Then kissing her on the cheek, said, "And, Carla, do you take me, Freddie, to be your wedded husband, to have and to hold, to comfort me, honor and keep me, in sickness and in health, to love and to cherish, for as long as we both shall live?"

"I do. I really do." Carla let loose of Freddie for just the instant she used to wipe the tears from her cheeks, and then said, "Now let's read the last line together."

And together, they proclaimed, "As God has joined us in marriage; let no wo put us asunder."

"Now, kiss me Freddie; I am yours forever."

Two days later early in the morning, and sitting at her desk, Marla heard the humming that meant someone was calling her. Touching her left eyelid, she heard, "Marla, it's Annette. How are you today?"

Touching her right eyelid, she replied, "I'm fine, Annette. What's going on in the big city?"

"Not much, I'm at the cabin and I just called to check in and see how you are doing. It's so quiet here; I think I'll have Pat take me out to the woods for a picnic."

Marla felt that some of the heavy burden had been lifted from her and she smiled as she said, "Annette, I think that's wonderful. Have Orange fix you something special and have a happy and peaceful lunch."

Hands on her cheeks, Marla leaned on her desk, exhaling with a sigh, and thought that now she could share with Annette her conversation with Carla. She didn't blame Carla a bit for grabbing Freddie and their self-marriage two days ago. She started a wicked smile as she thought I'm stirring up a lot of discontent with my pushing the truth on an ignorant populace. But I must do it. And I must get Annette to stop playing it safe and help. Oh course, she has what she wants: power, luxury, her own male, so why should she put herself in danger and help? Well, I'll meet her at our usual patch of woods for lunch and see what I can do. Really, I mean to see what she is willing to do, if anything.

"Thanks for inviting me to lunch," Marla said as she greeted Annette at their picnic area. "I have so much to tell you."

"Let's eat first. Orange made your favorite, so let's go sit on that log. Oh, you can tell me what you want to as we eat. Okay with you?"

"Sure, although what I tell you may upset your stomach a bit."

"Now Marla, nothing bothers my stomach, except not eating," said Annette as she sat down on the log.

"It looks to me like we are getting the message out to a few woz, you know, the message about there being two genders and how babies are made." Annette nodded her head and continued to eat. "And Gracie at my office found out about the marriage law."

Annette continued to eat, but she also started to frown, and after a drink of wine said, "She did? How?"

"Anna was telling me about it and Gracie reads lips."

"Is that as far as it has gone?"

"No. Gracie found the *Book of Rituals* from the Twentieth Century and showed it to another wo."

"Not good, but I suppose eventually everyone will know. We really have to control who knows what. We can't just openly go against Cynthia."

"Wait, I'm not through. This wo, Carla, took the book and the male she wanted, and they read the marriage ceremony and consider that they are now married."

Annette stopped eating and open-mouthed, turned to Marla "You mean that they did the ceremony themselves?"

"They did. So what should we do about all of this?"

"Marla, I knew that I should have kept that marriage law to myself."

"Annette, you are my superior; you made me from nothing, and I owe you so very much. But, with deep respect, I disagree. I think it's time to fight."

"If Myrna were still alive, I would agree with you, but with Cynthia, tomorrow we could be eliminated."

Marla put on her most serious face, looked straight into Annette's eyes, and then with a hint of a smile, said, "I have a plan."

"Tell me about it, Marla."

"You may remember that when you took me out of obscurity and made me a member of your staff, you said to me, 'Marla, the less you know, the safer you are.' Well, Annette, ma'am, the same goes for you now. I would not hurt you for the world; WOZ needs you."

Annette smiled and squeezed Marla's hand.

Marla continued, "All I want you to do is make certain that the marriage law is on the computer on a long lost file. And I want you to add to it, 'Any Wo of U One K or higher may perform the marriage ceremony if there are present two or more Woz of U Ten K rank or higher,' or something like that. Then just sit back and watch the fireworks."

"Oh, that's easy to do. I'll sign the original MOTHER MYRNA's name to it. That's my dear old Grannie, the old dear who started this whole mess."

A week later Pat, wearing his blond wig entered Marla's office. Addressing Gracie, he said, "I have a very confidential note for Marla," he said.

"Please go right in, and, Pat, your wig looks fine today," she said, laughing.

Marla eagerly greeted him as he said, "Annette said you wanted this memo, so here it is, and I have to hurry back before I'm missed."

"Thanks, Pat. I'll take care of it immediately," she said as he made his hasty departure.

Marla closed the door and then hurried to her desk and taking the letter opener freed the long awaited message from its envelope. Nervously she unfolded the single page and began to read:

Marla, this was an emergency law written because of the terrible death rate from radiation and because there were many married woz who demanded it. When the U-100s started taking males as 'servants,' this law was forgotten.

This law was passed by a vote of 82 to 18 on August 12, 2057 and signed by MOTHER MYRNA on August 14, 2057.

Session of 2057: General Code.
Article 402.

A. **Marriage is permitted between one wo and one male.**

B. **This law does not grant citizenship to the male.**

C. **Control of a married male is reserved for the married wo.**

D. **The married wo has the right to refuse the use of her male for sperm donation.**

E. **A marriage under the above sections may be performed and/or certified by any Wo, ranked U One K or above.**

F. **This article falls under section 32 of the Council of One Hundred Rules and may only be repealed by a three-fourths vote of the Council of One Hundred.**

Marla got up from her desk, went to the door and said, "Gracie, has that donor borrowed from that U-100 left yet?"

"No, he's still here."

"Good, then please ask him to come to my office."

"I'll go get him right away."

Five minutes later, Guy, Ursela's servant, appeared before Marla in her office.

"Sit down, Guy," Marla said. "Tell me, and be completely honest, would you rather be with Ursela, or would you rather stay here. Now, please tell me the truth; a lot depends on it."

Guy, tall, 21, red hair, smiled but said nothing. "Guy, I am U One K, but I started out as an ignorant common wo, and I understand a lot of things. I manage this farm, but that doesn't mean I approve of certain things. I want to change these things, but I need your help. Your help right now is to tell me the honest truth."

Guy sat silent for a few more moments, and then Marla said, "I can arrange for you to stay two more months here or I can send you back to Ursela in fifteen minutes. What shall it be? It's your choice."

"I want to go back to Ursela. She treats me fine."

"Now Guy, would you like it if never again you could be loaned out for donor duty?

"No offense, ma'am, but I'd rather not be a donor again. I don't mean you mistreated me, but ma'am, it's a dismal life here."

"Guy, would you say that maybe being a donor is giving up your soul, or do you understand the word soul?"

"I understand the meaning of soul, ma'am. I really do."

"You read, don't you?"

"Yes, ma'am, I can read."

"Then, Guy, read this paper."

A bit skeptical, a bit nervous, a bit curious he took the paper and read it; then he immediately read it again, grinned and read it a third time.

"Do you think that you understand what it means, not only what it means, but what it could mean for you?"

"I think it means I could live with Ursela the rest of my life, that is, if she wanted me."

"That's what it means. Now, Guy, I am going to write on a piece of paper where Ursela can find this on the big computer. Give this note to her and tell her to forget where she got it. I think things are going to change, Guy."

Guy grinned. "I think so too."

"You must see to it that she checks this out. The souls of millions of woz and males depend on it."

"I'll give her the law information and hope she will marry me,"

"If she doesn't, or even if she does, would you also tell your friends who are servants to members of the Council?"

"I'll do what I can."

As Marla and Gracie watched Guy leave, Gracie said, "I hope that he can be trusted."

"If he does nothing, we haven't lost anything, but we haven't gained anything either."   As the dust from his departing car settled, Marla said, "Well, let's have lunch."

Early the next morning Marla heard the humming and touching her left eyelid, heard, "Marla, this is Ursela; you probably remember you had my servant, Guy, at your farm for a while"

Touching her right eyelid, Marla answered, "I've never met you, but I certainly know who you are. What can I do for you, ma'am?"

"I've heard what an efficient farm you run and I would just like to visit there sometime."

"Any time, ma'am, anytime at all."

"This is not an inspection, Marla, just a visit. I know so little about starter farms. I was wondering if it would be all right if I come by this afternoon about three or four."

"That would be just fine, ma'am, just fine."

At ten after three that afternoon as Marla was straightening her office, a large, expensive car arrived in front of Building A. Gracie noticed the car, and then rushed to Marla's office. "Marla, ma'am, there's six woz out there, but I think there's really three Woz and three males wearing blond wigs."

Marla jumped up from her desk and hurried to the outside door, paused a moment, and then rushed out to greet the visitors. It was easy to tell the Woz as they were wearing wigs to disguise who they really were. As Marla approached, the tallest one stepped forward. "You must be Marla."

"Yes, ma'am, I am Marla."

"I am Ursela," and then pointing to the other two Woz, said, "And this is Iris, and the Wo in the red wig is Julia."

"I'm pleased to meet you," and then looking at each in turn, said, "Ursela, Iris, and Julia, I thank you for dropping by. Would you like to come inside and have something to drink, something to eat?"

Iris stepped forward and very seriously said, "We would, but first I need to know, are you U One K?"

"Yes, ma'am, my rank is U One K."

"Good, then you can marry us. Is that correct?"

It's working, shouted Marla to herself. "Wonderful, ma'am, I would be delighted to do so. Oh, all of you?"

"All of us," said Iris. "Could we do the ceremony under those trees by the field? And I think we should do it immediately, if you don't mind."

Marla could not control her enthusiasm as she said, "Wonderful, just wonderful. To save time if you would like to start for the trees, I'll run into the office and get the book that has the ritual I am to read." As Marla turned to leave she caught Guy's eye and saw him give her a big smile and then wink. It's working; it's working, she thought and ran to her office.

Seven minutes later Marla and Gracie arrived at the group of trees. "Who's this?" asked Julia.

"This is my helper, Gracie. She is U Ten K. Although you could be a witness for each other, I thought we should have a witness who is not part of the ceremony, so I asked Gracie. Would you rather she went back to the office?"

"No, she's fine," said Ursela. "But let's get this over with. None of us can afford to be gone very long."

Marla stood facing them and said, "Each of you face me and hold hands with your intended mate."

Ursela took Guy's hand; Julia took Jimmy's hand, and Iris put her arm around Dan and then held his hand. "Good," said Marla. "As you are in a hurry I'll make this as short as I can."

"Good," said Ursela.

Opening the Book of Rituals, Marla studied it a few seconds and then said, "Ursela, do you take Guy, Julia do you take Jimmy, Iris, do you take Dan to be your lawful wedded husband, to have and to hold, forsaking all others, to love and to cherish, in sickness and in health, for as long as you both shall live? If so, answer, 'I do.'"

Ursela, Julia, and Iris said, "I do."

Marla smiled and then said, "Guy, do you take Ursela, Jimmy, do you take Julia, Dan, do you take Iris, to be your lawful wedded wives, to have and to hold, forsaking all others, to love and to cherish, in sickness and in health, for as long as you both shall live?

All three males held up their free hands and shouted, "I do!"

Marla closed the book and with all of the energy of a young wo, said, "By the authority given me by the marriage law of 2057, I pronounce that you are Woz and mates. What God has joined together, let no wo put asunder."

After kissing each other the couples started to walk rapidly toward their car. "Come to the car, Marla," Iris said. "We just don't have time for a celebration now. But come to my townhouse this Saturday evening for a dinner party."

"I'd love to. Thank you."

"Oh, and bring your Mac, and your Gracie too."

A minute later Marla and Gracie were standing in front of the office and staring at an empty dusty road, wondering what hit them. After a few moments of silence, Marla turned to Gracie. "I think success has come our way," she said quietly.

Gracie nodded her head yes. Still staring at the empty road, Marla added, "But will it continue, or will it bring down the roof upon our heads? Nothing is free, so what will I have to pay for this?"

Saturday evening when Marla opened the door to the ballroom where Iris was having her party, she was shocked at the difference between what she saw inside and the solid, unfriendly exterior of this townhouse. As she entered the building, the cold, dark, stone exterior gave way to a brightly lighted foyer whose mirrored walls and marble floors announced that someone very special lived here. Even the spacious, elegant foyer did not prepare her for this party hall with its extravagantly dressed Woz.

Iris greeted her and guided her into the celebrants, dressed like... Marla didn't know how to describe it to herself. "This year we are having Twentieth Century Parties," Iris said. "We have pictures from old magazines and books to show how Woz were dressed then."

"Oh, and I came in my uniform," Marla said somewhat embarrassed. "But it's all the clothes I have, or have ever had."

"Don't let that bother you, Marla. We are interested in you, not what you are wearing."

"We Woz are wearing what was called fancy Cocktail Length Skirts in the Twentieth Century. Oh, we have these Twentieth Century parties every six months or so. And we let the males wear what was called dress shirts, ties, that sort of thing, not that anyone really cares what the males wear.

"Iris, ma'am, Gracie is waiting in the car with Mac, my male, shall I say, helper. Should I have her come in or just wait for me?"

"Have both of them come in. This is a party and we wouldn't want you to be without your male. Oh, are you going to marry him, or did you already?"

"Not yet; but he is special to me."

"Come, Marla, and have some wine. I'll send someone to bring them in. And I've got a surprise for you." Then glancing at the notebook Marla had under her arm, said, "Although I doubt it is a surprise. Woz here want to get married."

"I came prepared," Marla said, taking a sip of her wine. "Though it isn't a big surprise, it does make me very happy."

Iris took Marla by the arm and started to lead her into the crowd of Woz and males. "Come on, I want you to meet my friends."

Marla smiled and looked at Iris. "Fine. Perhaps as I meet them, they would sign the marriage list; then after the ceremony I would sign it and it's done."

"That's a good idea," Iris said as they approached a Woz standing in front of her male. "Linda, this is our wonderful guest, Marla."

Escorting Marla forward, she said, "Marla, this is Linda and she is one of my very best friends."

Linda offered her hand, which Marla took and squeezed very gently. "And this is my future husband, Henry," said Linda. Henry was smiling as though he had been crowned the King of England. "I am pleased to meet you, Marla," he said.

And for the forty minutes Marla went through the same procedure with seventeen more U-100 Woz and their males. Gracie and Mac had arrived by then and were well on their way to enjoying the wine in their crystal glasses. Gracie spotted Marla chatting with a tall red-haired Wo and her male and waited patiently for their conversation to end. When a long pause did occur, Gracie said quietly to Marla, "I have your *Book of Rituals* here in case we need it."

Aside, Marla said, "Good. Need it? Yes, that's why we were invited. Eighteen couples want to get married tonight."

"Great," said Gracie. "Did you ever think it would happen so suddenly?"

"I hoped that the possibility of their losing their males would shake them up. I was so surprised when Cynthia took the bait and drafted their, er, servants for starter farm duty," said Marla.

Mac smiled and then back away as Iris approached. "Marla," Iris said, "Are you ready to perform the marriage ceremony? We have eighteen eager couples waiting for your magic."

Marla laughed. "My magic, huh? Well, let's see what it can do. Iris, perhaps you would ask the Woz and their males to stand in front of me. Probably where we are is as good a lace as any here, don't you think?"

s, that should work," Iris said, and then turning to goers, in a loud voice announced, "Will all of you

Woz getting married please line up here. And hold your male's left hand with your right."

Eighteen smiling, almost grinning Woz lead their males toward Marla and stood before her eagerly awaiting the ceremony. Waiting for a few moments for the chattering to subside, Marla said, "All right. Gracie will give to you two pieces of paper containing vows. One paper is for the Woz to read when the time comes; the other is for the males to read. If you have any questions, please ask them."

The vow papers were passed out and read and no questions were asked. Marla wondered if there were really no questions or whether no one wanted to delay the ceremony, regardless of any problem which might arise later. Iris smiled and nodded to Marla who then opened her *Book of Rituals* and began to read:

"Dearly Beloved, we are gathered here in the sight of God and in the presence of these witnesses to join these Woz and these males in holy matrimony. It is not to be entered into unadvisedly, but discreetly and in the fear of God. In this holy estate these huz have come to be joined."

Marla looked up from reading her *Book of Rituals* and addressing the crowd said, "Will you Woz please say 'I,'" and then say your name, and then read aloud the rest of the vow written for you,"

Each of the Woz said, "I," then her name, and then continued, "Do take my male to be my lawfully wedded husband, forsaking all others, from this day forward, to have and to hold, to love and to cherish, in sickness and in health, as long as we shall both live."

After all of the Woz had cheerfully and loudly recited their vows they looked at Marla and smiled the smile.

"Wonderful," said Marla. "And now you males please state your name and read the vows written for you."

All eighteen males said their names and then recited, "Do take this Wo to be my lawfully wedded wife, from this day forward, forsaking all others, to have and to ho and to cherish, in sickness and health, as long as we both shall live."

Everyone was excited, now, smiling, grinning, laughing, and looking at Marla as she pronounced, "For as much as you Woz and males have consented together to be in holy wedlock, by the authority given me by the marriage law of 2057, I now pronounce you Woz and husbands." Then closing her book, she said with her tears flowing, "What God has joined together, let no Wo put asunder."

And then in a loud voice, she said, "Woz, kiss your husbands!"

After a few minutes of kissing and hugging everyone and anyone nearby, Iris managed to get their attention by saying, "All right, the table is set with food and drink. Let's celebrate and be happy, for no one knows what tomorrow may bring."

After the group of newlyweds and guests had chatted for a few minutes they gradually moved toward the large dining room with its elegantly set table brightly lighted by candles in their tall silver candle holders and the brightly glowing chandeliers hanging from the mirrored ceiling. Marla visited each newly married couple, congratulating them and asking each to sign The Marriage Register.

Johanna and her male approached Marla and thanked her for coming there to marry them. After signing Johanna said, "Marla, I didn't want to delay the service by asking a question, but I was, and still am wondering, what did you mean when you said, 'in the sight of God?' Who is God?"

"I know, Johanna, that the first MOTHER MYRNA and her friends hated males. And I read a lot about who woz thought God was. Maybe because God was considered male, God was ignored. And as Myrna said, 'Males cause all of the evil on Earth.'"

"So, Marla, what do you know about God?"

"From reading about life before WOZ, I think that God is the creator of everything. I think that the Cosmos is a violent and scary thing and God has created a beautiful haven for us. That's what I think, but I don't know very much. You know, a few years ago I was just an ignorant, common wo scrubbing floors, until some power took me and made me worth something. At least I hope that I am worth something. That's all I know, Johanna."

Before Johanna could respond Iris appeared. "Marla, would you like to stay for the party? It should get real interesting after dinner. And we have room for all of you to stay the night if you wish."

Marla smiled, and then squeezed Iris' hand. "I would dearly love to, but my duty is to take care of my farm. So I feel that I should go and take care of my duties. But I do thank you. And I do thank you for being able to marry these eighteen couples."

"You're wonderful, Marla. And just think, we now have twenty-one married Council members. When we get five more, we shall have twenty-six, enough so that the marriage law cannot be repealed.

Marla opened her notebook and handed a sheet of paper to Iris. "This is a copy of the marriage ritual. According to the law, any of you council members can perform it for a couple and they would be legally married. I love to do this, but so can any of you."

On the way home, Marla leaned on Mac's shoulder as he drove. Gracie curled up on the back seat of the car and slept. Arriving at the farm, Mac parked the car so that the car lights were aimed at the front door to the office. Marla woke up Gracie who groaned, "Let me sleep here in the car". But half asleep, Gracie struggled out of the car, into the office building and into to her room. Then she fell across her bed, groaned in relief and was gone.

Marla then started to get out of the car, but Mac said, "Would you stay put a minute while I park the car by the side of the office? It's full moon so we can easily see to walk to your door."

"All right, if you turn out the car lights, I would like very much for you to kiss me."

Mac laughed quietly. "Oh, the lights will be out; we don't want to excite the little woz and males, do we?"

"Mac, I'm not certain I really care. The way I feel now, I would kiss you in front of Cynthia."

As he kissed her, she whispered, "Honey, I feel it's now or never."

"I can't put you in danger, Marla. It's not only I fear for you because I love you, but you have been flirting with danger with this marriage business, like tonight. We can't afford to lose you. I would be devastated to lose you."

Marla put her arms around his neck and drew his lips close to hers. "Kiss me again, Mac, and then walk me to the door."

As they walked, Mac said, "The door equals reality. It separates slave from owner. But let's do it now; this is agony being here, knowing that I can never have you as really mine."

At the doorway they paused in a shadow with arms around each other. Neither said anything for a few moments, both asking themselves, should we or shouldn't we? Pushing her body against him, Marla whispered, "Mac, darling, in one of the books Annette loaned me, I read that people who were on their death bed rarely regretted what they had done. They regretted what they could have done, but didn't."

Mac backed away a few inches and looked at her, his face saying, "What do you mean? Do you mean what I think you mean?"

Marla looked down a moment and then softly said, "I fear Cynthia very much. But I don't want to lie on my death bed thinking that I could have, that we could have... but I have no right to put you in danger."

"Marla, I am yours to do with as you like. Oh, not because of the laws regarding primitives, but because you own my love for you"

"We are wasting time out here, Mac. You could stay with me until an hour before it gets light, then come out and sleep in the car until others were up and about. No one would know. Do you want to do that?"

Not giving Mac time to answer, she grabbed him by the hand and said, "Come on." Quickly she led him up the four steps to the doorway. Inside, Marla turned and locked the door and then in the dark, led him to her room. There, she locked the door and then opened the curtains to let the moonlight flow in.

As she turned to face Mac, she found that he was only a few inches away. In an instant they were welded together, and slowly moved toward her bed. Touching it, gravity took them falling onto her bed, still welded together. After a few moments Mac whispered, "I don't know how to best love you. I have really only touched you in my dreams. I have never seen a wo naked."

"Perhaps we could learn about each other by playing a game. I know; we could play an old game called Fumble."

"Fumble?"

"I read in an old magazine that it was a game played at parties in which all of the lights would be turned out. Then woz and males would crawl around and try to identify others by touch only. Touching anywhere was permitted. We could play Fumble and learn about each other's body."

Mac smiled and then placed his hands on the sides of Marla's face, kissed her and said, "You must be Marla."

"Just how can you tell? You haven't touched me anywhere. Maybe you are in the donors' dorm."

"You kiss like Marla. And besides, you don't have a flat chest like a male."

Marla smiled. "Better make sure, and don't judge by my shirt. Maybe I just stuffed several towels there. Do you think that you could identify me better by touching my skin?"

"I'm willing to try." Mac slowly slid his hand under her shirt and touched her nipples. And then he kissed them gently as he said, "I think I've found something here. Can you feel this, my dear Marla?"

"Oh, yes! But it's strange; I don't feel it there. I feel it lower, much lower."

Marla held him close to her with one hand; with the other she guided his hand lower. And then she said, "Oh! And what do I feel pushing against me?"

"You know what it is, sweetie. Haven't you ever seen a male naked?"

"No. I never have done sperm extractions. I've just seen drawings."

Softly, Mac said, "I'm going to take off my clothes and then gradually take off all of your clothes, gently massaging your whole body as I go. If after that, nature has not told us what to do I suppose that we shall just have to guess."

"I was always good at guessing games, my dear Mac."

Three hours later Mac was awake and thinking of what they had done. He had never been so happy in his life, yet he had never felt so guilty, putting Marla in danger. He noticed that Marla was asleep under a sheet, so he gently lifted the sheet and looked at her body. What good deed had he ever done to deserve being there seeing her, touching her?

Marla was far from asleep. I've done it, she thought. Cynthia can take my life, but she can never take the love given me by Mac. But then, have I put in jeopardy our whole revolt against this oppressive government? If so, then maybe I can never marry Mac and have a family. But what's done is done and I have no regrets. Nothing is free and I shall take what comes.

At four o'clock, Mac dressed and then woke Marla. "I am going to crawl out the window now and go sit in the car until it's light out."

Marla put her arms around his neck, pulled him down to her and then said very quietly, "Good night, my love, my Mac. Thank you for heaven."

A half hour later, Marla was rudely shaken awake by two huge males wearing blond wigs. Wondering what was happening, Marla barely was able to focus on them enough to attempt to ask. Before she could say a word, the largest one pulled her out of bed, pushed her against the wall, and then holding her there by pushing on her neck, said, "Marla 642080, by order of MOTHER CYNTHIA, you are under arrest!"

"What for?" she managed to say.

"Treason!

XXI. Caught

Early Sunday morning, the breeze was slight; hungry birds were chirping and a new day had started. Inside the jail, inside her cell, lying on the filthy floor, unable to feel the breeze, unable to hear the birds, Marla woke up. Mentally struggling to learn where she was, what the time was, she managed to remember where she was. Determined not to groan or make any sound due to her pain from being struck by the males, she concentrated on being able to touch her right eyelid though her hands were closely chained to the metal belt around her waist. After an hour of struggling but not succeeding, she decided to stop struggling with the chains, slide against the wall and rest her back. As she worked to forget her pains, the events of the early morning began to cloud her mental attempts to find a way out of this place.

She remembered the shorter of the males had opened the door to the outer office. He noticed Gracie standing in her doorway wondering what was going on. He immediately closed the door. "There's another Wo out there." Then turning to Marla, asked, "Who is that out there?"

"My assistant."

After a moment of thought, the larger male said, "You tell her that we are messengers from Annette and that she wants to see you immediately. Don't touch your eyelids. If you try anything funny, I'll kill both of you right here."

"All right, I understand."

"Good. Now straighten your uniform and we'll go out there," he said in a threatening voice. "Remember what I told you." And then took his hand from her neck. "Okay, let's go," he said quickly as he gave her a shove through the doorway.

At the outer office Marla looked at Gracie and said out loud, "Annette wants me to meet her right now." But without making a sound she moved her lips to say, "Help. I'm being arrested. Call Annette" I'm so thankful that Gracie can read lips. I knew it would come in handy sometime. But was she paying any attention to my lips?

Outside the office building, Marla said to her kidnappers. "Look, I know Cynthia wants me dead and she wants you to do it. But you are signing your own death warrant if you do."

"Yeah?" said the shorter one. "Who's going to know we did it? Think Annette can help you now?"

"Do you remember your friend, Simon?"

"Yeah, so what about him?"

"Well, I know something that you don't know."

"I'll bet, ha!"

"Well, I know he's dead."

"So do we."

"But I know who killed him and why. Do you?"

The larger male grabbed Marla by the neck again and held her against the closed car door. "Yeah? Well, talk, bitch."

Struggling to speak, Marla managed to say, "Air! Give me some air and I'll tell you how to save your lives."

The larger male let up on his grip. Marla gasped a few times and then said, "Cynthia sent two males to kill Myrna and her two males."

"Yeah, so?"

"Well, Cynthia doesn't like loose ends to anything. So she had Simon kill those two males. Then she told Simon to meet her one night by the river and she would pay him. He did, and she shot him and left him for dead. Now there was no one to tell on her, she thought."

"I don't believe it," said the shorter male.

"I know all of this because my driver, Mac, and I came along and found him. He was barely alive, but he managed to tell me that Cynthia shot him because he killed the two males who murdered Myrna."

"Why should I believe you?"

"He asked me to find his brother, Jack, and tell him to watch out for her. That's why."

"Yeah?"

"And he said to tell Jack, 'You owe me five dollars,' and then he died."

Jack turned to Greg. "She must be telling the truth. How else would she know about the five dollars?"

"You know Cynthia," said Marla. "She's mean. She had her own sister killed, and she hates males. So if you kill me, do you think she'll let you two live to talk about it?"

The males paused a few moments, and then Jack said, "Tie her hands behind her back, put her in the car, and deliver her to the jail."

"Yeah, and we'd better get a receipt for her."

When we arrived at the horrible stone jail, they brought me down to this old bomb shelter, threw me on the floor of this cell, locked it and left. No one has come down here since then. Well, I said, "Catch me if you can," and I'm caught.

At this moment Cynthia was having breakfast in the dining room of the mansion she had taken the day after Myrna had been murdered. She was eating slowly, enjoying every moment of her triumph over Myrna and Marla, and her soon to be triumph over Annette. She laughed out loud as she said, "WOZ will be all mine, all mine, and then look out, you sorry pigs."

Her dreams of glory were interrupted by her assistant, a timid young wo, who said, "MOTHER CYNTHIA, Iris called the office and wanted to know if she may call you. She wants to talk about some Wo named Marla."

"Yeah, tell her to call me at exactly nine; tell her I'll talk to her for ten minutes."

"Yes, MOTHER CYNTHIA,' the wo said and was gone.

At nine Cynthia heard the hum and touching her right eyelid said, "Hello Iris, what's on your mind?"

"I'm calling about Marla from starter farm number three. I heard that she had been arrested for treason. Is that true?"

"That's true. That bitch had the woz and the donors playing games together, dancing together. Then when she found out about the old marriage law she started soliciting woz to get married."

"I see. How are you going to try her?"

"It's not important, only a formality, then she won't be around to threaten us any longer."

"Let me remind you, MOTHER CYTHIA, that she is U One K, and must have a fair trial."

"She'll have a fair trial; she's alive isn't she? I will be the judge. She's guilty, so she'll disappear."

"She has friends in the Council, so I suggest that you try her before them. And don't forget to give her a defense lawyer."

"Okay, you can be her defense lawyer. By the way, Iris, I understand that you let her talk you into getting married. Is that so?"

"Well, I did have too much wine and it did seem like a fun trick to play on Dan."

"I'm going to order the Council to repeal that law anyhow. Well, your ten minutes are up. I'll see you this afternoon at the Council meeting. Oh, the trial? Shall we say in three days?"

Later Marla had dozed off when she heard someone call her name and looked up at the cell door. Peeking through the bars she could barely make out someone with a U-100 epaulet. "Iris!" she said. "Iris, you came to see me?"

"Yes, and it's a good thing I did. Now where is that stupid guard?" Raising her voice in anger, she yelled, "Guard, guard. Come here this instant."

A moment later a heavy, middle-aged wo equipped with a pistol under her belt appeared. "Yeah, I'm here. What do you want?"

Iris pointed to her epaulet. "You mean, 'How may I serve you, ma'am.' I am Iris, U-100, not a common wo."

Immediately the guard adjusted her uniform, stood at attention and politely said, "Yes, ma'am, what can I do for you?"

"This prisoner is U One K. So empty that bucket over there, but first escort her to the cleanliness room. No more buckets; every time she wants to go to the cleanliness room, she is allowed to go. Do you understand?"

"Yes, ma'am, but MOTHER CYNTHIA said ..."

"I'll be responsible for her. I am also her defense lawyer. Now take those hand cuffs off of her and escort her to the Cleanliness Room."

After the cuffs were removed, Iris took Marla under the arms and helped her to rise. "Marla, I'll wait here until you return."

Marla looked up, and rubbing her tearing eyes, said, "Iris, Iris, I thought I was forgotten."

"We'll talk when you get back." And then handing Marla a small bag, Iris said, "Gracie brought you some clean clothes, but they wouldn't let you have them until I arrived. Go clean up now."

Turning to the guard, Iris said, "Bring us two chairs. I need to talk to my client. And you need to go back to your desk at the end of the hall. Our talk is privileged."

Thirty minutes later as Iris and a clean Marla sat quietly talking, Marla said, "I don't know how I can ever thank you for coming. I was beginning to feel condemned and forgotten. I couldn't call Annette; I couldn't call anyone with my hands tied. How did you know I was here?"

"I had just finished breakfast when there was a banging on the front door. I hadn't quite recovered from the party last night so things were quite blurry to me. Dan looked out and recognized Mac standing there very impatiently. Mac came inside, still out of breath, but managed to say, "Cynthia's got her. She's got Marla!"

"Tell me what happened, Mac," I said. 'Dan, get Mac a glass of water.'

"Mac gradually got his breath back and after he took a few sips of the water, told me the following story:

"Cynthia knows all about the marriages and arrested Marla, Mac said. "Gracie told me that two males broke into Marla's bedroom and dragged Marla away. Gracie said that she tried to call Anna and Annette, but neither answered.

"Mac continued, 'You see, I was asleep in the car next to the building and I saw them drag her out of the building. They were going to kill her, but she talked them out of it; she said that if they did Cynthia would kill them to keep them quiet, so they just took her away.'"

"Where is she now?" I said.

"I followed and they took her to the downtown jail."

"Okay, Mac, I'll handle this now. You had better hide somewhere."

"Then he said that he would go to Annette's cabin. 'If you need me, call Orange and she will know exactly where I am.'

"Then Mac got in the car and left in a hurry. And that's what he told me about Marla."

"Right after that, Gracie called me and told me what happened. She tried to get Annette but she didn't answer. Well, here's what's happening. This afternoon Cynthia is going to try to force the Council to repeal the marriage law. She blames you for it and for soliciting Woz into getting married."

"What about my trial? I get a trial, don't I?"

"Yes. Cynthia wanted to try you herself, but I told her that you were U One K and she had to try you before the whole Council, and that's in three days."

Marla took Iris' hand, and then turned to her almost in tears. "But where is Annette? Did Cynthia have her killed? You know that Cynthia killed Myrna, don't you?"

"I thought she might have, but I had no evidence."

"Iris, if I tell you what I know about Myrna's death, it would put you in great danger. Let me testify and then call Jack and Greg, the two males Cynthia hired to kidnap and kill me."

"All right, but I have to get busy stopping her right now. I am going to get four more couples married this morning and that at least will make a tie vote, and I have prospects for two more votes against repeal."

Through her tears, Marla managed a slight smile as she asked Iris, "Why are you helping me. I'm so far below your rank?"

"Marla, you stuck your neck out for me, helped me to hold on to Dan. You are our only hope for a fair and honest country. Besides, I like you."

"I'm just a common wo who got lucky."

""Marla, I know who you really are. You probably don't, and for your own protection I think. I'll try to find out about Annette and I'll come see you tonight after the Council session. Oh, Anna is all right. I talked to her an hour ago."

"Thanks, Iris."

The chambers where the Council of One Hundred met was the completely restored State of Oklahoma congress building. Elaborate draperies and fine walnut heavily upholstered furniture were found in abundance. The floor of the hall held one hundred desks, one for each of the Council members. The front of the hall was elevated and contained a paneled desk fifteen feet long. Three large chairs with crests were behind that desk.

As members gathered Cynthia approached each Wo, and not with subtle words, suggested that it would be unwise for anyone to vote against repealing the marriage act. She said to Johanna, "You are the president of the Council, so you should realize that it would be extremely unwise for any U-100 to vote against repeal of the marriage law, that is, if that Wo wants to hold on to her servant-husband, if you know what I mean."

"Yes, Cynthia, I know what you mean. But, Cynthia, what harm does it do for a few Woz to have a tighter hold on their males?"

"The harm is..." and then she stopped short, took a deep breath and then shouted, "I don't like it! I am U-1; you council members are only U-100. I am MOTHER CYNTHIA and I rule this country. I own this country. I own you!"

Johanna timidly said, "Yes, Cynthia."

Cynthia then stood on the platform, looked around, not smiling, and then said in a loud voice, "All right, let's get started."

As members took their seats, Cynthia went behind the large desk, picked up the gavel and struck it on the desk top. "All right, let's not waste time. We're here to vote to repeal the marriage law. All in favor push the aye button on your desk."

Clicking noises were heard and then all looked to the vote counter on the wall which read for repeal 75, against 25. Cynthia banged the gavel again and said, "By a vote of 75 to 25, the Marriage..."

"Not so fast there my dear sister," shouted Annette who had just entered the room. "As U-2, I am entitled to vote and I vote no. So now you don't have the 75% majority and the repeal is defeated!"

Cynthia grabbed her gavel, and yelling at the top of her voice, threw it at Annette, but missed. Leaving the podium and storming toward the door, she turned and waving her arms wildly, shouted, "You are not U dash two. You are U dash nothing!" At doorway, she turned, pointed her finger at all of the Council members, and then screamed, "All of you are U dash nothing. I own you. I own everything and you will regret this day." Then pointing her finger at Annette, said, "And the trial of your pet, Marla, will be tomorrow."

That evening Iris visited Marla again in her cell. "You should have seen Cynthia in a rage, screaming at Annette, then at the Council, then at Annette again."

"The loss of the repeal really got to her, huh." said Marla, trying to smile a bit.

"You know, Marla, her temper tantrum really showed she knows she has lost. And she didn't make any friends that way either. Council members don't like to be threatened or hear someone screaming at them."

"But I'm still locked up, and I'm still going to trial, and I still could lose," said Marla, sadly.

"But you're not going to lose. If Cynthia knew what I know, she'd take poison tonight. And this time tomorrow all of our problems will be over."

Marla tried to smile a bit as she quietly said, "Yes, one way or another."

Just before ten Monday morning in the Council chambers, members were gathered in small groups awaiting Cynthia. "Did you hear that several of the married males simply disappeared last night?" Ursela asked Marlene, one of the Woz who was married last Saturday night at the party.

"What do you think happened to them? Did they run away in fear of being eliminated by Cynthia?

"Well, I really don't know, but Guy slept with a pistol by his side last night."

The door opened then and Marla, Iris, and Annette entered, went to a long table facing the podium, and sat down. A few moments later, Cynthia dressed in an elegant uniform with a new, large, colorful, golden epaulet entered and went directly to the podium. She stood there quietly and motionless for a moment, and then banged the gavel and said, "Let the traitor's trial begin."

Looking at the Council members seated at their desks and then facing Marla, she said, "How do you plead, you little bitch?"

Marla stood and facing the Council said, "I have done nothing wrong, nothing illegal."

"I'm glad you said that, for I will prosecute you myself. No need to trouble anyone else."

"You can't," and "No," and "Not legal," was heard among the mumbling of the members reacting to Cynthia's statement.

Cynthia paid no attention to them as she said to Marla, "Stand up and answer my questions."

Marla stood and stared at Cynthia's forehead at a place just above her nose. Marla knew that one could stare at this spot, and by not looking directly into the other wo's eye, could stare down that wo. It was usually quite unnerving.

It didn't seem to affect Cynthia as she said, "What is your name?"

"My name is Marla."

"What is your complete name, traitor?

"Marla 642080."

Quickly, Annette stood and said, "That's not her complete name, it's…"

"Not important. Sit down"

"Who is your mother?" Cynthia asked sarcastically.

"I was told her name was also Marla."

Cynthia left the podium and walked to within five feet of Marla, and taunting, asked, "And what happened to your dear sweet mother?"

"After I had been taken from her at the age of eight, I was told that she had killed herself."

"Why did she do that?"

"I don't know. I was only eight years old then."

"How did you feel when you were told she killed herself?"

"I cried. She was good to me."

"And that's why you worked your way up to U One K, so you could take revenge for your mother's death?"

"I was a little child."

"And you got this idea to ruin WOZ by introducing males into our society, pushing woz to marry, and destroy us, didn't you?"

Marla looked down and slowly shook her head no. "I only want woz and males to have their souls back. Nothing I did was illegal."

Cynthia raised herself to her full height, and with a broad smile said, "Well, you have just admitted that you committed treason, so I find you guilty and sentence you to elimination."

"Just a minute there, sister dear," Annette shouted as she approached Cynthia. "You don't have the power to even try her. She has done nothing illegal, and she is not who you think she is."

Before Cynthia could answer, Iris stood and pointing her finger at Cynthia, said, "I am her lawyer, and by Council rules I am permitted to speak. Even you must permit that."

Cynthia looked at the angry faces of the Council members, and then went back to behind the podium and said, "All right, have your say and get it over with."

"Iris stood and facing the Council members said, I have a few witnesses to call. First, I wish Anna to testify."

"What for?" said Cynthia sarcastically.

Anna stood beside Marla as Iris asked her, "Do you know this Marla who stands beside you?"

"I certainly do," she said, and then turning to the members announced, "She is my daughter."

There was general mumbling for a few moments, then Anna continued, "I did not commit suicide after she was brutally taken from my arms. I was born Marla, but when my roommate hanged herself, I assumed her identity and was sent to 100 K school in her place."

"You lied to get promoted, so why should we believe you now?" Cynthia yelled at her.

"Iris stood and then said, "Because we can prove who she really is." Reaching for two papers on top of the desk behind her, she produced two DNA print-outs. "Holding up one paper she said, "Here is a print-out of Anna's DNA taken yesterday" Then holding up the other paper, said, "And here is a print-out her DNA sixteen years ago when she was called Marla. They are identical, so Anna and Marla, the defendant's mother, are one and the same Wo."

"Why should I care about that anyhow?" said Cynthia.

"Because, my dear sister," said Annette, "The use of last names was never prohibited. Our grandmother, the original MOTHER MYRNA, Vice President of the United States, was named Myrna Johnson. This means that our mother, MOTHER MYRNA II, was also named Myrna Johnson. So you, and I, and my daughter, Anna, and young Marla are named Johnson. You are trying to eliminate Marla Johnson, whose rank is really U-4."

There was general applause from the Council chamber as Cynthia slumped in her seat on the podium. But after a few moments, she stood and said, "That makes no difference, she is guilty of treason."

Annette, still standing, said in a loud voice, "But the Council can't try her. By law, she can only be tried by three judges, all of whom must be U-10 or higher. So the judges can only be Anna, you, and me. That means you lose because we vote two to one for acquittal."

Cynthia shouted, "You dumb bitch, I am U-1. I am MOTHER CYNTHIA, and what I say goes,"

At this point, two males were brought into the chambers. Cynthia turned her face away when she noticed them. Johanna, who was seated at her desk, stood and announced, "We have other business today, now that Marla has been acquitted. As president of the Council I would like to question these two males. Does any Council member have an objection to this?"

Cynthia stood and yelled, "I object."

"Sorry, Cynthia, I overrule you," said Johanna. "But you can put your objections in writing and I will think it over tomorrow. Please sit down again." Then facing the members of the council, Johanna announced, "Iris, you may proceed to question the males."

"Thank you, your Madam President." Then addressing the two males, she said, "What are your names?"

"I'm Jack," said the taller one, "And he's Greg, ma'am."

Turning to the shorter one, Johanna said, 'Greg, you and Jack were sent Sunday morning to arrest Marla, is that true?"

"Well, yes ma'am, sort of."

"What do you mean by sort of?"

"Well, MOTHER CYNTHIA told us that if she struggled, or if we even thought she might struggle, we could use all the force necessary to take care of her."

"What did she mean by take care of her?"

"I asked her that and she said, and these are her exact words, 'A corpse doesn't struggle,' in other words, she didn't want her taken alive."

"Why didn't you kill her?"

"Marla told us that Cynthia would then kill us to keep us from talking."

Hearing this, Cynthia screamed, "I am U-1. I own you. I own WOZ, and I'll kill you just like I killed Simon and the other males. I can do what I want." And then she threw her gavel at Johanna, slumped down in her chair, and broke into tears.

Annette stood and facing the guards at the door, yelled, "Arrest Cynthia for the murder of three males and MOTHER MYRNA. Take her and lock her up." As Cynthia was taken away Annette turned to the Council members and said, "I never wanted to be U-1, but in light of today's events, I shall assume the office temporarily until after Cynthia's trial. Does the Council object to my temporary taking over?"

No one objected.

Marla slowly sat down. Turning to Annette and Iris, she said, "Annette, then you are my grandmother. Is that right?"

Annette put her arms around Marla, then around Anna. "Yes, and Anna and I hid you from Cynthia, just like I hid my Marla. But she almost messed things up when she took the identity of Anna. And you, young Marla, it was not by chance that I intercepted your letter to Myrna asking for promotion. When Anna told me what you had done, I immediately got the letter and decided I must put you under my wing. That's why I took you to my house and why I didn't want you to go to U Ten K School."

"And why you told me everything you knew about males and the history of WOZ."

Annette hugged her, and then walked to the podium, held up her hands for silence. She paused a moment, took a deep breath, and calmly addressed the Council members. "Members of the Council: I suggest that we adjourn until tomorrow at ten. We all need to rest and contemplate what needs to be done. I'll see all of you here tomorrow. Rest well."

Early Tuesday morning Annette heard a hum and touching her left eyelid heard Johanna say, "Annette, something terrible has happened."

Touching her right eyelid, Annette said, "Tell me." After listening a few minutes, she took away her hand and sat quietly on the side of her bed. As she walked toward her cleanliness room, she said quietly, "What a waste. What terrible things we do to others and to ourselves"

Promptly at ten Johanna opened the meeting of the Council of One Hundred. "Before we start our business of the day, Annette would like to say a few words," she said and then sat down.

Annette stood and facing the Council, said, "My sister, Cynthia, who was under house arrest, took poison last night and died almost instantly." There was much indistinct verbal response from the Council members, and then Annette continued, "In light of the events of the past few days, perhaps we should adjourn for a few days and think about what has happened and what we can do for our country."

Johanna stood and asked for a vote on adjournment and it was decided to adjourn until the next Monday.

Annette invited Johanna, Iris, Anna, and Marla to have lunch with her to talk about the situation. "Cynthia was a

Wo who did not react well to failure," said Annette during lunch. "As a child, she either got her way or she would not eat, she would not talk to anyone, sometimes for days. I guess she wanted to be supreme ruler of WOZ or dead."

"What made her that way?" asked Marla.

Annette shook her head. "I really don't know. All babies are born pure and innocent. Then the world happens to them and some turn out so sweet and others turn out so mean. Why? Myrna and I wanted to do our best for WOZ; Cynthia simply wanted to use her position for personal pleasure and gain. And she hated males. She believed as our grandmother, Myrna, did, that all of the evil in the world was caused by males. But my sister, Myrna and I knew WOZ built on sand, couldn't last and we had to change."

"Yes, change, Mom," said Anna, "But how?"

"We can't do it overnight," said Iris. "There would be a revolt with those who have grown accustomed to power over common woz and males too."

"I know," said Annette. "I have a few ideas of what we can do. Let me work on them and I'll present them on Monday. I also would like a small family service for Cynthia. She did some really bad things, but she was my sister."

"You're certainly quiet, Marla," said Iris.

Marla looked at Johanna, then Iris, and then Annette and Anna. "I was just thinking that three years ago I was just a common wo scrubbing floors, wondering if anything would ever happen to me." After a pause for a moment, she added, "Well, it looks like it did."

"May I come to the service, Annette?" said Johanna. "Cynthia did several nice things for me."

"Any member of the Council is welcome to come if she wants to."

Annette stood and walked to a table nearby. She took some papers from the table and handed them to her guests.

I have printed out my proposals for a short tem and ng term government. I shall send these proposals to all members of the Council by computer this afternoon. I would like for each member to think about what I have written and we can discuss everything next week."

"I'll see to it that everyone works on this, MOTHER ANNETTE," said Johanna.

At the doorway Annette bid everyone good bye with these parting words. "Starting now, I do not wish to be called MOTHER ANNETTE. I wish to be called Protector Annette, as I think we need someone in charge as we change a few things."

"I think that I shall call you Grandma Protector," said Marla.

"Don't you dare. Well, not in public anyway."

Monday morning the Council gathered together to listen and discuss Annette's proposal for changes in the government of WOZ. Every Council member was present and had the written pages of Annette's changes on her desk. Annette stood before them for the first time as Protector Annette, and as everyone became quiet, Annette said, "My Council members, ladies, that's a term from the past, but I like it. Basically, I propose that a committee of Council members be appointed to write a new constitution for the country of WOZ. I strongly suggest that a few from the upper ranks, such as the U One Ks, U Ten Ks, and some educated common woz and educated males be represented also.

"I strongly suggest that this committee intensely study the Constitution of the United States, the Declaration of Independence, the writings of Thomas Payne and others.

"I strongly suggest that WOZ become a democracy, and that safeguards are in place to prevent the government from crossing that line between protecting the population and controlling the population.

"I very strongly suggest that males are defined and accepted as huz, not primitives.

"I am legally MOTHER ANNETTE, but upon completion of a satisfactory framework of government for

WOZ, I shall step down and become a private citizen, giving up all inherited claim to rank."

There was a pause for a few seconds and then most of the members applauded, though others sat on their hands or walked out. Annette stepped down from the podium, then stepped back up, held up her hand and when the applause ceased, she said, "I am marrying Pat at my home today. The fun starts at six and I hope all of you will come celebrate with us."

XXII. January 1, 2107

Standing on a raised platform in front of thousands of citizens of WOZ, a smiling Wo held up her hand to quiet the crowd. Annette and Anna stood on each side of her; and next to them stood Johanna and Iris. Directly behind her stood a male, carrying a small toddler and holding the hand of another small child. The young Wo placed one hand on the Bible, raised the other hand and said, "I, Marla Johnson, do hereby swear that I shall faithfully execute my duties as President of the United Huz of America, and that I shall protect and defend its Constitution, so help me, God."

After hugging and shaking hands with the others on the platform, Marla held up her hands and the cheering crowd gradually became quiet. Marla took several sips of water and then going down to the next level of the platform stood alone. And then, without notes, began to speak:

"Before I talk about our future, I would like to thank and congratulate all of those who have worked so hard the past five years to establish our democracy. Not only did they strive to make our new country one in which both genders have equal rights, but for many, the cost was high. We owe the many Woz of all ranks our gratitude for giving up their privileges so that we may have a country with a future. None of this could have happened if it hadn't been for Annette establishing a protectorate so that some very cruel laws and attitudes could be corrected. As most woz were educated and very few males were educated, I wish to thank her for establishing the very temporary Department of Male Education. When 95% of all males and all woz are reasonably educated now there should be no reason to keep this department. I especially want to thank Protector Annette for her guidance and for stopping the aborting of the male unborn, and killing of sperm with the Y chromosome. We should have nearly equal numbers of males and woz in seven years, by the time my term is over.

"It was not so long ago that I was a common wo scrubbing floors. Everything was given me. I had a bed; I had two sets of uniforms; I had access to a cleanliness room; I had food, especially packaged for my rank." She paused a moment and then said, "Which was, of course, no rank at all. But I didn't have to worry about looking for a job; I didn't have to worry about being sick. I had as good health care as the government thought I needed to scrub floors. What more could I possibly have wanted? And it was all free! It cost me nothing... nothing but my own soul. I was a worker ant; I was a machine. I knew only to work, eat, and sleep. I did not know about living"

After thunderous applause, Marla continued, "I knew nothing of males; I didn't know they existed. Males were like ants also and did their duty furnishing sperm, not knowing what it was. They ate very well, not because anyone cared about them as huz, but because they were basically farm animals. They, too, were robbed of their souls.

"Woz was invented and run by a group who wanted a perfect world. They looked at the evil around them, and then believing that males caused all of the evil in the world, eliminated all males. So they invented WOZ, their perfect world, but others' perfect hell.

"As you know, they kept a few males for themselves and a few for sperm. But everything must be paid for; nothing in life is free. One hu's perfect world was paid for by another hu's hell. This perfect world had a price; No wo must ever know that males exist as most woz would want one. If the word got out, there goes their perfect world."

Marla paused for a moment, took a sip of water and then said, "So how does one build a perfect government to run this perfect world? I doubt that it can be done. But what we can do is balance protecting our huz against owning them. No more big lies, no more depriving the huz of their dreams, no more gender discrimination. I believe in equal civil rights. I do not believe in special civil rights for some but not others."

Marla paused as she looked at the crowd, and then shouted, "I believe in our new country. I believe in our United Huz of America!

"One more thing I intend to do; and that is help WOZ to be family orientated again. The government, any government can control huz to a certain degree. Parents, good parents, have the power to mold the next generations to become the parents' dream, but not if the parents abdicate their responsibility, or if the government usurps it. My administration is dedicated to protecting you and giving you the opportunity to work on your dreams.

"My grandmother, Annette, my mother, Anna, and I, Marla, all renounce any inherited right to govern this new country. I was elected to be President of The United Huz of America, but I shall serve only one term; I shall not live off of the huz. When my term is up, I shall go with my husband, Mac, and our two little boys to a newly declared safe place in the formerly desolate country and begin to farm."

THE END